P9-CDS-999

3/18

SEA WITCH

SEA WITCH

SARAH HENNING

KATHERINE TEGEN BOOKS
An Imprint of HarperCollins Publishers

Katherine Tegen Books is an imprint of HarperCollins Publishers.

Sea Witch

Library of Congress Control Number: 2018933269
ISBN 978-0-06-243877-5

Typography by Carla Weise
18 19 20 21 22   PC/LSCH   10 9 8 7 6 5 4 3 2 1
❖
First Edition

To Nate and Amalia—
the only ships in my sea.

And to Justin—
*next time there will be
more car chases.*

I have sea foam in my veins, I understand the language of the waves.   —Jean Cocteau, *Le Testament d'Orphée*

PROLOGUE

Two small pairs of boots echoed on the afternoon cobblestones—one pair in a sprint, the other in a stumble and slide. A blond girl, no older than five, dragged a raven-haired girl an inch taller and a year older down the sea lane toward a small cottage.

The dark-haired girl's lungs were sputtering, each inhale a failure.

She was drowning on dry land.

As the house came into view, the blond girl opened her mouth to scream for help but before any sound could come out, the other girl's mother burst through the door. Like she knew what had happened—she always seemed to know what they'd done.

"Evie!" the mother cried, cradling her daughter in a heap at her chest and running toward the cottage. "Anna," she said to the little blonde, who was panting from carrying her friend so far, "fetch the royal physician—"

"But—"

"Go!"

The girl didn't protest again, fine boots clacking against the cobblestones as she regained speed.

When her mother shut the cottage door tightly behind them, the raven-headed girl knew the physician's medicine wouldn't heal her.

Only one thing would.

"Gianni!" The mother called, and the girl's father poked his head out of the bedroom, his face slack with the sleep he wasn't allowed on his latest whaling trip.

"Evie . . . what—"

"A broken rib. Maybe a punctured lung." She laid the girl in her bed and ripped the girl's bodice to her navel. Blood under the skin showed black across the expanse of the little girl's ribs, fissures like spiderwebs crossed from spine to sternum. The mother tried to read her daughter's dark eyes. "What happened?"

The girl licked her lips before inhaling just enough air to speak. "I saved Nik."

That was true. And the little girl was proud. Daring to smile despite the pain.

They'd spent the morning together—the blonde, the raven-haired girl, and their boy—running through the waves, climbing rocks, dancing in the sand. But then the afternoon came and it was time for them to part. The boy sent back to his castle, the little girls home—the younger one to her mansion, ten times the size of the other girl's tiny cottage.

Mischievous and sunburnt, they ran in protest, the boy leading the way, holding the girls' hands as they raced across the stepping-stone rocks that led into the cove. They giggled and shrieked as they hopped from rock to rock, the boy's minder chiding them from the shore.

But one rock was slick with moss. The boy slipped—falling backward, the base of his skull aimed directly at a crook of solid stone.

In a blink, the little girl made her choice.

She threw her body between the boy and the jagged edge of the rock. Her back took the hit with a huge crack. Her head snapped back, her skull missing impact by a hair. Just as she hit, the boy's head bounced onto the pilled cotton of her bodice rather than smashing into the rock.

It was a thing of magic that she'd made it in time.

They were caught then. The boy's minder yanked them back onto the beach and told them in stern tones to never do that again. Then the old woman hauled the boy away without a good-bye, leaving the girls on the sand.

As they turned for home, the little raven-haired girl stumbled, the shock wearing off and the pain beginning. It radiated up her back, around her rib cage, to the front of her dress. She couldn't catch her breath, each inhale stopping short. The little blonde said she'd walk her friend home but by the time they made it to the sea lane, the raven-headed girl couldn't stand, all her weight on the blonde's shoulders.

"Oh, Evie . . . ," the girl's mother said. As if she'd seen it all. Immediately, she sent her husband for her bottles. Her inks. Not that one. This one. She laid the girl in her bed and lit a fire with a snap of her fingers.

And tried every healing spell she knew.

It only took seconds to know none of them would work. The girl's breath withered until it was almost nothing at all.

The mother wept, wishing for her sister—the strongest witch. Healer of Kings, reviving those in power who turn a blind eye to magic when their lives depend on it, but banish it when it doesn't. She was the reason the physician might come at all—though he would be too late. As would Hansa, a day away, healing yet another noble.

The girl's father pressed his hand into his wife's shoulder and wiped away her tears. Then he squeezed his daughter's hand, already growing cold, her circulation failing.

"I'll go fetch the minister—"

"Not yet," the mother said, determination ringing in her voice. The girl's mother stood at the edge of the bed, her shoulders now pin straight, her voice calm and direct. "There is one more spell I can try."

With gentle fingers, she painted octopus ink across the little girl's cheeks, down her neck, and across her chest. Then her mother laid her hands gently over the girl's chest.

"Don't you worry, Evie."

The words she said next were old and dark, and the little girl didn't understand them. They made her blood crackle like the fire across the room. Stole the air from the cottage. Made her mother shake, violently, as she held her hands to her daughter's skin.

The little girl couldn't do anything but watch her mother,

her veins singing. Soon, her mother's palms on her skin became more than damp. They began to burn.

And then the pain stopped. Air rushed into the little girl's lungs, and her chest rose. She exhaled, long and deep.

At that the girl's mother smiled—just before her own body began to seize, her eyes rolling back in her head.

It was too much. The mother's chest compressed, a long breath pushing out—but no inhale following.

"Greta! Greta!" The girl's father placed his hands on his wife's face, his palms burning and flying away, suddenly red.

The prickle in the little girl's blood spiked with fear. She struggled to pull herself to sit, her mother's hands sliding away as her form slumped over and her pale cheek smashed into the bedsheet. The little girl didn't hesitate, reaching for her mother's potions. She turned her mother's head to face upward before smearing ink across those pale cheeks, her little fingers blistering with the touch. Her own skin was pink and warm and full of life as her mother's skin turned as white as snow, as hot as ash.

The girl was smart, though. She'd watched her mother enough. She knew how these spells worked. Magic was barter—the right words, actions, potions for the right result.

She put her hands on her mother's face and began repeating those strange words.

Words of life.

"Evelyn, no!" Her father didn't move, just screamed, fear freezing him to his spot at the foot of the bed.

But the little girl had fumbled her way through the words

enough that her own skin began to grow hot. The pain returned. Her breath became shallow. Then her mother's eyes flew open, showing beautiful hazel instead of the whites.

It was working.

Her father looked from his wife to his daughter. Those words were dark. Old. Powerful. He knew this as much as he knew his native tongue.

Her mother's lips began moving. She took a deep breath. "Gefa!" With this single command, she stole the words right from the little girl's mouth. Dark words and dark magic and all sound gone from the girl's powerful tongue.

Still, the child kept going, chest heaving—she was yelling but could not be heard. Tears as dark as night flowed down her little cheeks. Black coating her vision, the girl began to wail without sound, her whole body shaking.

And, with her last wisp of energy, the girl's mother looked to her father.

"Bring Hansa home. Tell her. Promise."

As he nodded, her mother whispered one last spell, and the little girl's screams filled the air, black tears dripping onto her ruined dress.

"No, Mama, no!"

The little girl grabbed her mother's hand, still burning to the touch, and saw the light flee from her hazel eyes.

1

THE SEA IS A FICKLE WITCH.

She is just as likely to bestow a kiss as to steal the breath from your lips. Beautiful and cruel, and every glimmering wrinkle in between. Filling our bellies and our coffers when she is generous. Coolly watching as we don black and add tears to her waters when she is wicked.

Only the tide follows her moods—giving and taking at the same salty rate.

Still, she is more than our witch—she's our queen.

In all her spells and tantrums, she is one of us. The crown jewel of Havnestad, nuzzled against our shores—for better or worse.

Tonight, dressed in her best party finery, she appears calm, anger buried well below her brilliant surface. Still, there's a charge in the air as the stars wink with the coming

—1

summer solstice and the close of Nik's sixteenth birthday.

Formally: Crown Prince Asger Niklas Bryniulf Øldenburg III, first in line to the throne of the sovereign kingdom of Havnestad.

Informally: just Nik.

But "just Nik" isn't quite right either. He's not *just* anything to me. He's my best friend. My only friend, really.

And now he's dancing with Malvina across the deck of his father's grand steamship. That is, if you can call her violent tossing and whirling "dancing." My stomach lurches as Nik comes within inches of tipping over the rail after she forces an overenthusiastic spin. I wish she'd just give it up.

Malvina, formally Komtesse Malvina Christensen, is a perpetual royal suitor. She and her father have been vying for King Asger's attention for years, hoping he will make the match. Yet despite Nik's good-natured patience for her dancing, I have my doubts there will be a royal wedding in their future.

I want to look away from the pink silk blur of Malvina, but Nik's eyes are begging me to rescue him. Pleading. Silently calling my name across the distance—*Evvvvv- vieee.*

I am the only one who can save him. Every youth in town is here, but no one else can cut in on a girl like Malvina. For the others, there would be consequences— lost invitations to galas, the oldest horse on the weekend hunt, a seat at the table next to one's senile great-tante instead of the Komtesse. For me, there are none of those things. You can't fall far in society if you're not part of it to begin with.

After another aggressive turn, I finally stride onto the makeshift dance floor, ignoring a chorus of smirks as I go—they've seen this play before. Malvina will be the victim, I'll be the villain, and Nik will let it happen. It can be a messy business, being the crown prince's confidante; enduring small humiliations is only a fraction of the cost. But I won't apologize for helping him. We all make compromises in friendships, and having Nik's loyalty when no one else will even look me in the eye is worth every criticism I face.

I tap the girl on one sturdy shoulder, screw my face into exaggerated panic, and point to the eight-layered, blue-sugar-spackled monstrosity she insisted on crafting.

"Oh, angels, Evie! What is it?" Malvina barks.

"The cake's icing—"

"*Fondant,*" she corrects, as if I've spit on her oma's grave.

"The *fondant*—it's bulging."

True panic colors her features as her feet refuse to move. Torn between dancing with Nik and rescuing her masterpiece from a bulbous fate, her eyes skip to my face for a moment, incredulous. She fears I've purposely stolen her turn. It's just the sort of thing the girls of Havnestad think I would do—the ones whispering in the shadows about us now. Except in this case, they're right.

"Do your duty, Malvina. It was lovely dancing with you." Nik bends into a slight bow, royal manners on display, not a hint of displeasure in his features.

When his eyes cut away, Malvina sneaks a glare my way, her disdain for me as clear as her worry that I'm actually telling the truth. She doesn't need to say what she's thinking, and she won't—not if she ever wants to dance with Nik again. So, when Nik completes his bow, she simply plasters on a trained smile and leaves him with the most perfect curtsy before running off in a rush of golden hair and intent.

Now Nik bows deeply to me as if I'm his newest suitor, his mop of black hair briefly obscuring his coal-dark eyes. "May I have the remainder of this dance, my lady?"

My lips curl into a smile as my legs automatically dip into a polite curtsy. *My lady.* Despite how good those words feel, they're enough to earn me the ire of everyone on this boat. To them I am just the royal fisherman's daughter abusing the prince's kindness, using him for his station. They won't believe we're just friends, as we've always been, since we were in diapers. Before I knew what I was and he knew who he was meant to be.

"But of course, Crown Prince Niklas," I reply.

He meets my eyes, and we both burst out laughing. Formality has never worn well between us—regardless of Nik's training.

We settle in and begin to waltz across the deck. He has a good foot on me, but he's practiced at leaning in—whispers are often our most convenient language.

"Took you long enough," he says, twirling me through the last bars of the song.

"I wanted to see how long you'd stay dry."

He gasps with false horror in my ear, a smile tingeing it. "You'd send your own best friend swimming with the mermaids on his birthday?"

"I hear they're beautiful—not a bad present for a teenage boy."

"They also prefer their presents not breathing."

My eyes shoot to his. I can feel the slightest tremble in my jaw. Today would've been our friend Anna's birthday too. It still is, though she is no longer here to celebrate it. She was exactly a year younger than Nik. We'd each had our share of close calls in those days, the great and powerful goddess Urda seeming to want us all for herself. But we lost Anna. I glance down, feeling tears hot against my lash line, even after four years' time. Nik sighs and tugs a curl off my face. He waits until I finally glance up. There's a soft smile riding his lips, and I know he regrets pulling us from a place of joy to one so fraught. "Well, thank you for saving me, Evie. As always."

It's as good a subject change as any, but it's not enough—and we both know it. I take a deep breath and look over Nik's shoulder, not trusting myself to say more.

I swallow and try to concentrate on the party. Everything here has been borrowed for Nik's celebration—the ship, the free-flowing hvidtøl, the band, two servants, and a coal man—and it's beautiful. I focus on the miniature lanterns ringing the deck, the golden thread of my single fancy dress catching their glow.

Suddenly, Malvina hoists herself onto the dessert table, still frantically trying to control the cake's growing bulge. I expect Nik to laugh, or at least knock out a very royal snort, but instead he's looking over my shoulder, portside, at the sea. I follow his eyes, and my heart sputters to a stop when I make out a swift schooner, the familiar line of a boy—a man—adjusting the sail.

"Iker . . ." His name falls from my lips in a sigh before I can catch it. I meet Nik's eyes, a blush crawling up my cheeks. "I didn't know he was coming."

"Neither did I." He shrugs and raises a brow. "But Iker's not exactly one to confirm an invitation. Missed that day at prince school. The lecture about being on time, too."

"I believe it's called 'fashionably late,'" I say.

"Yes, well, I suppose I wouldn't know," Nik says with a laugh.

The little schooner closes in, and I see that it's only Iker—he hasn't brought a crew with him from Rigeby Bay, not that I'd expect him to. He's a weather-worn fisherman trapped in a life designed for silk and caviar. He redirects the mainsail perfectly, his muscles tensing tightly as he aims straight for his cousin's form.

Nik leans to my ear. "There goes my dancing partner."

I punch him on the arm. "You don't know that."

"True, but I do know how you've looked at him since my cake had about ten fewer candles on it."

I roll my eyes, but I can't help a smile creeping up my lips. He's somewhat right, though now isn't the best time to argue that the way I looked at Iker changed from brotherly to something else entirely about four years ago, not ten.

I clear my throat. "I'm sure Malvina won't mind—she's almost finished with your cake," I say, nodding in the direction of the blue monstrosity but never taking my eyes off Iker as he readies to throw up a line to the steamer.

Nik hugs me close and dips down to my ear. "You're such a ravishingly loyal friend."

"Always have been. Always will be."

"'Tis true." Nik grins before waving a long arm above his head. "Well, if it isn't the crown prince of Rigeby Bay!"

"And here I hoped to surprise you," Iker says, laughing. "Can't surprise a lighthouse of a man on his own boat, I suppose."

Nik laughs, standing even taller. "Not if I'm turned the right way."

Iker laughs even deeper. There is salt in his hair and few days' worth of scruff lining his strong jawline, but he strides across his deck with the elegance of a prince. He glances up at me, his eyes briefly betraying a hint of doubt about the sturdiness of my frame, but tosses the line to me anyway. I catch it, securing it with a knot I learned from Father.

Iker hauls himself up the rope and onto the ship. He manages to land on the small patch of deck just between Nik and myself. Behind us a crowd has gathered.

"Happy birthday, Cousin." Eyes laughing, Iker claps Nik on the back and brings him in for a hug, his toned arms fully encasing Nik's spindly-yet-strong form.

When they release, Iker's eyes go right to me. They're the clearest of blues—like ancient ice in the fjords of the north.

"Evelyn," he says, still retaining an air of formality from his upbringing, but he then shockingly pulls me into a hug.

I freeze, eyes on Nik as he and everyone else on the ship stares. Iker doesn't seem to notice or care and pulls me tighter, his arms wrapped around my waist. Warm from ship work, he smells of salt and limes. His shirt is freckled with water droplets, onyx on the starched gray fabric—the sea leaving her mark.

When the moment is over and he lets me go, an arm lingers across my shoulders. I try to ignore the question nagging me, the one I'm sure everyone else is asking too. *Why me?* We've known each other since we were children, but he's never shown me this kind of affection before. I'm not his type. I'm not *anyone's* type. Yet Iker continues to act as if it's all completely normal. He turns to Nik, to the crowd, and grins that perfect smile.

"Good people of Havnestad," he says, his voice commanding yet sincere. Then the grin grows wider. "Let's give the prince a celebration so hearty, he'll never forget it."

2

I FEEL AS IF I'M LIVING IN A DREAM.

Still warm from Iker's strong embrace, I twirl across the dance floor in his arms.

I tried to tell Iker we shouldn't, but he wouldn't hear of it. "Let them talk," Iker said. If only he knew how much they already did.

I can sense Malvina's eyes following me. *Yes, Malvina, this is what it looks like when someone dances without fearing for his life.* But I try not to think about her. I want to remember this moment, even the smallest details. Everything about him wears like oiled leather and loved muslin. His hands are rough and worn from the sea, and yet they are gentle, his thumb delicately caressing mine.

My twelve-year-old fantasies were never this detailed— hardly anything beyond me in a grand purple gown and Iker in his royal finery hand-in-hand on a stroll through the palace gardens. The reality is so different, so intense, and I'm not sure I'm handling it well. I know I'm not. Can he feel my palms sweating? My heart beating loudly against his chest?

"I saw you from my deck, you know," he whispers in my ear. "Before coming aboard. You've never looked more beautiful, Evie. And I've never begged the gods to steer my ship faster."

I don't know what to say, my voice seizing in my throat. I look around instead, trying to organize my thoughts. The sun has completely set, the last strands of light gone with our plates in a rush and clatter of tiny quail bones, torsk tails, pea pods, and strawberry hulls. And though the entire ship deck is still lit by a ring of miniature lanterns, the remaining shadow is enough that it almost feels as if we're alone.

Just a boy, a girl, and the sea.

The song ends and he hugs me tight. When he pulls back, he runs his fingers along my jawbone. "I shouldn't have stayed away from Havnestad so long," he says, capturing one of my curls between his fingers. "You have the same hair you did as a child." His gaze lifts to mine. "The same starry-night eyes."

I struggle not to look down—down to where he's still wound a lock of my hair lightly between his fingers. I bite my lip to silence the sigh there. His fingers wind tighter around the curl. It almost seems as if he doesn't know he's doing it—this boy made of smiles and grand gestures doing something so small it's escaped him.

Iker's eyes drift to the band members who have circled around a bench where someone has begun to play a guitaren. Though we can't see him, the shiny, precise plucks are a dead giveaway that the musician is Nik. He's always been the kind to pick up any instrument and immediately know exactly how to play it, ever since we were children. He's strumming the song I used to sing on the docks as a girl to wish my father safe travels on his fishing trips. Nik said it always got stuck in his head.

Iker drops the curl.

Clears his throat.

Adjusts his body so that we're not touching in so many places.

It's over. I know it. Perhaps fantasies are only meant to come true for a moment. Surely a trick of the gods.

His eyes linger on the band when he eventually speaks, but his tone has changed. "Evie, I love visiting Havnestad, but I don't like to step on my cousin's toes."

Now my voice isn't right. *Why did Nik have to play that song?* I swallow. "But you aren't," I say, hoping he can't hear the pleading in my tone. "Besides, I don't think Nik would mind seeing more of you, and there *is* the Lithasblot festival coming up in a few days."

"Ah, yes, when you people go nuts for Urda, throw

bread at anyone without a double chin, and run in circles until you pass out."

"*You* people?" I say and give him a jab. Iker may be from across the strait, but he's just as much an Øldenburg as Nik. Their family has ruled Denmark and Sweden for four hundred years. They know better than anyone not to discount the harvest the goddess has bestowed on us. "Don't poke fun at the games. We take them very seriously."

"Oh yes, a life-or-death game of carrying around the heaviest rock."

"Or running the length of a log. All useful skills." I laugh, happy to have lightened the mood again.

Iker turns to me. "If I stay for this Lithasblot extravaganza, you must promise you will scramble across some recently murdered tree for my entertainment."

"If that's what it takes, then I promise," I say, dipping in a mock curtsy.

A laugh escapes from my lips, but Iker's attention is locked on my face. Almost as if he can't help himself, his thumb grazes my cheekbone again, down my jaw and to my mouth. The touch of his finger to my lips sends color rising in my cheeks as I meet the glacier blue of his eyes.

"Iker, I—"

"Goooooooood people of Havnestad!" Our heads whip around as Nik's voice booms across the length of the ship. He is still holding the guitaren, but now he has a crown fashioned of lemon wedges squashed on his wavy flop of hair. There's a huge smile tugging at his cheeks, and his long arms are thrust high into the air. He's actually doing quite the unintentional impression of Iker, though only after a few mugs of King Asger's special brew. "As your crown prince, I hereby issue a royal decree that we sing *for me* on this, the sixteenth year of my life."

"Hear, HEAR," yells Iker, followed by the rest of the crowd, which has suddenly crept back into the corners of my vision.

"Excellent. Ruyven has sent the signal for fireworks. But first, a so—" Nik's voice cuts out as Malvina's strong hand jerks him down so her lips can meet his ear. The other hand is gesturing behind them, toward the cake. Nik stands back up slowly and resets the guitaren. "The lovely lady Malvina has informed me we are at a loss for candles." Nik points the instrument's neck at me, feigned formality still thick in his throat. "Evelyn?" He raises a brow.

I raise one back.

"Come on, I know you know where they are."

And I do. Exactly where Nik left them when he "borrowed" the king's boat for the first warm day after a long, ice-filled winter.

"Yes, I do, good prince."

As much as I don't want to leave Iker's side, I step away, the warmth of him clinging to my skin for a ghost of a second as we separate. I snag a lantern that's dipped low on the line ringing the deck and move away from the crowd.

Boots clomping on the stairs, I disappear belowdecks to the captain's quarters. The space is much larger than something that should be a captain's anything—the whole place is nearly bigger than the home I share with Father and Tante Hansa. The miniature lantern struggles to keep up with the vastness, illuminating a halo barely beyond the hem of my party dress. It's utterly annoying.

Glancing up the stairs, I confirm that I am alone; no one followed me below. My back to the door, I reach a hand into the lantern. Softly muttered words of old fall from my lips as my fingers pinch the tip of the candle. *"Brenna bjartr aldrnari. Brenna bjartr aldrari. Pakka Glöð."*

The candle begins to glow with the full force of one three times its size.

It's a small act—something so subtle I probably could've done it in full view of everyone above. But even something as run-of-the-mill as a strengthening spell is dangerous here.

Women burned for far less under the Øldenburgs of yesteryear.

My relatives burned for far less.

Which means there are things about me Nik and Iker can never know.

Besides, I already took a risk tonight when I silently urged Malvina's cake to shed its sugary skin. I hadn't tried something like that since I was a child, but it worked well enough. Strengthening the candle in the open would have been pushing my luck, though, and I've never had much of that to begin with.

Now the cushion of light is more than enough. I ease my way through the vast space and toward the pair of chairs under one of the starboard portholes, a chessboard painted into the oak table between them.

I'd watched Nik stuff the ship's allotment of extra candles into the table's drawer while helping him clean up evidence of his warm-weather get-together. Not that his father wouldn't know about our little celebration—dishonesty has never sat well in Nik's royal mind—he just hadn't wanted to leave the castle's harbor crew with more work.

With rescued candles and matches in hand, I grab the lantern and spin toward the door. But suddenly in my peripheral vision, I catch two flashes of shocking white and blue. I spin back around to where a small halo of light beacons through the porthole.

My heart sputters to a dead halt as I realize I don't know of any fish with markings like those.

Like human eyes.

Lungs aching for me to remember how to breathe, I raise the lantern to the porthole, my mind churning to account for everyone onboard the ship. Yes, everyone had been there when I descended the stairs.

Yet, when the halo of light reaches the thick glass, a friend's eyes are there, deep blue and framed by luminous skin, water-darkened blond waves, and a look of surprise on parted lips.

"Anna?"

But in the instant I say her name into the damp cabin, the face vanishes, and I'm left staring into the indigo deep.

My lungs release and draw in a huge gulp of air as I race to the next porthole, my breath coming in rapid spurts as I repeat her name. But there's no sign of her beautiful face at that porthole or the next two.

I stand in the middle of the king's great cabin, heart pounding, breath burning in my lungs, as a heavy sob escapes my lips. Tears sting my eyes as I realize that even with Nik's brotherly friendship and Iker's new affection, I'm still just a lonely fisherman's daughter.

A lonely fisherman's daughter wishing that I could have my sweet friend back. Wishing hard enough that I'm seeing ghosts.

Wishing so very hard that I'm losing my mind.

3

I WIPE MY EYES WITH MY WRIST, THE CANDLES AND matches still clutched in my fingers. A couple of deep breaths, and I will myself through the door and up the stairs, my legs leaden.

"The good lady has returned with the candles!" Nik shouts when he sees me, his voice half-singing in tune with the guitaren.

"And the matches, my prince," I hear myself say in a much steadier voice than I'd have thought possible.

"My dear Evie, always rescuing her prince from his own lack of forethought."

"Someone has to, Cousin," laughs Iker, rising to his feet while Malvina snatches the goods from my arms. Immediately, she bustles behind Nik, spearing the beautiful layers of fondant with the fat ends of the tapers. No thank-you from her, even though for anyone else, her trained manners would require it.

Nik begins the song before they're all lit. His voice soars above us all, even over Iker's baritone. As usual, I just mouth along to the words—my singing voice was ruined the day I lost Anna. Tante Hansa says I'm lucky that is all the sea took. Nik has his eyes shut and isn't even facing his cake, the flames flickering and twisting behind him, manipulated by a strong wind from deep within the Øresund Strait.

My gaze follows the wind into the dark distance. Just past the edge of our wake, the indigo skies go pitch-black, the furrowed edges of an angry line of clouds moving in at a furious pace.

"Iker," I breathe.

". . . *Hun skal leve højt hurra . . .*" Nik hits the final line of the traditional birthday song and turns to blow out the candles, opening his eyes just as the first of the fireworks shoots off from the beach. Bursts of white and red stream across the sky in quick succession, illuminating Havnestad below and the ring of mountains surrounding the city proper.

"Iker," I repeat, my eyes still upon the clouds closing in. He turns, hand still set heavily about my waist, and I point to the storm line as a tendril of lightning strikes the water just beyond the confines of the harbor.

A flash of recognition hits his eyes as they read the distance between the rain and the ship. "Storm!" he yells, a clap of thunder cutting off the end of the word. "Everyone belowdecks! Now!"

But, of course, our party turns toward the storm rather than away, human curiosity flying in the face of safety. Iker, Nik, and I rush into motion as the first fat drops of rain splatter onto the deck.

Nik begins directing the crowd belowdecks. Iker is up at the wheel, working to right the ship toward the harbor after sending its previous driver—the coal man—down below to feed the steam engine.

With the rain already sheeting, the boat tips as I climb the stairs to the stern. I cling to the rail. There is no magic I can do in the open to stop this, which makes me grateful to be the salt of the sea and the daughter of a fisherman. I'm not helpless in the least.

Thunder rumbles deep and rich directly overhead. The cake's candles and the lanterns ringing the ship have been blown out by the blustery wind, and I'm thankful when a flash of lightning cracks across the sky just long enough to show me the scene.

Iker—getting the boat going in the right direction, his feet planted and muscles straining.

Nik—trudging up the stairs after barring the door down below, his crown of lemons fed to the sea by the flying wind.

The cake—tipped over and beached on its massive side as the boat lurches starboard.

Another clap of thunder sounds as I reach Iker and help him hold the wheel. Iker is strong enough to steer it by himself, but the boat's line noticeably straightens when I help him maintain control.

"A birthday pleasure cruise!" Iker yells across the booming skies as I smile at him through clenched teeth. His eyes dance even as every tendon in his neck strains to keep our course. "All clear skies and fancy drinks. Isn't that what Nik promised?"

Muscles already screaming, we both focus on the lighthouse at the edge of the harbor, still minutes away. A heavy wave crashes along the deck, taking the remainder of the cake with it. Nik manages to hold tight to the stair railing, his white dress shirt plastered against his skin.

"We're too slow," Iker yells into my ear between peals of thunder.

I nod and grit my teeth further as a gust of wind pulls the ship portside, yanking the wheel with it. "I've got it," I say. "But we won't go any faster unless—" I nod toward his prized craft, a present from his father.

Iker nods, heeding my suggestion. "Nik!" he yells over the whipping wind and angry waves. "My schooner! Help me cut it loose!"

Somehow Nik hears him and immediately pulls himself portside, where Iker's little boat is adding too much weight.

Another wave tips up the ship, sending us starboard. Boots sliding, I manage to keep us steady, pinning the wheel in place with all my weight. On the main deck, Nik has made his way over to the portside rail. He hooks one long arm around the rail to steady himself, and then works furiously with his free hand on my knot. Iker is on his way there.

The boat lurches again, and I close my eyes, willing land to get closer. When my eyes open, we might be closer to Havnestad's docks, but only by a few feet. I twist my head to the side and see that Nik nearly has the knot free.

A whitecap splashes over the side, drenching Nik. He shakes his head, wavy hair splaying out to the side. He rights himself, the slick railing and new floorboards doing him no favors in traction or leverage. With one final pull, the rope is completely loose, and slides over the side of the ship. Nik, much stronger than he looks, hangs on as the steamer's equilibrium changes with the loss of Iker's schooner.

"Three hundred yards to the royal dock!" Iker yells, making his way to the wheel. I look from Nik back to land. The lighthouse is indeed finally closing in, the blaze atop the tower looming just below the steely thatch of clouds.

But not as fast as the biggest wave we've seen yet.

Black as the sky above, the wall of water splashes hard on the portside, sending Nik to his knees. I call out for him to stay down—a lower center of gravity is safer—but my small voice is swallowed up in the storm.

He stands.

A charge of lightning rips across the sky.

The ship tips, pulled down with the weight of the wave, rocking Nik headfirst into the deep.

4

"NIK!"

I scream his name as loudly as I can. The boat rights itself, but there's no sign of him along the portside. Only wet wood and sea foam where he once was.

"NIK!" I wail again and let go of the wheel, passing Iker and sprinting toward the stairs to the main deck.

My mind moves faster than my wind-battered body, a string of thoughts running together in the murk as I dash forward, not caring or paying attention to the wind, the rain, the course, or even Iker.

No.

You CANNOT have him, you wicked sea.

Your mermaids will have to take someone else.

Nik belongs to me.

"Evie!" Iker yells. "Don't! Come back! It's not—"

"NIK!" I lunge down the stairs. The deck boards are

slick under my boots, but I race to the spot where Nik fell. The wind whips my curls about my face as I squint through the rain and night at the churning sea below. "NIK!"

I yell his name over and over, my voice becoming raw and weak, to the point where it's barely a whisper. Finally, we reach the royal dock. I drop onto the wood before Iker and the coal man even have time to anchor. I scan the horizon for any sign of a long arm, a flop of hair, or a piece of boot.

Iker heaves himself over the railing and onto the dock next to me, leaving the coal man to free the rest of the passengers from the captain's quarters. "Evie," he says, his voice much calmer than it should be—the sea captain in him overruling his bloodline. "Look there." He points to just this side of the horizon, where the stars have returned, unhidden by the clouds. "The storm's almost over. Nik's a strong swimmer."

I nod, my hopes pinned on the reason in his eyes. "But we still need to find him," I say. Everything my father taught me about the sea kicks in, and I point to a spot in the churning waves. "We were about there." I move my outstretched fingers in a sloping line in the direction of the wind, following the line until it lands on the cove side of Havnestad Beach. "Which means he will most likely be . . . there."

I don't look to Iker for confirmation—I just take off

down the dock, tear onto the sand, and race across the shoreline in that direction.

"Nik!" I choke, my voice still raspy and hopeless against the wind. Iker is on my heels for a few strides and then ahead of me in a few more.

Havnestad Cove is part jutting rock, part silty beach. There's a rolling W shape to it, and a few large boulders form footstep islands toward its center, before the waters become too deep. In good weather, it's a beautiful escape from the rest of the harbor. In bad weather, it's a hurricane in a birdbath.

Iker points to the biggest island—Picnic Rock. "I'm going there to see what I can."

The wind is already calming, the rain tapering off. Even the lightning seems to be behind us, disappearing with the storm into the mountains. The swiftness of such a powerful storm confounds me. The magic in my blood prickles at the strangeness, but I have no time to think of things beyond this world.

I tilt my chin toward a mass of rocks farther along the shore, the point that makes the W by jutting deep into the middle of the cove. It's just tall enough that it blinds us from the remainder of the beach.

"I'll climb up there and take a look on the other side."

"Wait!" Iker says, his face weary. For once, he doesn't seem to know what to say. He reaches his hand through my hair and pulls me close. My heart is pounding.

"Iker, we ca—" The words are whispers on my tongue—
that we can't delay, that he shouldn't slow me down—when
he tips my chin up and his lips are on mine.

I breathe him in, long and deep, and for a moment
we're not on a gritty beach, soaked to the bone, searching
for Nik. We're somewhere far from here. A place where
class, title—none of that matters. Somewhere that surely
doesn't exist outside of this instant. Another trick of the
gods.

He pulls back, and I'm stunned still, staring into his
cool eyes.

"Be careful," he says.

Shaken back to reality, I pick up my waterlogged skirts
and run along the coastline to the wall of stone. The swift
clouds have almost reached their end, their tail nearly
directly above the cove entrance. Starry night reigns above
the massive sea beyond, calm waters with it. My eyes are
constantly scanning the waves, looking for any sign of Nik.

But there's nothing.

I steal a glance back at Iker. He's already made it to
Picnic Rock, hoisting himself up. I breathe a sigh of relief
that the stormy churn didn't wash him away and turn back
to the approaching boulder just steps ahead.

I've climbed this giant rock hundreds of times since
childhood, as have most of Havnestad's youth. I know
the placement of the fingerholds with my eyes shut; my
boots automatically drift to the perfect places to wedge

themselves before taking another step up. The rain has all but stopped now, and the crag of stone is mostly damp, not slick.

I lug myself on top and scan the waters again, squinting at every irregularity, struggling to use the limited moonlight to make out what is yet another coastal rock and what might be Nik. I close my eyes, dread piling at my feet as I pivot toward the hidden portion of the cove. When my eyes spring open, I have to blink again to make sure my mind isn't playing tricks. A flash of bright-white fabric swims on the distant sandy line.

My heart swells with hope. I scramble down the rock and onto the other side of the beach. My feet work overtime to propel my body forward as the wet sand swallows my boots with each step.

Lightning radiates over the mountains, illuminating the sky for a flash—long enough for my brain to register the outline of Nik's body against the sand.

And the form of a girl hovering over him.

"NIK!" I yell, my voice coming back to me.

In response comes Iker's baritone from behind, "Evie!"

But I don't wait for him. I don't even turn in Iker's direction, keeping my eyes only on Nik and the girl leaning over him, her body still mostly submerged. Without another stroke of lightning, I can't make out much more than her long, long hair—so long it drapes over the white of Nik's shirt.

The girl's head tilts up in the moonlight as if she's just now noticed me running toward her at full speed. The lightning returns in a burst, and though my legs keep moving, my heart skids to a stop.

Large blue eyes. Butter-blond curls. Creamy flush of skin.

It's the girl. The one from the porthole.

Anna?

No, it can't be.

Recognition seems to fill the girl's eyes, and her features skip from contented calm to a pure rush of panic. Panic that sends her straight into motion. A gust of wind pushes her hair over the curve of her shoulder as she takes one hasty and last glance at Nik's face before heaving herself fully into the water.

"Wait!" I yell as best I can, but it's useless with her ears deep under the waves.

In less than a breath, I get to Nik and crash to the sand next to him, pulling his chest to mine, my ear to his mouth. A rush of air from his lips touches my cheek as Iker yells both our names from behind.

Nik's lungs work in great rasps, but they work. His eyes are closed, but he seems to be conscious.

"Evie . . ."

"I'm here, Nik. I'm here."

A ghost of a smile touches his lips. "Evie . . . keep singing, Evie."

Confused, I begin correcting him. "Nik, I'm not—I don't . . ."

My mouth goes dry. I scan the waters for any sign of the girl. The girl who looks like Anna all grown up. The girl who must like to sing the way my friend did as a child.

At first, there's still nothing. Just ever-calming waves and starry night, backlit by the summer solstice moon.

But then, just at the edge of the cove, I see it.

Blond hair gone silver under the clear moon, peeking up for a swift moment before the girl dives back underwater. A trail of sea spray flies up in her wake—and with it comes something more.

The perfect outline of a tail fin.

FOUR YEARS BEFORE

The sun was out, as fierce and as hot as possible in Havnestad. It wasn't as fierce or hot as it is in other places, but memorable to those in the mild-mannered Øresund Kingdoms, much more accustomed to Mother Nature's cold shoulder than her steamy smile, though it was the height of summer.

Two girls, one with waves of blond, one with curls of black, pranced along the shoreline. Their voices lifted toward the naked June sun, carried aloft by a deep wind from within the strait.

A boy, already as tall as a man, trailed them, piccolo to his lips, writing a tune for the girls' merry lyrics.

Despite the sun, the main beach was clear, the majority of Havnestad hauling fish and hunting whales at sea, the bustle of a modern economy weathering a boom. They would flood the shores with catch and tales soon enough, returning that night for the days-long Lithasblot festival and the midsummer full moon. For now, the whole stretch of sand belonged to the two girls and their boy.

The waves, heavy and exuberant, churned in the strong wind, tossing themselves at the girls' ankles—bare without anyone there to correct them. The boy's boots were on—his feet were gangly and hairy in a way they hadn't been last summer, and he didn't want the girls to see. He stayed on dry sand, just beyond the waves' reach, coal-dark eyes pinned on the girls' delicate toes, which also seemed to have changed in a year, but only maybe in the way he couldn't look away from the flash of skin beneath their skirts.

They went on like that until the girls suddenly stopped—singing, prancing, everything—so suddenly that the boy bumped into the raven-curled girl's back. She laughed it off, but both girls' eyes were locked on the sea. Watching the whitecaps with wonder, adventure flashing in their eyes.

The one with the blond waves and ocean-blue eyes spoke first. "She's angry—foaming at the mouth."

"Are you calling the sea a rabid dog?" asked the raven-haired one. "She wouldn't like that much."

"I suppose not."

A black brow pitched above eyes blue like midnight. "Touch the sandbar and return to shore?" She smiled, lips pinned in a slight twist. "Dare you."

The blond girl considered it, chewing on her lip, reading the waves. Finally, in answer, she began unlacing her dress's bodice.

The boy sat on the sand behind the girls, playing the piccolo so they'd think he was distracted, not paying an inch of attention to them as they stripped to their petticoats. Even in surreptitious glances, their shoulders and arms were things of beauty, smooth as the marble statues his mother had commissioned for the tulip garden. So beautiful they made his cheeks hot. He knew he should not look—it wasn't right, not at the age they were getting to be—but still, he watched.

The blond girl watched back, her eyes finding him, cheeks pinking as her clothes fell to the sand. The raven-curled girl thwacked her on the shoulder, dark eyes big and knowing. No secrets between friends, except those in plain sight.

When the girls were ready, they stood, dresses neatly folded, and pointed slim fingers toward the sea.

On the count of three, they were gone.

5

I DON'T BELIEVE IN MERMAIDS. I DON'T. THEY ARE JUST an abomination ancients like Tante Hansa dream up to keep children from doing especially dim-witted things. *If you touch that hot pot . . . if you eat that whole cake . . . if you take that candy . . . the mermaids will steal you away.* We're superstitious, children of the sea, but we're not gullible.

Mermaids don't exist.

But I know what I saw. I know *who* I saw.

Nik, for his part, doesn't seem to remember much. He thinks I rescued him. He thinks I sang to him.

It's been more than a day, and I still haven't told him that he's lost his mind if he thinks that's what happened. Mostly because I don't have an answer to what really did. None of it makes any sense.

No, I don't believe in mermaids.

But I do have a strong belief in friendship—more than anything in this world.

I believed it with Anna.

And I believe it with Nik.

Iker—I don't know what to think of Iker, though he's standing right before me on the royal dock, borrowed crew packing a borrowed ship behind him.

"Come—the sea calls." Iker brushes away a few of my curls and cups his hand about my ear as if to amplify the sea's ancient voice. He leans down, his cheek brushing right against mine, his lips warm next to my skin as he whispers, "Evelynnnnn."

His enthusiasm makes my heart skip, and I wish I could go, but Father is leaving this morning as well, and he hates the idea of me being aboard a different ship while he is at sea too. He's superstitious to a fault, even if it's just for a quick trip up the Jutland and back before Sankt Hans Aften and the opening of the Lithasblot festival. Iker is enchanted by sightings of a large whale—one that would feed Rigeby Bay for weeks in both meals and trade. I hate it, but I know Iker must go—the seafaring season waits for no one, not even a prince.

"I'm so very sorry to disappoint," I say. And I am. This time with him has been strangely magical, even if all we've done is sit with Nik, telling stories to make him smile as he recovers.

"Too late, the sea is already disappointed—your skills during the storm were top-notch. You're a sailor she needs upon her waves." His eyes flash, the curve of his mouth serious. Vulnerable, even, as strange as that is. But I don't—I can't—let myself think that it's he who needs me and not the sea. Reality doesn't work that way.

"The sea will have to wait."

"And so will I." He bends down to kiss me then, and though it's the second time, it's still a shock—a deep dive into ice-capped waters.

"You don't have to go," I say when we part, my voice small and slurred.

"What's that?" he says, pretending not to have heard. "You don't have to stay?"

He grabs my hand in both of his and begins to tug me toward the ship, full of crew waiting for his instruction. "Splendid, let's get going—you steer; I'll sip portvin and keep an eye out for the whale."

I laugh and let him tug me a little farther up the gangplank than I should. In my heart, I don't believe in Father's superstitions. And yet I have superstitions of my own. Nik is still recovering. I can't leave. What if he took a turn for the worse while I was gone?

No, I must stay.

Iker will come back. He says he will.

I know he will.

Something changed that night on the steamer. More

during the storm than in the huddled moments before—we'd seen each other in our element. The salt of the sea, the both of us. And despite choosing to stay, it is the very last thing I want Nik to know about. Most especially the kissing. But it shouldn't be too hard to keep a secret from my best friend—after all, I've been keeping my magic from Nik his whole life.

I step down from the gangplank and onto the dock. With a wave and a shout to his crew, Iker is off, taking our secret leagues away as I tuck it deep within me. I watch as he leaves the harbor, standing there just long enough to glimpse him turning back, my hand ready to wave. And then I set out for one more good-bye and my daily duties, Tante Hansa's amethyst heavy in my pocket.

No, I don't believe in mermaids. But I am willing to believe in whatever it is that happens when I kiss the amethyst to the bow of my father's ship before an expedition. What happens when I cast the spell I created using centuries-old magical wisdom.

It's only been a few weeks, but already it has worked, bringing in far more catch than by this time last year. I smile when I see the fishermen celebrating on the docks now. After four years of suffering through the Tørhed, a barrenness so severe the town's fishing fleet decreased by half, these hearty cheers are welcome sounds. I haven't heard them since before Anna's death; the grumbles from tired fishermen coming ashore to restock on salted meat and limes have filled our ears instead.

After three years of the Tørhed, King Asger knew that praying to the gods was no longer enough. Havnestad had to find a new way to stay afloat. The royal steamship was ordered, and any man not at sea was put to work building the boat from late summer to first frost, shaping wood, and fitting sheets of metal to the smokestack.

But even that ship, hammered together by the strength of this fine town, was not enough to keep all of Havnestad's bellies fed. The steamer was a one-time measure. Even the crown can't afford a new ship every year.

I had to do something.

So, as I've done since the summer of Anna's death, I stole into Tante Hansa's room while she was off playing her weekly turn of whist down at Fru Agnata's shack. Hansa's bedroom is a stifling place, with the fire lit every night, even in the summer. Dried roses line the walls in a ring as high as she can reach—the hundreds of them a testament to her belief that their scent and beauty are superior to the tulips so popular throughout the Øresund Kingdoms.

Beneath the line of roses, in a corner opposite the flue, there's a sea chest draped in shadow and an ancient moose hide. Inside is everything the Øldenburgs fear, all they have banished by law: gemstones, age-stained books, cobalt bottles sealed with pinches of cork and wax. The very same items Tante Hansa used on me when I resurfaced in Nik's arms four years ago, Anna nowhere to be found. When I'd been in bed, nearly dead myself, watched over by Hansa and spoon-fed elixirs tasting of perfume and age. And aged they certainly are, passed down in shadow generations for centuries. Someday they will belong to me, I suppose.

That day I took a purple stone—one so small that I hoped it would escape Hansa's notice, but big enough to have an impact. I snagged one of the tattered books with crumbling spines, too, fishing it out from where it was packed under a cake of beeswax and a marble mortar and pestle.

Hours after lights out, I crept down to the beach, but well beyond Havnestad Cove. As the shoreline thins, becoming one with the rocky mountain, sharp boulders jut out from the sea. The water is deeper there and the waves choppy, but in between the shadow of two large rocks is a swath of sand. Overhead, stone from the edge of Havnestad has formed into a perfect arch, the result of Urda coaxing the sea into this crevice for thousands of years.

This place doesn't have a name, as far as I know. I've never seen anyone come here, and it's hidden from view on the beach and by the boulders from the sea. I've taken to calling it Greta's Lagoon, after my mother. She would have liked a place like this. Deep in the shadows of the lagoon is a small cave barely large enough to fit two, but it's plenty big to store the few tinctures and inks Tante Hansa has entrusted to me.

I moved away the few small boulders I use to hide the entrance and lit a candle. With the amethyst stone cradled in one hand, I slid the book under the meager light. The words were ancient and yet familiar, recalling our great goddess, Urda, and the power she bestows on the land and sea. As the waves splashed against the rocks outside, I read the scrawl over and over, swirling the spells across my tongue. It took until nearly daylight, but finally I could feel the magic tingle in my blood.

After nearly three months of practice, I spelled Father's boat for the first time.

Three days after that, he came home with his first whale in more than two years. It was thin, but fat enough for all the joy that came with it.

Now the spell is a must.

The need to keep Father safe and prosperous is thick in my veins each morning when I wake, jamming my heart with anxiety until I can do my job. My part.

Even when I've done my duty and he's away for days, I come to the harbor and spell any ship docked and still. The fishermen are used to seeing me daily now. They don't seem to find it strange that I'm always there, letting my closed palm trail along the salt-worn bodies of ships, old and trusty.

And today is the day I begin to do more. Along with what I *cannot* claim, I have been working away on something I *can*. Something all of Havnestad will recognize as helpful and not some fate of Urda.

"Evie, my girl!" Father is hauling a crate up to the deck of his whaler—*Little Greta*, also named for my mother. There isn't a single crate of supplies left on the dock beside the ship. I've only just caught him. "I wasn't sure you'd come."

I laugh lightly, fingers tight over the gem in my palm. "Just because I want you to stay doesn't mean I'll miss you going."

Father's mouth settles into a tart line, the sun spots marring his forehead crinkling up to his black hair—he's Italian by birth, though he's Danish through and through.

We walk up the gangplank together. He drops the crate two feet from the innovation I know will make these desolate seas that much easier to fish—a permanent cure my magic cannot provide. Mounted proudly to the mainmast, half-harpoon, half-rifle, my darting gun looks as shiny and perfect as I'd hoped.

Father hugs me close. "My Evelyn, the inventor."

"It was nothing," I say, though we both know that's not true. It took me the whole winter to create one from an old rifle and modified harpoon, but if my calculations are correct, the contraption will send out both a bomb lance and a tether harpoon, narrowing the chances of a whale escaping. If all goes well with Father's maiden voyage, we might be able to transform the way Havnestad snags its whales.

"It's not nothing. It'll be a revolution."

I tilt my face up to his, brow raised. "It'll still be a

revolution if you wait a week."

Father bristles at the sore spot between us. He's not the only fisherman headed out during the festival, though far more are staying than leaving, bolstered by their recent luck—my recent help. But he's the only one I care about. And, as the royal fisherman, he's the only one King Asger cares about as well.

"There will be other Lithasblot festivals, Evelyn. If you've been pelted with bread once, you've been pelted with bread a thousandfold."

"But—"

He cuts me off with rough fingers on the point of my chin.

"But nothing. I have to seize my luck while it's there." Father's grizzled old thumb settles on my bottom lip. "I'll return for the close of the festival—the ball."

Despite my disappointment at yet another good-bye, I form a tight smile after his words. "If you've seen me once in my only nice dress, you've seen me a thousandfold."

He leans in and gives me a quick kiss on the cheek, his beard both soft and rough against my skin.

"Take care of Hansa, my dear."

I hug him to my chest, the cloying scent of pipe tobacco catching in my lungs.

"If only she'd allow such a thing, I would."

He releases me with a single squeeze of my forearm. I turn for the gangplank, one last look at both him and my first stab at whaling innovation. When I'm back on the sun-ruined wood of the dock, Father yells for his men to hoist up the gangplank and anchor.

Before he's gone, and with the sailors distracted by departure duties, I take my chance and press my little stone to the ship, right under my mother's name, painted in block letters across the stern. My eyes flutter to a close, and I whisper my spell into the breeze coming in off the Øresund Strait.

6

IT'S A PERFECT NIGHT FOR BURNING WITCHES.

That's what Sankt Hans Aften is, after all. A celebration in the name of ridding people like me from this earth through flames, drowning, banishment—whatever seemed right at the time.

Today, thankfully, witches are only burned in effigy. It's the traditional opening of Havnestad's version of Lithasblot. Ours is the earliest in the Øresund Strait, but we're also the longest festival, five whole days, drawing people from all around to watch the games, sing songs in celebration of Urda, and taste plates of tvøst og spik: black whale meat, pink blubber, and sunny potatoes. Even through the Tørhed, the people of Havnestad have always been willing to sacrifice their limited food supply to honor the goddess.

As the bonfire grows hot, shooting tendrils of flames high into the salmon-toned sky, the festival is ready to begin. First is King Asger's speech of love and gamesmanship.

Now Nik's speech of love and gamesmanship.

For on the night of that treacherous storm, Nik, thankfully, still came of age. And as tradition demands, he must take the reins of the festival—near-drowning is not an excuse.

Thus, since regaining most of his strength, he's been shut away, pacing the halls of the palace with his father's words on his lips. I've heard him run through it twice—before his birthday and after, and both times he was excellent, if not a hair too fast. Still, that's just because this is new to him. I know he'll be amazing.

But Crown Prince Asger Niklas Bryniulf Øldenburg III, first in line to the throne of the sovereign kingdom of Havnestad, does not share my assessment.

Nik is nearly white with nerves. His long fingers shake as he tugs his hair flat. This day is already hard for the both of us—the fourth anniversary of Anna's drowning—and with the pressure of the speech added atop that, Nik looks as if he might keel over.

I don't hesitate to snag a hand and press my fingers around his. Somehow, seeing him so nervous calms my own reservations—about my innovation's trial run with Father, about the fact Iker has yet to arrive. I squeeze Nik's fingers. "You've done nothing but practice for the past week. You'll be just fine."

"But I'm not cut out for this, Evie."

"Of course you are! You're cut from the Øldenburg cloth. Kings for a thousand years." I lean in, my face consuming his vision. "This speech is in your blood."

Nik turns red and averts his gaze. "I think that particular blood spilled out of me when I bashed my leg on that rock at ten."

I nearly laugh, thinking of Nik passing out at the sight of his own blood. Right in the middle of a trail leading up Lille Bjerg Pass. Anna and I stripped off our stockings and tied them tightly above the gash across his shin before bracing him between us and hobbling down the mountain.

"Think of your birthday. You didn't seem at all nervous while you sang on a bench with lemons in your hair."

"That wasn't the whole kingdom. This is."

"So? What's a few more faces?"

He lets out a very royal snort. "Since when does a 'few' mean a hundred times more? And maybe my disastrous birthday is not the best image to calm my nerves."

"Oh, don't be dramatic."

Nik cocks a brow. "Oh, but you're not plenty dramatic when you make moon eyes at the harbor, scouting for a certain sailor from Rigeby Bay?"

I say nothing, my wit tied to a stone in the pit of my stomach. Despite myself, I squint out at the water, my heart willing Iker's boat to appear. But the sea beyond the harbor is clear, all the visiting ships and off-duty whalers already in port.

Nik sighs, and I know he's beating himself up for such a quip—and again I'm thankful he knows nothing of the kisses Iker and I shared. He squeezes me close again, the nervous tremble subdued. "He'll be here. Iker makes his own rules, but he never breaks his word."

That was the last thing he said to me before Queen Charlotte pulled him away for his final speech preparations. I sink to the sand and sit, a little doll in my lap dressed in black and white. Ready for the ashes. I can barely force myself to play along. And without Nik by my side, this year I play along alone.

I suppose I *could* join the castle workers—I've known them since I was a small child. But I'm not truly one of them. And the other girls my age? Well, they're never really an option—they've made that much clear over the years.

Maybe banishment wouldn't be such a bad thing—I could just break out my magic as we burn our little witch dolls and leave this place for good. But then I'd leave Nik for good too. And implicate my entire family.

So, I sit alone—the secret witch, the prince's friend who doesn't know her place.

I am well within eyeshot of Nik as he readies to speak—in the event that his courage has retreated up Lille

Bjerg Pass—but far enough to the side that I have a clear view of the sea in my periphery.

He will come.

He said he would.

You shouldn't care anyway.

I turn my attention back to the royal family. And to the flames I must face before Nik's big moment.

There's a traditional speech honoring this "celebration" too. And though the king may have ceded his duties to Nik, Queen Charlotte would never give up her chance to speak out against the horrors of witchcraft.

The queen is a beauty by any measure, all fine bone structure and swanlike grace. Her hair is curled and coiled atop her head, a deep blond halo around a crown of sapphires and diamonds. When she steps forward in the sand, she looks every bit a painting in the firelight.

In her hands is her ceremonial first doll—clothed in blood red.

As if the death of every Dane in the past six hundred years was the fault of a witch.

As if the Øldenburgs hadn't burned hundreds of women with flimsy proof.

As if "the witch hunter king," King Christian IV, hadn't been proud of the name he earned and of the lives he ruined.

"Good evening, dear ones." Queen Charlotte smiles to the crowd, and it's like ice cracking under pressure. "On this night, we not only celebrate the beginning of Havnestad's Lithasblot, but we remember the hardships endured by our ancestors."

In the shadows, my knuckles turn white as I clench the doll in my lap. This part is almost worse than tossing a replica of myself into the fire.

"We live in safety and harmony in the Øresund Kingdoms because of the courage of King Christian IV. We live in safety and harmony because of the laws he put in place. Witchcraft has no place except in the depths of hell."

The queen hoists the red doll above her head so hard its little witch's hat falls, the fire sucking it into the flames. "Shall there be any devils on our shores, know you do not belong here nor in this world." I swear her eyes find me in this moment. "The light will win, and you shall be swallowed deep into the flames and returned to your horned maker."

The crowd erupts, and Queen Charlotte spins on the spot, tossing the witch into the bonfire—royally ousting us because our power is a threat to her own.

We are to form an orderly line circling the fire, but I can't do that. I won't do that. Instead, I stand and toss my doll over the heads of those charging forward, eager to murder little wooden models of me. My mother. My aunt. My father's family.

I look for Nik then, who follows suit with a smile on his face. Somewhere Tante Hansa is laughing, her distinctive cackle hitting my ear. I know it's a ruse to protect us, but I don't know how she can pretend to enjoy it so much. She even goes so far as to have the most colorful doll, meddling with pastes and dyes until she can ensure its little outfit will be the brightest on the beach. This year, hers is a stunning orange, thanks to a customer who unknowingly added to her fun by paying her in turmeric.

It's ironic: the same townspeople who come to her when they burn their skin, grateful for her ancient medicinal treatments, turn little wooden replicas of our ancestors to ash each year on this date. And she just laughs in their faces like it's nothing. As hundreds rush the fire, I sink back down to the sand and wipe my hands on my skirts. It's just sweat, but it almost feels like blood.

When every last witch has been tossed, the crowd retreats. Nik has stepped a measure in front of his parents to the most prominent spot on the sand, the bonfire at his back. Even in the ochre light, his skin is unnaturally pale. I make my gaze as heavy and focused as possible, not even so much as blinking until he catches my eye. I give him a smile and a nod.

You'll be splendid.

His lips curl up, and he clears his throat with a deep breath.

"Good people of Havnestad, welcome to the opening night of Lithasblot, when we honor Urda and give thanks for her blessings and bounty, be it from the sea or from land."

The fire crackles happily behind him, the tallest flames licking at the stars. Despite the crush of people, only that crackle and the lapping of the sea fills in the practiced pause in the traditional speech. We all know it by heart—and could join Nik in its recital, if it were appropriate. Most days, he's one of us. Just Nik. But tonight he's our crown prince, and our duty as subjects outweighs our familiarity.

So we are quiet.

Nik glances up at his pause and meets my eye again. I nod him forward even though his color has suddenly returned.

"These next four days are a celebration. Games, races, songs, and feasts in our goddess's name. Let us not forget that it is all for her. It is fun. It is merry. But it has a utility—a reason. Urda."

There is an audible gasp in the crowd—Nik has gone off script. He's speaking from the heart, and I couldn't be prouder.

"Last year, we did the same as we will do this week," Nik goes on, his voice gathering strength. "We pelted our thinnest with bread. We sang to Urda. We watched as I carried the heaviest rock down the beach."

At this, he flexes a bicep and flashes a smile—all his

nerves replaced with bravado. A few chuckles carry through the crowd, but there is only one heavy guffaw—issued by Tante Hansa, from her corner at the table reserved for the ancients.

Nik rounds on her with a pronounced grin and then pulls his brows together. His tone swings back to serious. "Yes, I am aware my scrawny feats of strength are quite hysterical. But those are on display daily"—he grins again—"and they are not why we do this year after year. We do this for Urda. And some years she teaches us a lesson and reminds us of her power."

Nik pauses, the air heavy and silent. Not even the bonfire dares to crackle.

"My father stood on this exact spot a year ago and recited the very same speech he has said for thirty years. Which his father before him recited for thirty years before that. Yet we were in the thick of the Tørhed—the third year running. And did it improve when we came together to sing songs about Urda until our voices were rough and fingers bleeding on our guitarens? No. Did it improve when I defeated all you weaklings in the rock carry? No."

Only Tante Hansa is brave enough to cackle this time. But no one turns her way. All eyes are on our crown prince. Even the king and queen are hanging on his every word.

"Let us remember that though we celebrate her, Urda owes us not a morsel. Just like the tide that laps our shores—her tide, her shores—she can take as swiftly as she can give."

Nik pauses, his coal-dark eyes on the harbor over our heads. I realize he's referencing Anna too. Honoring her as something Urda claimed for her own, the sea doing the goddess's bidding.

"So, let us honor Urda this week, not just celebrate her name, but truly honor her. She is our queen—forgive me, Mother. The land that gives us bounty. The sea that brings us our supper as much as coins in our pocket. She is more than a goddess—she is us. Havnestad. And all the people within it. Without her, we are nothing. No magic can trick her. No words can ply her. No will can sway her. She is queen, and we are simply her subjects."

He comes to a full stop, eyes on the waves beyond the crowd, posture firm and tall—regal.

Perhaps stunned by his originality and honesty, it takes the whole of Havnestad a few moments to process that he's finished. I stand and begin to cheer and clap. Nik's eyes find me, and there's a wink of relief that brushes across his features before my view of him is blocked—every last person leaping to their feet, hoots at their lips and applause gone wild. And somehow it feels as if he's leagues away.

7

It's impossible to see him after that.

All the people want to shake his hand. Tell him how awed they are by his thoughtfulness. About how poised he was. How kingly he sounded. How impressed they were and are.

Nik is swallowed by their affections.

And though I wait on the beach for him to resurface, he doesn't. Whisked away for the night in a crowd of his subjects. Every other creature eventually peters out for the night too. A rush and then a trickle in exit until it's just me, a hot pile of kindling, and a few poor souls who have lost the battle of alertness to free hvidtøl and a patch of soft sand.

I stand, legs stiff in my boots, eyes toward the harbor, breathing in the sharp, salty air. My throat tightens and tears threaten my eyes.

He's going to be king, Evie.

I want to laugh at my foolishness for thinking I'd always have him. Of course everything is going to change.

The moon is so bright that I can see the length of the beach without any other aid. Too bright for my dark mood, but maybe a walk will do me good. Clear my head. I should be happy for him, after all.

I make my way down the docks first, taking the worn planks in careful steps as ships large and small clank and bump at the sea's discretion.

Naturally, the royal dock is the largest in the harbor— with room for the king's giant steamer, my father's craft, and a dozen other royal ships, boats, schooners, and skiffs. There's a pole at the end that is empty, though—the spot where the king's steamship should be.

I stare at the water there for a moment, wishing for the second time tonight that his boat would materialize among the gentle rolling waves. Just suddenly appear with Iker aboard, a shine in his eyes and laughter on his lips. That he'd jump off the bow before anchoring, not able to hold himself back from me a moment longer. That he'd pull me in deeply into his arms for another kiss.

I blink and the thought has vanished.

The pole is still untethered.

There is not a single ship on the horizon.

I step off the dock, my back to the waves that took Anna, my head and heart throbbing with the wish that she would return, too. That I'd have my friend back. That I wouldn't feel the need to pin my hopes on boys who I should've known all along would only care about me until they hit that invisible line in the sand—blood—and then let me down. Though maybe, being highborn, Anna would've felt the same way.

I am too restless to run home to bed. To nod and smile at Hansa's drunken tale of her grand evening with her grand friends—as if those friends didn't just burn thousands of *us*. So I walk along the water to the cove side, the moonlight guiding my steps, catching on the shimmering flecks of sand to create a brilliant path along the shoreline.

I don't have a plan, and I don't need one. I just need a chance to wear myself out enough that I fall asleep unencumbered by the sadness dragging my heart down to my ankles.

I do have friends who aren't royal. I do.

I have the kids from school who tolerate me for Nik's sake, but only really when their prince is around. But for the most part, all I see when I greet their faces is the disapproval reflected in their eyes.

That girl—couldn't save her mother.

That girl—lived while her best friend drowned.

That girl—thinks her father's job gives her keys to the castle.

That girl—thinks herself more than a passing fancy for the playboy prince.

I meet the first rocks of the cove and stand there, letting the salt air toss my curls about my face. The wind here always seems so cleansing—like it sweeps away grime both physical and mental with one exhale from the Øresund Strait.

Tonight the cove is calm. The waves lap gently about the shore, kissing both the sand and the rock formations with the same delicate precision. There is no one else in sight, and this dress isn't anything special—nothing I have is special—so I yank off my boots and stockings and place them carefully on a patch of beach not likely to be touched by the tide. The sand sticking to my toes, I hop onto the first footstep island and leap from stone to stone until I make it to Picnic Rock.

Though it's damp from the recent high tide, the slab isn't so wet it's uncomfortable. I gather my skirts, pull my knees to my chest, and sit there with my eyes closed, letting the sea's charge wash over me.

Finally, my heartbeat slows, and I can feel exhaustion creeping in. But I can't sleep here. I force myself to stand on stiff legs and grab my things. There's barely a breeze, but a tingle runs up my spine. I cross my arms over my chest, but I can't get rid of the cold. I squint into the night, at the shadow where the sea meets the rock formation splitting the cove, when I swear I see a flash of white skin.

"Hello?" I call, my body shivering.

Only the wind answers, gently gaining strength from well past the harbor and deep within the sea.

I am suddenly awake, and I turn my attention again to the rock wall. But there's nothing to see but shadow and waves.

Maybe it was the octopus who's made the cove his home, taunting me the same way he taunts Tante Hansa, who would like nothing more than to bottle every last drop of his ink.

But probably not. My eyes are playing tricks on me again.

Just as they must have on Nik's birthday.

"Perhaps you need to avoid the cove when the moon is strong, Evelyn," I mutter. The moon can do funny things to a witch.

I can hear it now, another strain in the chorus of pity: *That girl—seeing apparitions in the moonlight.*

FOUR YEARS BEFORE

The boy heard the splashes, one right after another, and stood, piccolo forgotten, eyes only on the sea. He held his breath, waiting for the first one to surface. They were both strong swimmers, but the raven-curled girl made a habit of winning.

It was a hundred yards to the sandbar. A worthy swim on any day, but as the boy surveyed the sea again, he knew this was not just any sea. These were not just any waves.

The sea was angry.

The boy held his breath and took a step toward the water, careful not to get too close—his mother had often lectured him on the damage salt water could do to his fine leather boots.

The blond girl surfaced first. She pulled in a deep breath and then went back under, the sandbar in her sights, still seventy-five yards away.

The boy scanned the water for dark hair. Took a breath. Squinted right at the spot where she should've surfaced. Still nothing.

The blonde bobbed up again. Now ten yards closer to the sandbar and not looking back.

No dark hair to be seen.

He took another step forward. A wave took full advantage and marked his foot. On reflex, he glanced down. Yes, the leather was completely soaked. But he didn't care. Eyes immediately back on the sea. Heart pounding. The wet boot already coming off.

There. In the distance, thirty yards out. Not the crown of a raven-haired head.

A single hand, reaching for air.

The boy dove in, full breath cinched in his lungs, and opened his eyes. Nothing but the murky deep and the sting of salt.

Thinking of the girls, of the hand, he surfaced early. He would keep his stroke above the waves, his head close to the surface. He was a strong swimmer, and his new height had not diminished his natural strength, but the undertow was fiercer than he'd ever felt, constantly tugging at his pant legs. A force from the deep pulling him toward the harem of mermaids all Havnestad children were told lived at the bottom of the sea.

At the surface, he saw nothing. Not a strand of hair, nor a flash of hand. But he knew where they were. He knew where he must go.

Twenty more yards and he opened his eyes to the sea again. Looked down. Where the undertow had pulled him.

Black hair curled up like a cloud of ink, pale fingers stretched toward him. Her face hidden. He dove, hoping it wasn't too late.

Lungs burning for air, he surfaced, one arm hooked under her shoulders. The force of the swim had pushed the curls from her face. Her features bordered on blue, and he couldn't tell if she was breathing.

All he knew was that he had her.

"Come on, Evie. Come on." He prayed to the old gods as well as the Lutheran one when he had the breath, his body fighting the tow for them both, the shoreline distant but in his sights.

Moving forward, he turned his head as much as the weight and struggle would allow, hoping for a flash of blond safely at the sandbar.

He saw nothing.

On the shore, he called as loud as he could for help. He set Evie on the sand, brushing back her curls, ear to her mouth.

No breath.

He rolled her over and pounded on her back. Salt water streamed from her lips and nose, dribbling onto the beach.

People came then. Men from the docks, women from the sea lane. They crowded around, speaking in whispered tones about the girl. They never had nice things to say about her, even with her this way.

The boy told the men that there was one more. Pointed them toward the sandbar and empty waves. Barked orders of rescue. The men listened. Because of the boy's name.

The boy blew air into the girl's lungs and pounded her on the back again, moving her hair out of the way to make more impact. More water came forth, this time in a great gush, along with the rasp of a breath.

Her eyes blinked open, dark and worn.

"Nik?"

"Yes! Evie, yes!"

Smiling briefly, he hugged her close then, even if it was inappropriate, with her bare-shouldered in her petticoat and him a prince. But he didn't care because she was alive. Evie was alive.

"Anna?" she asked.

They turned their eyes to the sea.

8

HAVNESTAD THRUMS WITH ENERGY.

The brightness of summer and the thrill of Urda's festival combine to create the kind of charge one usually witnesses with a coming storm. It has me up early, feeling light and free after such a black night.

As I walk down to the harbor, amethyst in my pocket, I see Nik's carriage pass by. I wave my hand, but I can't tell if he's seen me. He's surely headed into the valley to visit the farmers in his father's stead, a Lithasblot tradition. We give thanks to Urda but also to those who work our fields.

The ships in port are empty, but I run my closed palm along their lengths, spelling them though they won't be headed anywhere this day or the next. On a morning as glorious as this one, it is not hard to conjure the words for Urda, yet I can't help but think back to Nik's speech. *No magic can trick her. No words can ply her. No will can sway her.* Is my spell a trick? A panic suddenly seizes me. My heart beats fast and my feet feel like lead. The dock begins to spin before my eyes. Is this my punishment? I close my eyes to right my balance. I'm being silly. My magic is not meant to deceive. My words are intended to honor Urda, honor her sea. Bring life. Surely she knows that. My heart rate starts to slow and I leave the docks. I need a distraction.

Nik isn't supposed to return from the farms until midafternoon, and while the streets will soon be alive with festival visitors, the real party doesn't get started until suppertime, when Nik will have to judge the livestock. So I walk down Market Street and gather a late breakfast, paid for on Father's account—fat strawberries, a stinky half-wedge of samsø, a jar of pickled herring we call slid, and a crusty loaf of rye bread so dense it could pass as a sea stone—and return to the Havnestad Cove.

It's quiet here, just a few couples trailing along the rocks, none taking any notice of me. I remove my shoes and stockings and place them in the same spot as yesterday, and I hop between the smaller footstep islands to the big one, Picnic Rock earning its name yet again. The strong sun and calm tide has made the rock almost completely dry, so I lie on my back, face to the sky, and shut my eyes.

Though I don't want it to, my mind shifts to Iker. He still hasn't returned. I am already anxious, and the same panicky feeling quickly returns.

What if something's gone wrong?

What if the steam stack exploded?

What if the whale crashed into the ship's hull upon capture?

Am I at fault?

I know I'm being ridiculous, but worst of all, we would never know. All of us are here, for once our eyes inward instead of turned to the sea.

That sends my mind into a downward spiral about Father, and then suddenly a shadow falls across the backs of my eyelids, the direct sun blotted out by a passing cloud. It's as if the weather worries too—

"Excuse me, miss?"

That voice.

My eyes pop open, searching for the face of a friend who I know in my heart is long gone.

But there, leaning over me, is the girl.

The girl from the porthole.

The one who rescued Nik.

Yet that can't be right, either. I really am losing my senses today.

I sit up and rapidly blink my eyes in the sun, but when they refocus, the same girl remains. She shifts back, long blond hair swinging.

Her face is like the singsong of her voice—so much like Anna's, but more mature. The smattering of freckles around her nose is familiar too. She wears a gown that's nicer than all of mine put together, and her shoes shine with new leather.

Shoes. Feet. No fin—she can't be what I saw. My stomach sinks, but I don't know why.

"This is quite embarrassing, but . . ." The girl's eyes fall to the strawberry in my hand. "I haven't eaten in more than a day."

I'm so stunned, I just hand over the strawberry. She isn't ready for it and bobbles it in her fingertips before taking a bite. I shove my whole meal toward her.

Anna loved cheese and fruit.

"Oh, no, you don't have to, I—"

"I insist," I say, and I'm surprised that's what comes out because there are so many other words on my tongue. So many questions. But I'm almost terrified to ask them because I know what word will fall out—*Anna*.

The girl eats, and I try to figure out what to say next.

Did you save Nik?

Were you a mermaid?

Are you Anna?

Don't you remember me?

All would make me run if I were her. So, as she chews a hunk of rye bread, I open the jar of slid.

"Do you feel better?" I ask.

"Yes, much. Thank you. I'm so sorry. I'm done."

I shake my head and tilt the open jar toward her, the

little herring bobbing in their brine. "Eat, please."

She sees the fish and recoils, waving her hands in front of her face. I pull out a herring and eat it myself, yanking the bones out by the tail before discarding them into the cove. She looks at me as if I've just bitten off her ear.

I used to do the same thing to Anna. She didn't like slid either. I smile, but on the inside, the sadness is suffocating. I have to stop looking for the dead in the living.

"Are you sure you aren't still hungry?" I try. "There's more cheese."

"No. I'll be fine." A sob swallows the word *fine*. Her brow furrows and the skin under her lashes reddens; there are no tears, but she looks exactly like she should be weeping.

My hand flies to her shoulder to comfort her. When the girl catches her breath, she begins talking again, her voice almost a whisper. She doesn't seem to mind me touching her. "I ran away from home."

"Oh, Anna—"

The girl's eyes fly to mine. "Annemette. How'd you—"

"I didn't . . . I just . . . you remind me of someone I used to know."

She coughs out a sob-laugh. "I wish I were that girl."

"No you don't," I say quickly as this girl—Annemette—wipes her nose.

"Was her father a liar? Weaving tales about where he's

been and what he's done, selling off all our livestock and not bringing a coin home?"

I shake my head because I don't know what to say.

"I've had to sell half our fine things to pay his debt and put food on the table. I couldn't take it anymore. I took off running over Lille Bjerg a day ago."

Her words are off. They seem forced. I can't help it—I stare at her face. I've seen thousands of faces since Anna failed to surface, but I've never seen one so similar. Never heard a voice with the same timbre. If I hadn't touched her, if this girl weren't clearly made of flesh and bone, I'd think she was a ghost.

She scrubs her face with her hands, nails clean and shaped. Her eyes blink open and then she takes my hands. "I'm terrible. Here I am, barging in on your breakfast, stealing your food, dumping my problems in your lap, and yet I haven't even asked your name."

"It's Evie," I reply.

"Evie," she repeats, testing my name out on her tongue. "British?"

"Evelyn, yes. My mother fell in love with the name in Brighton."

"I can see why." Annemette smiles, her teeth clean and straight, like that of a princess or a dairymaid.

I tell myself again that she's not Anna. She's not even the girl from the porthole or the beach or anywhere else. She's a farm girl from the other side of the pass. My cheeks grow hot. Annemette squeezes my hands. "Thank you for your generosity, Evie—it's a gift. Truly." Her eyes sting red again and her lip trembles. "I doubt I'll be so lucky again."

I don't know what to do with this openness. This odd feeling blooming in my stomach. "You really have nothing and nowhere to go?"

Annemette waves her hands across her body. "Only my clothes and my pride."

I can't explain this girl or my feelings or why I have the need to believe her, but I do. And I want to help. "Come with me."

9

THE LITTLE HOUSE THAT MY FATHER BUILT ISN'T THAT far from Havnestad Cove—it's practically waterside itself, the cottage at the end of a lane in the shadow of Øldenburg Castle. It backs up to a thatch of trees that buffer it from a rocky cliff jutting out into the sea.

"It's so quaint," Annemette says.

"It's home," I answer, and push through the front door. It's been a long time since I've introduced someone to our tiny cottage. When I was little, we'd often take in children while their parents were away at sea. But that stopped after Mother died.

At the hearth, Tante Hansa is stirring something—by the smell of it, most likely the ham-and-pea concoction she brings to every Lithasblot to place beside the roast hog we have on the second day of the festival. Because "there can never be enough swine in this sodden fish market."

Hansa's back is turned, and I feel the need to announce that we have company—it's never safe for a witch to have no warning.

"Tante Hansa, I'd like you to meet my new friend."

Hansa wipes her hands, and I know by the set of her shoulders she was stirring the soup without a spoon. Domestic spells aren't spectacular, but they're her favorites because she'd never planned on having a family of her own—and Father and I are more work than she'd like to admit.

When she turns, her face is pulled up in a smile, clear blue eyes flashing with the delight of catching me at something remotely unusual. Hansa is my mother's older sister by almost two decades, the time between them filled with brothers who lost their lives to the sea's moods much too young. She is as old as the grief of burying all her siblings suggests. But I have never been able to put anything past her.

Which means her reaction to Annemette is the same as mine. Only she actually says what she's thinking.

"Why, Anna, returned from the deep, have we?"

Annemette's mouth drops open as if she's lost her tongue, her jovial attitude gone as well.

"*Annemette*, Tante," I correct. "She's from the valley. A farm."

Hansa takes a step forward and raises a brow—quite the feat given the blood-drawing tightness of her hairdo.

"Is that so?" Hansa looks her up and down. "Those hands haven't seen a day of hard work in all your years. That fair face hasn't seen the sun. And that dress is worth more than the best cow in the valley." She takes a step forward and grabs Annemette's smooth hand. "Who are you really?"

"Tante, please, leave her be, she's had a rough trip—"

"Hush. You only see what you want to see." She turns back to Annemette, staring at the girl as if she could bend her will as easily as she tamed the soup. "So, again I ask—who are you really?"

Annemette's eyes have gone red around the rims again, but she doesn't cry. If anything, there's an edge of defiance in the cut of them. Like she's accepted Hansa's dare for what it is. But when she speaks, she says the last thing I'd expect.

"Your soup is boiling."

But the soup is more than boiling. The pea-green liquid hisses as it rolls in violent, unnatural waves over the iron pot's rim.

"Ah!" Hansa cackles. "I've seen your type before."

I'm stunned. *Her type?* Is Annemette a witch?

I stare at her.

Another witch. My age. Next to me.

Of all the things I can't believe about Annemette, this might be the most unfathomable.

Something cracks open in my chest as the secret we've

held so tightly as a family flies into the soupy air. I stare at this face so familiar and yet so strange, and my mind whirls. Anna was not a witch, but Annemette certainly is.

Annemette nods, and the liquid returns to a gentle simmer.

My aunt's spotted hands grasp Annemette's again, but this time there's a funny light in her eyes, all her skepticism gone. "Evie, child, you've made quite an interesting friend indeed."

It's a long while before Tante Hansa allows us to escape, having thoroughly quizzed Annemette on her family. In the funny way of things, we both claim lineage to the town of Ribe and Denmark's most famous witch, Maren Spliid. Tied to a ladder and thrown into a fire by King Christian IV 220 years ago, she became as much a lesson as a legend. Her talent was inspiring, but ultimately her audacity was her undoing. Her death and so many others under the witch-hunter king scattered Denmark's witches like ashes in the wind. And our kind never recovered—our covens fractured, magic kept to families and never shared.

Given the time and distance, it shouldn't be a surprise that there's more than one magical family in Havnestad related to Ribe and Maren, yet I still can't believe it. We've been alone for so long.

After Hansa is finally satisfied with her family tree, Annemette and I head outside. We walk into the woods behind the cottage, where we're shaded from every angle, including from Øldenburg Castle and its sweeping views, and start to pick our way down toward the sea.

The ground is covered in gnarled roots and branches, a danger for anyone not looking where they're going. But I know this steep path better than anyone, and I use this moment to steal another glance at Annemette. Her family may be from elsewhere, but her face still belongs here.

Anna did not have any magic in her blood, at least as far as I know. She had two "common" parents and a grand-mother who loved her more than the sun. Her parents left shortly after Anna's funeral. Took their titles and moved to the Jutland—miles and miles from this place and the daughter they lost. Her grandmother is still here, but she's gone senile with grief, the loss of her family too much for her mind. I see her at the bakeshop sometimes, and she calls every person there Anna. Even me.

"What?" Annemette says, catching me looking as we pass between twin trees, slick with sap.

I can't tell her what I'm thinking, but I do have ques-tions for her. "It's just . . . how did you know we were witches? If you'd been wrong, we could've reported you. You could've been banished."

She dips her head to avoid a branch. "I could just feel it."

Like Tante Hansa did.

"I must not be much of a witch," I say. "I couldn't tell. I

mean, now my blood won't stop singing, but an hour ago? No." There's so much I don't know about the magic in my bones.

"I'm sure you're a fine witch, Evie."

It's a nice thing to say, I suppose, but not necessarily true. Tante Hansa teaches me only the most mundane of spells. But I read her books and Mother's books, and I know there is so much more. With a few words and her will, Annemette brought out all that possibility into the open.

"How did you do that? The soup, I mean."

Annemette just shrugs and hooks a hand on a tree, swinging around it like a maypole ribbon. "It was just an animation spell," she says as if impressing Tante Hansa was nothing.

The ease, the comfort, the understanding she has about her magic makes my blood tingle with envy. It's so much of what I want. It took me months of studying and toying to create the spell to combat the Tørhed and even then, I'm not sure it actually works. My evidence is only anecdotal, and Fru Seraphine has taught me better than to use anecdotes as true measures of success.

In a few more steps we reach the sliver of rocky beach blind to Havnestad Cove, my own shortcut to Greta's Lagoon. I try to calm my heart from beating so loudly, but I've never gone to the lagoon in daylight and I'm nervous. I steal a glance up the beach. It's deserted as far as I can see, everyone off preparing for tonight's festivities.

"Careful," I say as we reach the end of the beach and the two large rocks. "The water is deep here."

I take off my stockings and shoes and wade in. As I reach the sand, I turn around, but she's still standing by the rocks. "Here," I say, wading back out and extending my arm. "Take my hand. I'll help you."

With tentative steps, she walks forward and grasps my hand tight. I smile at her. "Come on. It's okay."

Once we're in the right spot, I push aside the small boulders that obscure the entrance and steer her inside. Although it's daylight, the cave is still steeped in shadows. I light a candle. Various mundane tools hang from juts on the wall, and on the floor, oysters sweat in a bucket—my latest failure. On a ledge in the rock wall are my tinctures, bottles full of octopus and squid ink, jellyfish poison, and powdered crab shells.

"You've made a lair."

I laugh. "'Secret workshop' might be a more accurate term."

"Oh no, this is a lair." Annemette's hands move automatically to the ledge. She holds each bottle up to the light, admiring the slosh or swoosh of the contents.

Her boot nudges the oyster bucket. "And what are your plans for these little fellas?" She scoops one up and holds it in her hand as if it's a baby bird and not an endless source of frustration for me.

"They're barren, but I'd hoped to spell them into

producing pearls to be crushed for—" Annemette stops me cold with a wave of her hand. She mumbles something I don't understand under her breath, her eyes intent on the oyster in her palms.

Within moments, the oyster swells to a pink as vibrant as the sunset and springs open. Inside is the most gorgeous pearl, perfectly round with an opalescent shimmer.

"It's beautiful," I say, though the word doesn't do it justice. It's otherworldly, unnatural. I want to touch it, but I'm frightened of it all the same. It seems . . . alive.

Annemette's grin grows mischievous. "Too beautiful to crush, I think." With a simple Old Norse command— "*Fljóta*"—she sets the pearl afloat over her palm. Then, without saying a word, she commands a few lengths of thread—repurposed and therefore unspooled—from the nails on the wall. Next, she covers the thread and pearl with both hands, shielding from me the magic she's clearly working with her mind, her eyes set on her work. Seconds later, her hands part to reveal a perfect pearl necklace.

"Turn around and pull up your hair," she says.

I do as she says and she draws the thread around my neck, draping it so that the pearl lies at the base of my throat. I don't own any real jewelry and have never even tried any on, save for my mother's wedding band—Father keeps it tucked away in a little chest, along with letters and drawings and other tokens from their life together.

I touch the pearl and look up at her, but she is busy

working on another oyster and more string. After a few moments, Annemette ties her own pearl necklace around her throat.

"And now we match," she says.

My throat catches. I remember Anna saying those words to me that time we made necklaces from wooden beads the tailor was giving away. They were crude and childlike, yet still special. We promised to never take them off, but I couldn't bear to look at mine once Anna was gone. It's now in a small box underneath my bed.

I force a smile at Annemette. My pearl sits in cool repose against my neck, pulsing with vigor. It's a curious feeling that is not altogether pleasant, and I wonder if the pearl will always beat like this. Oddly, I find myself hoping that it will.

"Can you teach me?" I ask, the words spilling from my lips.

"What is there to teach? You're a witch, aren't you?"

"I . . . Tante Hansa hasn't taught me anything like that. Everything I know is like a recipe to make cheese—fail one segment and the whole thing falls to curd."

Annemette scrunches her nose. "It shouldn't be that hard." She picks up an oyster. "Here. Try. *Fljóta*."

Annemette sees the reluctance cross my face and tilts her head. "It's just a command. Say it with confidence and you'll have the magic do the work."

With hesitant fingers, I take the oyster in my hand. It's

as gray and barren as ever, and stinky, too, a tinge of rot to it. *"Fljóta."*

The oyster shakes in my fingers but doesn't lift. I can't seem to make that connection like I do when I spell Father's ship. There's something missing.

"You control the magic, Evie. It's yours. Take it."

There's a note in her voice that's like a jolt—like pushing me off the dock and into the water.

I square my shoulders and stare at the frustrating, rotting little thing. I feel my mother's blood deep inside me. The blood of Maren Spliid. The blood of the stregha hiding within my father's "common" façade. I feel the spirit of Urda, outside, inside, all around me, creating the natural energy we draw from. I spin these feelings with all the want inside me—the want to have the sort of power that could've saved Anna and my mother. The kind that can truly end the Tørhed for good, not just mask it with a daily spell. The kind that Annemette seems to have.

"Fljóta," I say with all that want. With the wound that lives deep in my belly from the day I lost Anna. The day I almost lost Nik too. When I wanted more than anything to use my magic to make it better.

The oyster hovers.

"Líf," Annemette whispers. Life. I should give it life.

"Líf," I command. The oyster begins to change colors, its gray shell warming to pink and then to the burnt orange of dawn.

The oyster grows hot. Hot enough to match its new lively color. Its warmth licks at my palm.

In a moment, the oyster pops open, the most perfect pearl at its center.

It's beautiful. Again, it's almost too beautiful to crush for the magical poultice I'd planned, but there's so much magic I now want to make with it.

Annemette laughs. "And that, my friend, is how you command the magic."

Although the spell is over, I can still feel the magic pulsing through my veins, a blue fire so hot, it's cold. It's unlike anything I've ever felt before. I don't want it to stop, but I know there's a danger in sipping from this feeling too long.

I set the oyster on the table I use for my inventions, fashioned from a piece of driftwood I found on the beach. It's littered with more bottles and vials, but I clear some space and hold the pearl in my fingers. Unlike the pearl Annemette made, this one is still warm to the touch, not icy hot. The magic responds differently to the two of us, I suppose—I don't know. But I want to learn.

It's time I really embrace who I am. Tante Hansa has kept me in the dark for too long. My mother was an established healer by my age.

"Annemette, will you stay and teach me?" I ask.

"I can't," she replies quickly, her mouth drawn tight, but trembling. She turns and braces her arms against the cave's opening, watching the tide come in and out.

But I don't understand. Why is Annemette so upset? Why must she suddenly leave?

"You *can* stay," I insist. "You're safe here from your father, and we have more than enough room. And you'll be with us. With a family that cares for you and *understands* you. You don't have to run away to find that. To be yourself."

Annemette meets my eyes with a look I know, and with every force of a Viking spell, she says it again.

"I can't."

She bends down and runs her hands through the sand, letting it fall between her fingers. "I can't stay here."

It's her. I can't deny it now. She's not trying to deny it either. The look she gave me is the one I saw on the beach. The one that I saw on the girl's face as she loomed over Nik. Before diving into the water and disappearing, only a tail fin popping up from the waves.

"You can't stay," I say.

She nods, her eyes nervous.

"You're not a witch, are you?"

She shakes her head no.

"You're a mermaid."

10

"HOW IS HE—THE BOY?" ANNEMETTE SWALLOWS HARD and takes a step toward me.

I instinctively take a step back, bumping into the table behind me and knocking a corked vial of octopus ink on its side. I'm not sure if it's Tante Hansa's old wives' tales telling me to run or the fact that Annemette is clearly more powerful than any folktale could have ever described. My hand reaches out and grasps the vial before it rolls and smashes to the floor. The pearl at my neck throbs. I want to leave, but her face looks pained, and I can see now that she's been holding this question in since she arrived.

I realize she's not here for me or my magic. She's here for Nik.

In my stunned silence, Annemette goes on. "Is he all right? He was breathing when I brought him ashore, but I didn't have time to—you came and then that man, and I had to go. I need him to be alive, Evie. Please, say something!"

I nod. "He's fine. You saved him." My throat tightens and tears sting my cheeks. If it wasn't for Annemette, I'd be dressed in mourning clothes. "He's totally healthy. Strapping. Probably milking a goat at this very moment!"

Annemette practically collapses in my arms. "Oh, thank goodness! When he fell into the sea, I caught him, but the tide and the storm was so strong, I—"

"Stop. I shouldn't know," I say. "You shouldn't say any more. It's too dangerous for me to—"

"But you aren't any more welcome here than I am," she says, pulling herself upright. "Your magic is just as forbidden as mine." And when my eyes meet hers and they're clear and hard, I realize we've made an exchange. A dangerous one.

I know her secret and she knows mine. Breaking this trust would ensure our mutual demise. I slip the vial of ink I'd been clutching into my dress pocket.

We will only survive our secrets together.

"I promise I won't say a thing," I assure her, a hint of regret in my voice.

"Thank you," she says. "My lips are sealed too." She weaves a slim finger through her blond hair, twisting a long wave into a curl. "What's his name—the boy?"

"Nik. His name is Nik. And he's my best friend. I'm so glad that you were there. I saw the wave too late, and he was gone." I realize for the first time that after saving Nik over and over again, even if it was only on the dance floor, there was nothing I could have done that night. That he'd have saved me from the sea, but I would have failed him. My smile falters and I look down to the gray oysters at our feet. "I wish I could repay you with more than a few scraps of food and a pearl necklace."

Annemette loops a finger in mine. It feels strange, too close, but I don't want to push her away. "I didn't do anything special," she says. "Mermaids are not the monsters you humans think we are. I could not just let him drown."

Drown. Like Anna did. Like I thought Anna did.

At this moment, Annemette looks so pretty. So innocent. She raises her eyes to meet mine.

"Would you like to meet him?" I ask.

"Please," she says.

~

We leave my "lair" and make our way back through the rocks, Annemette still nervous as she heads out first. So strange and sad to see a mermaid afraid of the sea. As I go, I pause in the water for a moment—I want to take a last look at the cave to make sure all is hidden—and that's when I feel them. At my feet, three dead minnows bounce between my ankle and the boulder—surely knocked out of the sea by a wild wave and smacked into the rocks. I shake my head, remembering the last time such fish floated at my feet, but I can't think of that day. Not now.

On the shore, Annemette and I dry off and put on our shoes. Then we head back up the trail through the forest. Once the trees spread out enough and we have room to walk side by side, I feel as if I can finally ask her more. "So, have you always been a mermaid?"

Annemette gives me a look. "Have you always been a girl?"

"Yes," I reply. "But you're no longer a mermaid. At least, I don't see a tail. Perhaps you weren't one from the start."

She laughs, and I almost draw back because she sounds just like Anna again. Our elbows bump as I check myself, wishing I'd just asked her directly what I wanted to know.

"Sorry to disappoint you," she says. "Born a mermaid, hopefully not forever one." She dances gracefully into an arabesque pose.

I stop walking. My brows pull together. My courage rises. "But is it possible, for a human to drown and become a merperson?"

She shakes her head and I reset.

"How long can you stay like that?"

Annemette glances down for a moment and then her eyes are up and locked with mine. "A few minutes," she says, her back leg still high in the air.

"No, I mean, how long can you stay *human*?"

Her eyes shift at the word. She stands up straight and stretches. "Not long," she says after a pause. "At least not as I am. But it depends."

"Depends on what?" I push back.

"I promise to tell you," she says, though I can see in her hesitation that she doesn't quite trust me. Her face turns pale and she almost looks scared—lost, even. "It's just that I have to see Nik first, or none of it will matter."

The little pearl pulses against my neck—*lif*. Her magic is strong, but good. She saved his life. The least I can do is make an introduction. I glance quickly at the sun on its descent toward the mountains. "We should get going. The Lithasblot festivities will start soon," I say. "It's our harvest festival. People come from all over. They've even heard of us in Copenhagen, I swear."

"Sounds fun," Annemette says. "And Nik will be there?"

I nod yes. If she tries anything, I have Tante Hansa's and my mother's magic in my blood. She grasps my hand tight.

"Let's go."

~

When we come upon the beach where tonight's festivities are, the palace staff and some local villagers are still setting up. We're a little early. The livestock stage is being nailed together, and a hundred or so people are milling about fixing decorations, laying out food, and tending the bonfire, where soon a giant hog will be trussed up on a spit.

"It's not Copenhagen, but it is a kingdom, I suppose.

As the sun goes down, the beach will be so full you can barely see a grain of sand."

"We have some pretty good parties on the sand where I come from too."

I laugh. "I'm sure you do."

Suddenly Annemette walks up to the fire and holds out her hands. I forget that she's never seen fire like this before.

"Whoa there, young lady," says Herre Olsen, the tailor, pushing Annemette back before I can get to her. "Any closer and you'll soon be roasting with the hog."

"Thank you," Annemette says with a curtsy. "I'm sorry."

"Who are you here with?" he asks.

"I'm visiting for the festival with—"

"Me," I interject, steering her away from the scowl on the tailor's face. "Thank you, Herre Olsen."

"We need to give you a better backstory," I whisper, guiding her toward the castle grounds.

The townspeople like to talk, especially about me, but the king and queen will need something substantial if their son is going to be seen speaking to her. A lowly girl without a house name is not good enough; I would know.

We decide to give her the title of a baron's daughter, the same title Anna had: *friherrinde*. A friherrinde from far away—Odense—come to see our unusual Lithasblot. Her chaperone has fallen ill, and Tante Hansa is tending to her.

I'm filling in as her chaperone and guide. Yes. It'll work. Another lie added to the list. I suppose there's some truth behind the town gossips whispering that I spread false-hoods, saying the prince should not trust me. But telling the truth to gain their approval is not a risk I'm willing to take.

"When will we see Nik?" Annemette asks, tired of reciting her story to me.

"Don't worry." I point to the giant stone monstrosity on the hill. "He's waiting for me up there."

Annemette follows my finger.

"Øldenburg Castle," I say. "Five hundred years old and as drafty as a sailboat."

I guide her to the queen's garden, which is rich with tulips of every color. Annemette proclaims each one the most beautiful thing she's ever seen until she gets to the next one. And the next. "I love to garden," she says.

Her mouth drops with a gasp when we get to the queen's pride and joy—statues of her family, each taller than a horse, circled up among the tulips. The king and queen are fashioned as they were on their wedding day, the marble smooth and glistening from the years. And there, next to them, is the latest version of Nik—eleven feet tall and chiseled as if lunging across the bow of a great sea vessel.

"Is that . . . *him*?"

She stands on her tippy toes, fingertips not even get-ting so far as his tastefully unbuttoned collar.

"Yes, yes, that's him."

"He looks different than I remember. Drier, I guess." She laughs.

We crest the steps and there, already waiting and watching Havnestad Harbor, is Nik. He's freshly washed after his trip to the farms, the light crown he's forced to wear for festival days pressed down over his wet hair. I always think he looks ridiculous all fancy in Havnestad's customary blue-and-gold suit, but Queen Charlotte is from the fjords up north and very traditional. She insists he emulate his official portrait for the high holidays of the Old Norse.

"Evie, there you are," he says, catching me first in his line of sight as he turns from the view. When his eyes land on Annemette, his face freezes on her features. All except his lips, which are still moving ever so slightly. "And you've brought a friend . . ."

I smile and guide her toward him. "Your Royal Highness, this is Friherrinde Annemette. Annemette, this is Crown Prince Niklas."

A light zips through Nik's eyes as he meets Annemette's gaze. At first I think that he recognizes her—that he instantly realizes she's the one who saved him. Or that he sees the old friend we lost, the first half of this girl's name ringing in his ears.

But almost immediately it's clear that he's thinking of neither, because he does something I've never seen before.

He blushes *hard*. Honest-to-Urda heat is rising in his cheeks, and it's so intense that he has to glance at me before looking down.

He thinks she's beautiful.

And she is—she's gorgeous—but this . . . this is unprecedented.

I'm ashamed to admit the pang of jealousy radiating in my chest. So often, I'm the only one who has Nik's attention, and he's never looked at me like *that*. But I suppose if he had, we wouldn't be friends. Is this how he feels when I'm with Iker? Ugh, I do not want to think about Iker. I smile at them both, standing awkwardly between them, wanting to run away but afraid for what might happen if I did.

"Enchanted," he says when the words finally kick in, the blush still hearty along his cheekbones. "How do you know Evie? I thought I knew all of her friends."

I cut in to answer him. "Her chaperone became ill on their trip from Odense. Tante Hansa is seeing to her. Annemette very much wanted to attend a proper Lithasblot festival, so I've become her guide." I touch her arm. "And meeting the crown prince is quite the way to start, isn't it, Annemette?"

She grins. "Yes, it most certainly is."

Nik's color begins to normalize, his training rushing in on a white horse to rescue him. His humor, too. "Well, I am quite the carnival show. Over six feet tall and solid muscle." He raises a wiry arm and pats the bicep. "I have a gaggle of followers trailing after me like ducklings, just so I can open sticky canning jars."

I wink at Annemette. "It's true; I'll have no one else open my troublesome jars." *There,* I'm being a good friend. To them both. I'm okay with this. Really, I am.

Annemette continues to smile but looks a little confused. She knows a lot about this world, but not so much that she might know a canning jar from a regular one. I smile at Nik and do my best to save her. "So, are there jars on the agenda at the moment, Crown Prince Niklas, or shall we go gawk at some livestock?"

"You really don't have to call me Crown Prince Niklas—just Nik," he says, eyes on Annemette. "Evie's just joking. I don't care much for titles." He touches his crown and then blushes again. "Crowns, either . . ."

Annemette nods. "What do you care for?"

"Music, mostly."

"I love to sing." I swallow as she says this, my eyes unable to see anything other than the friend she insists she's not. The girl who had the voice of an angel—ask anyone in Havnestad.

But rather than looking heartsick, Nik begins to blush again. A sheepish smile spreads across his face. "Then I shall use my princely power to borrow an instrument later and accompany you."

My stomach churns. This is perfect. Just perfect.

We stroll down the steps and into the garden. I see him duck away for a moment and pluck a pink tulip from the end of the row, where the queen won't notice it. Annemette dips down to smell her favorites.

I step away and watch as he strides up to her lowered form, flower behind his back. When she stands and turns, he pulls the pink tulip from where it's hidden and lowers into a slight, princely bow.

Annemette's mouth drops open into a wide smile and her eyes snap to his.

"Really? I can have it?"

"What good is being a prince if I can't pluck a tulip from my own garden?"

"Oh, thank you! This one is my favorite."

"You are most welcome, Annemette." Her fingers snatch it away, and she lifts it to her nose, inhaling deeply.

When her eyes open, I catch them and smile. "To the festival, shall we?"

11

NIK CHOKES DOWN WHAT MUST BE HIS TENTH spandauer, the flaky sweet pastry sticking to his lips. As we walk around the festival, Nik is stopped at practically every turn to taste each table's offerings. Whether it's cheeses both old and stinky, berries and stone fruit from the valley orchards, crusty breads of rye and barley, split-pea delicacies attempting to rival Hansa's famous soup, or the tables and tables of desserts, Nik is required to try them all. He assures the vendors that whatever he's just shoved down his gullet is the best in all of Havnestad, possibly in all of the Øresund Kingdoms.

"Save me, Evie," he grumbles after his last bite.

Why don't you ask her? I want to say as Annemette walks next to me, but instead I hand him my mother's handkerchief. "Take small bites and then use this."

My mood hasn't much improved, though I'm trying.

It helps that Annemette's porcelain face has gone gray, the seafood our town is known for churning her stomach. We pass by tables selling pitch-black whale meat and pale-pink blubber, lobster bright red and still warm from boiling, soft-fleshed crab, salty salmon roe, even slices of slow-roasted eel.

At the next table, Annemette grabs my hand and leans into my ear. "Why do you kill all the sea life if the other options are so vast?"

I shrug. "It's our way of life. Havnestad lives and dies by its nets and harpoons." I suppose I should be sympathetic, but it's hot, and all this stopping and going has made me even sourer.

Her brow furrows. "But there is so much else to eat."

She leans in, her whisper growing softer as Nik tries to shake off yet another local culinary wizard. "My father always tells us to stay far from the surface, scares us with tales of our kind being split in two by harpoons, talks about humans as the scourge of the seas, always hunting and killing. But this . . ."

"It's the way it is, Annemette," I say as gently as I would to a child. In some ways that is what she is, even if she's my age. The time she's been in my world can easily be measured in hours. "We are all surviving as best we can. We don't mean harm to the sea life, or the pig, or anything else."

"I was unprepared."

"I was unprepared to meet a mermaid today," I whisper, my words just an inch from her ear. "But I did."

She laughs into the falling night. Nik glances over at us, and I raise a brow at him and purse my lips. He grins at Annemette but then catches my eye again and I know he suspects I'm feeding her girl talk. And I'll just let him go ahead and think that.

Nik tears himself away from the latest onslaught, a plate thrust into his hand, fried torsk dripping with fresh fat, heat rising from its body, head still on, beady little fish eyes staring vacantly into space.

"Fru Ulla insists this is the best torsk in all of Havnestad—possibly all of Denmark, to hear her tell it. If you seek a true Lithasblot experience, Annemette, this is where to start."

I touch the plate and press it toward his chest, where it is safely out of the way. "She doesn't eat fish."

Nik laughs. "Who doesn't eat fish? We're Danes—"

"Allergy," I say. "If she has fish, she'll blow up like one of those French flying balloons."

"It is terrible," Annemette says, coming to life and puffing out her cheeks.

The questions die on Nik's lips. Without hesitation, he drops the plate into the open hands of a chubby little boy, who grins wide-eyed and then hurries after his family. "Then it will be my sworn duty to protect you from Havnestad's affinity for sea life."

Annemette's eyes skip to mine and then back to Nik's in one swift motion. "The brave crown prince you are, indeed."

Long after the fire has died down and the largest bull from Aleksander Jessen's farm has been crowned this year's winner, Nik, Annemette, and I sit on the end of the royal dock, eyes on the ocean and music in the air.

Nik plays a basic rhythm on the guitaren and Annemette chooses the words—picking old sailors' songs that they apparently know under the sea as well as we do on land. This one is their play on "Come, All Ye Sailors Bold."

"The king trusts to his sailors bold, and we shall find them as of old—for father, mother, sisters, wives, we're ready now to risk our lives . . ."

I sit beside them with my eyes on the waves, surprisingly enjoying the clear quality of Annemette's voice. It's as beautiful as Anna's ever was, rich and high, with a lovely air of innocence built into the base of each note.

"For Danish girls with eyes so blue, we'll do all that sailors do. And Dannébrog upon our masts, shall float as long as this world lasts . . ."

They are sitting so close together that the fold of her skirt is touching his trousers. Neither seems to mind, and if anything, they drift closer as the minutes pass. I am on

Nik's other side, and with each song, laugh, and snippet of conversation, the gap of roughhewn dock grows between us.

While I'm glad that Nik is happy and that Annemette seems to have found what she was looking for, I can't shake this gray cloud of self-pity, engulfing me like a fog descending on the harbor. It was so easy for Annemette to make that connection with Nik, and no one thought anything of it. There were smiles all around as they walked arm in arm, each townsperson remarking on her beauty, how nice they looked together. I stalked beside them. The chaperone.

I know in this moment that I will never find what they have if I stay in Havnestad. I merely speak to anyone outside my station and there are calls to lock me up in the brig. I wish Iker were here, but it's clear that even if he is by my side, it'll always just be a childhood fantasy. He may not care what the others think when he's with me, but when it comes down to it, he'll marry a highborn daughter, and that will be that. I will be alone again.

If only Anna were here. The true Anna. Maybe things would be different.

The tune comes to a natural end, Nik and Annemette falling into each other in a fit of laughter.

"You have the most lovely voice, Mette," he says, using a shortened version of her name I didn't know she preferred. I wonder when she told him to call her that. Or maybe he just did it, feeling an instant familiarity with her that I don't have.

"Much obliged, Nik." She bends at the waist. A sitting curtsy. That's a new one.

"We must do this again tomorrow, Mette. Please tell me you will be here tomorrow."

"Yes, yes, of course I will be." Annemette's face beams in the moonlight.

"Excellent. Shall I send a coach round to your room in the morning? Where are you staying?"

"With me," I say, the lie we planned ready. "Her chaperone is quite ill."

Nik's brows furrow with concern, or maybe it's doubt. He grows quiet for a moment, and I'd wish he'd speak.

"But then Mette might grow ill," he says finally, and I release the breath I didn't know I was holding. "And you too, Evie. You both can stay at the palace. I insist." He turns to me, grin in place, though my face must reflect sheer shock. We're best friends, but the line in the sand between us has always been the palace. I've never stayed there—Queen Charlotte even sent me home the night he nearly drowned. "I'll message Hansa and have your trunks brought round."

No. That won't work. Because then he'll know Annemette has no trunk—she has nothing but the clothes on her back. "No worries, I'll get them!" I blurt. "Hansa is too busy to pack her things."

Nik nods, having gotten what he wanted, the trunks a mere formality.

Annemette grasps my hands and looks me in the eye. "Thank you," she says. There's a sincerity in her voice, tinged with desperation that I haven't heard since she first asked if Nik was alive.

Right. She saved him, and she came here to see him. She had her reasons.

I could kick myself for being so petulant and bitter all night, even if only I noticed. But at least I, too, have achieved my aim. Repaying her good deed with their introduction. And it seems to be worth a lot to her. To both of them. Yet still my stomach flutters, the dock moving as if I'm adrift past the strait, alone on the open sea.

12

I DON'T WANT QUESTIONS. I JUST WANT TO GET UP TO the castle before the queen finds out about Nik's invitation. Our lie about Annemette's noble heritage passed Nik's scrutiny, but he wanted to believe us. His mother, well, I wouldn't put it past her to know the name of every noble this side of Prussia.

At the cottage, I blow through the entryway like I'll hurtle through the back window, through the trees, and off the cliff, but at the last moment, I veer down the hall and into my bedroom.

My grand entry does not escape Tante Hansa, despite the fact that she was surely deep in her thoughts as she distilled octopus ink by candlelight.

"Was that a tempest or my sister's child bursting through the house?" she asks, coming down the hall.

I ignore her, shutting my door before plowing through

my chest of drawers for all the proper pieces of a wardrobe—stays, undergarments, stockings, boots, dress. I shove in the latest book of magic I stole from Hansa's library—*Myths of Maritime*—too. There might be something in there about mermaids that would be worth a look.

Within a minute, Hansa opens the door. Immediately, her arms cross and her brows pull together. "You aren't going to smuggle your entire closet out in that trunk, my dear."

"Who said I was smuggling it?"

Tante Hansa takes a step forward, lips drawn into a perturbed line.

"The bloomers poking out the front."

Sure enough, the ruched ankle of an undergarment is sticking out of my trunk like a dead man's tongue.

Hansa tilts her head a bit, one brow now impossibly raised. "Are you going to tell me why you are rushing in and out of here with enough clothes for an entire week at sea? It wouldn't have to do with your new friend, would it?"

The thought skips to the front of my mind to tell her. If anyone would believe that Annemette is a mermaid, it would be Tante Hansa. But I can't tell.

"Well, child? Have you formed the perfect bluff in your pretty little head? You've had more than enough time."

"It's not a bluff. Nik's asked me to stay at the castle—Annemette, too."

That earns me an ancient Hansa chuckle. "His festival

duties have the boy in such a tizzy that he needs to sleep with moral support down the hall, does he?"

"Something like that," I say, though I know Tante Hansa isn't buying it.

The brow arches higher. "Are you certain that cad from Rigeby Bay hasn't arrived with promises on his lips and a night's lodging at the castle?"

Heat creeps up my cheeks.

In my dreams.

"Iker still hasn't arrived." *I'm not sure he will at all*, I add in my thoughts, but I manage to keep my features plain despite the pang I feel in my chest. "And Nik has requested my—our—presence tonight in his stead."

"Oh, he's *requested*, now, has he?" Tante Hansa peers down her long nose like a blue heron. "So princely after one canned speech that he's now *requesting* the presence of his little fish-rat friend?"

"You know Nik's not like that. Besides, *you* come when you're called—'Healer of Kings,' is it?"

"Don't make this about me, child. I know what *I'm* doing." She laughs again as I lug the chest toward the door. Annemette will be nearly finished with the grand tour by now. If Nik's been ratted out by a member of the staff, the queen won't go to bed without addressing him.

"Are you finished with me?" I take a step toward the door she's blocking.

"No, I'm not finished with you." She crosses her arms

for a moment, looking stern, but then backs away from the door, leaving a sliver for escape. "But you are just as stubborn as your mother, and if you fight me as long as she would have, I'll be in this doorway until dawn."

I take another step toward her and lean in as much as my belongings will allow, planting a kiss on her papery cheek.

"Good night, Tante Hansa."

I stride past her, past her smelly inks, and out the door. I'm not one step beyond the threshold when I hear her call, "Don't grant all the prince's requests, darling girl. Men are always asking for more than they should."

⁓

Though I'm not with Father on one of his fish deliveries, it seems too strange to walk through the main entrance of Øldenburg Castle. There are some things that are just not for me as a commoner. Malvina Christensen and her ilk might think I don't know my place, but I do. It's evident every day.

I'm angling through the tulip garden, the trunk dragging along at my feet, when I hear my name.

It's nearly midnight, but Queen Charlotte looks just as regal as ever, still in the full evening gown she wore at the festival, crown nestled in her perfectly styled hair. I catch Nik approaching behind her.

"Evelyn," says the queen, the distaste in her voice not hard to miss. "Niklas told me you'd be joining us." She eyes her son, and I know he had to fight for me to stay. "It was gracious of Friherrinde Annemette to suggest you stay in the same room."

"She's very gracious indeed, as are you for having us, Your Highness," I say. The queen nods as if I've passed a test—I know how she prefers to be praised.

"My pleasure," she says, and steps away. But then she pauses and turns. "Please stay within this wing."

I nod. Yes, I know my place.

Once the queen is gone, Nik rushes to my side.

"Let me help you."

"I've got it." But just as I say it, he's snuck a hand on either handle and hoisted the thing to his chest, as effortless as can be.

"You shouldn't. You're still recovering!"

"I'm fine. It's practice for the rock carry—I have to defend my title."

"Since when do you care about winning so much?" I goad him so we don't have to talk about his mother.

"Turns out a taste of victory is all I needed to care."

"Or the need to impress a girl. Speaking of . . . where is she?"

Nik takes a step toward the door, and I rush ahead of him to open it. "Mette was so enamored with her room; it was so sweet, I didn't want to disturb her. Besides, Mother . . ."

His voice trails off as a guard comes to help, taking the

trunk from Nik's hands. Nik grabs the edge of the door above my head, relieving me of my duty. For a moment, I stand there trying to read his face, because it's not as clear and open as I'm used to seeing. His emotions are all muddled, like Hansa's magical ink swirling across the surface of water.

Nik looks over at the guard. "Take her trunk to the Baroque Room, please, Oleg."

Oleg nods, and Nik pulls me back outside and onto the steps. He sits down on the top step, and I follow. His shoulder nestles next to mine and his voice is low.

"Apparently coming of age means more than giving speeches," he says without preamble, his eyes on his hands.

My heart starts pounding and my hand finds his shoulder. "Nik . . ."

"Mother is pleased because Annemette is the first of her 'girls' to arrive."

My mouth goes dry. I should've seen this coming—among so many other things these past few days. Annemette must have passed the queen's scrutiny, my aid unneeded.

"She had her ladies send letters to every high house in Denmark, inviting every princess, komtesse, and friherrinde to the Lithasblot Ball and God knows what else. Now that I'm sixteen, I should be courting, but Mother thought it wise to bring the girls to me."

"Oh, Nik—" I start, but then he stares up at me, and

the look in his eyes makes my throat catch.

"Lured them in with Iker's presence, too . . ."

Of course: the playboy prince, two years older, with brave tales of the sea. I bet every last girl with a title is on a steamer right now.

"Two princes for the price of one—we're the market special," he says. "No wonder Iker's still at sea."

He's careful to smile at his joke—he's trying to save my feelings. But I can't grin back, not even a little bit. I want so badly to turn to stone like the statues in his mother's garden. There must be a spell for that, no? At least then I wouldn't have this rot of disappointment creeping up inside me. It turns out knowing better doesn't always help. It makes it worse.

It's funny, though—maybe *funny* isn't the right word, but Nik and I are both trapped. I'll forever be the fisherman's daughter, caught in a web of whispers and lies spread by those too scared to open their eyes and see beyond what's in front of their faces. And Nik—he'll be locked in by royal traditions, forced into a loveless match with someone only out for the crown. Nik will always be in the shadow of the castle. And nothing I can do will save him from that.

Except, if the queen already believes Annemette's story, surely Annemette is better than these komtesses flocking to our shores. She does seem to make Nik happy. I know it's only been a day, but even I'll admit that I've never seen Nik smile as much as he has with her. It's not everything, but it's a start. And she's not after his crown. That I know. She genuinely cares. She *saved* him. Besides, it might serve us all well to finally have some magic in the palace, to perhaps bring an end to Queen Charlotte's brutal warnings and doll burnings. Maybe as a trusted friend to both the crown prince *and* princess, I wouldn't be relegated to the kitchen door. My family would not have to live in secret. If Annemette makes Nik truly happy, we can both be free. *Stop, Evie. You're getting ahead of yourself.* But a smile pulls on my lips all the same.

"Let's go inside," I say to him. "Everything will be okay. Annemette is waiting."

13

I WAKE IN THE BLUE LIGHT OF THE MORNING AND SIT straight up. I thought a night in the royal wing, on the most comfortable mattress I've ever slept on, would do me well, but it hasn't. I'm anxious.

I've smuggled a mermaid into the palace, for Urda's sake!

In the bed across the room, Annemette sleeps, a ruffle of blond waves piled about her face. One foot has escaped the bedspread, five toes stretching lazily toward the ceiling.

It's easy to forget that she's never slept in a bed before. I throw off the covers and tiptoe to my trunk, left by Oleg next to the double-sided wardrobe. And there, beneath my underthings, is the book I threw in at the last minute. Though the name isn't too suspect—*Myths of Maritime*—I suppose it's lucky we arrived so late in the evening that the maid couldn't unpack the trunk. I should've been more careful, though.

I crawl onto the plush red window seat and hold the book up to the new day's light, thumbing through the pages for anything about mermaids. I know all the lore from childhood, of course. I can still hear Tante Hansa's voice reciting the tales over the campfire.

Mermaids call sailors into storms, their siren songs and beauty too difficult to ignore. Probably a myth. Annemette is beautiful, but she didn't force Nik into the sea, and I'd be able to tell if she was using magic on him now. I think.

Then there's *Mermaids can conjure storms with a blink, sacrificing sailors to please the all-powerful sea.* I hope to Urda that this is not true. A shiver runs up my spine as I think of Father and Iker.

But the one that always made me and Anna scream was: *Mermaids steal naughty children and feed them to the sharks for protection.* Ha! I'll let Tante Hansa have that one. It kept me from making lots of unwise choices, though I suppose not nearly enough. If only Anna and I had truly listened.

None of this lore is easing my rattled nerves. The only positive mermaid tale I know is the one I saw with my own eyes: *A kind mermaid may swim you to shore.*

But there has to be more written about mermaids than a few childhood warnings.

After much reading, I finally find a section on

mermaids, following an intensive discussion of the kraken. It doesn't say much—there's just slightly more detail than the descriptions I know by heart. I focus in on one paragraph.

Accounts of mermaids at the surface often come with tales of rescue—the saved sailor opening his eyes just as the mermaid dives back into the waves. The maids are always described as staying within the water, unable to leave the sea completely.

That was exactly how it happened. Maybe there will be more on what happens next. I turn the page, expecting a section on a mermaid's ability to change into human form. But there is nothing. No description, no account, no guesses at all.

I stare at Annemette. She can't be the first mermaid to change into a person. She can't. It just must be so rare there's not an accurate tale to pass on.

Possibly feeling the weight of my eyes on her, Annemette shifts, her arms stretching high above her head. Her eyes blink open and she sees me watching her. I expect her to startle, to forget where she is and what she is, but she doesn't. Instead, she just yawns.

"I could get used to this." She rolls fully toward me. A slim finger points to her calf. "But is it normal that this part just aches? Burns. And my toes are . . . tingly."

"Pins and needles?" I offer.

"More like knives," she replies without hesitation. "But I'll be fine." She pushes herself up a little and yawns again.

I set my book between my nightdress and the windowpane. "Maybe it's a side effect. You know, of your transformation," I say. And now's my chance: "Have other mermaids ever turned into humans before?"

"I'm not the first," she replies. She stands and turns her back to me as she opens the wardrobe, revealing a closetful of dresses.

"Where'd those come from?" I ask, my mouth agape as I walk over to the wardrobe.

"I conjured them last night while you were sleeping."

I want to scold her for doing something so reckless, but they're incredible. Silk day dresses in pink, cerulean, and deep purple, each with little white collars and pearl buttons. I clutch at my necklace and wonder if those pearls pulse like mine. The evening gowns are even grander. Full skirts and long trains, gold embroidery, and even beading. They're going to think she is the wealthiest friherrinde in the whole region.

"Do you like?" she asks. "Hopefully they will do the trick."

I nod eagerly. "What trick?"

"Allowing me to stay," she says, clutching a Havnestad-blue dress with mother-of-pearl inlay. "Don't you want me to stay?"

"Of course I do, Mette," I say, trying out the nickname for the first time. And I realize I mean it. Not only so she can save Nik from his mother's misguided intentions, but to have a friend who knows magic, who knows the real me. I didn't know how much I wanted that until I met her. "How long do you have?" I ask, hoping she'll give me a real answer this time. "I want to help."

"The magic lasts four full days," she replies. "I have three left."

My face falls. "That's it?"

"But three days becomes forever if, before midnight on the final day, my true love has fallen for me, too."

Too.

Nik.

Forever.

"I love him, Evie. I really do." Annemette flops on the bed, no longer the shifty girl holding everything back. More like the girl I used to talk with about boys and gossip in her own grand room. "He's why I came back. I know he can love me. Didn't you see us last night?"

"But what if he doesn't?" I ask. She turns and stares out the window, out at the sea far below.

"What is it?" I come to her and sit on her bed. "Tell me, Mette."

She shakes her head and buries her face in her hands. When she responds, it's as if she's repeating something she read in a book—and maybe she is.

"To come to land in human form a mermaid must complete a magical contract—her life as a mermaid for four days on land." She pauses and shudders, her chest heaving slightly. "She may not return to the sea after those four days, for she can never again be a mermaid."

My stomach practically tumbles to my feet. "Wait . . . you *die*?" What kind of dark magic did she do? Nik is wonderful, amazing, the best guy I know—but to risk her life for someone she barely knows?

She sits up and nods. "I know. It's crazy. But you don't get it. He's what I've been missing. I knew he was mine when he fell into the sea. Into *my* arms. And to be human? Evie, you don't know how lucky you are."

I don't even know what to think. Of course I want her to live, and I want them both to be happy, but how can this work? Falling in love in four days seems . . . unrealistic, to say the least.

I temper my words carefully. "How can you tell when he truly loves you?"

Annemette's face goes dreamy again. "True love's kiss is all I need."

I almost laugh. Now it's unrealistic *and* ridiculous. So much so, I'm completely incredulous. "A kiss, really? Your life for a kiss? That's it? That's some magic."

"It's the feeling in the kiss. I'll know. The magic will know."

I think of Nik on the steps—enchanted, yes, but in

love? No. Not yet, anyway.

I walk back to the window seat. I need space to breathe, to think. If Annemette hadn't risked her life on this, I don't know how I'd feel if Nik really did fall in love in three days. The whole thing just feels wrong—her life depending on Nik somehow awakening powerful magic, simply by having enough love in his heart for a girl he's only just met. One I like, one he likes, one I'm forever grateful to. But I just don't know . . . there has to be another way to keep her alive without forcing Nik to *love* her.

When I look up, Annemette is rushing toward me. She squeezes onto the window seat beside me and takes my hands. The color has drained from her face.

"Evie . . . I'm not encroaching, am I?" Worry furrows her brow. "You were searching for him that night . . . he was waiting for you at the palace last evening. He isn't . . . ? You don't . . . ?"

"I'm not in love with Nik, and he's definitely not in love with me." I've had to say this exact phrase many times, most recently to Malvina. "We're just best friends."

She breathes out a sigh, hands fluttering as she smooths her hair. "You seem so close, and I didn't even question . . . you must think I'm horrible."

"Not at all! Nik and I have been inseparable for years." I struggle to make eye contact here, her closeness again overwhelming. "It's a common mistake."

Relief washes over her, and she sinks back against

the window seat cushions. "Do you have someone, then? Someone who makes your heart beat so hard you think it'll pound itself out?"

Iker's face flashes in my memory, a wide smile reaching the ice of his eyes. I bite my lip. "I do—I did. I don't know." Annemette is staring at me for more, so I reluctantly go on. "You saw him—the other boy on the beach that night." She nods in recognition. "Well, he's Nik's cousin, the crown prince of Rigeby Bay. But it doesn't matter, Mette. He's away at sea, and we have more pressing things to consider. *Three days . . .*"

"Oh, Evie, you're such a good friend," Annemette says, pulling me into an embrace.

Three days to fall in love. Three days to live. Three days until the ball every noble lady in the Øresund Kingdoms will attend. I shake my head. Finding true love is hard enough without the competition.

14

I DON'T KNOW HOW SHE ACTS SO CALM AS WE WALK down to meet Nik for breakfast. It must be the sea in her veins, flowing against the tide no matter what the weather. My entire body might as well be one giant bundle of nerves tied up in a sailor's knot on her behalf, but Annemette walks out onto the sun-drenched balcony off the third-floor ballroom looking as enchanting and confident as anyone could, her blue dress casting her eyes a deep ocean hue and her butter-blond hair shining in the sun.

We blink into the bright light and are met with a spectacular view of the harbor. I know our corner of the sea so well, but it's different from this angle, nearly the whole coast in sight. It's an empowering view, to be able to see all that you rule over. The current is moving faster than usual for this time of year, and I turn my back, not wanting to dredge up old memories.

"Good morning, ladies. Won't you have a seat?" Nik stands and pulls out the chair to his right. "Mette?"

Annemette blushes and takes the coveted place. I push my nerves down and greet him with a wink as he pulls out my chair. It's then that I see he's a bit red himself, that blush from last night back again at the sight of Annemette. Nik, the romantic. A good sign for sure.

True to his word of protecting Annemette from the evils of our seafaring diet, Nik asked the palace kitchens to avoid the traditional breakfast herring and traded up for summer sausage, sweet rolls dripping in fresh butter, and raspberries flush with dew. Served with it is black tea, hot and fragrant.

My stomach growls at the mere vision of all this food. It had been churning all morning, my anxiety getting the better of me. I am starving.

"Goodness, Evie. Do you have a tiger hidden in your bodice?" Nik laughs into the delicate china of his teacup.

"You know me, always smuggling wild animals to breakfast," I joke.

"I'd expect nothing less from your dark magic." Nik laughs again, and he has to put the cup back into the saucer to keep from spilling it over his shirt.

Meanwhile, Annemette can't hide her surprise. She stares at me, confused. After all that fuss I made about how we must keep our magic a secret here, the crown prince, of all people, is laughing over it.

"Nik should know better than to spread dangerous rumors like that." I gently elbow him. This is a game we play, Nik and I. Joking about the "magic" in my family—even if his joke is closer to the truth than he knows. "My tante, Hansa—"

"She turns men to toads and makes a soup out of them," Nik says, brows shooting dramatically under his hair. Annemette laughs, which only encourages him. "It's a great bit of luck you didn't have her pea soup last night."

Annemette's lips drop open.

"It's green for a reason." I wink at her.

Nik and I burst into a fit of laughter, and it feels good to relax. His fingers scramble to touch the bare skin at her wrist. Maybe this will work.

"We kid, Mette," Nik goes on. "Tante Hansa is a marvel of a medicine woman—she's saved my father a few times when our own doctor failed, and I'll never forget it. She'll take great care of your chaperone—but she can't turn men into toads." Annemette nods, a quizzical grin pulling up against her pink cheeks. Nik lowers his voice, conspiracy thick in his tone as he turns his back on me. "Though I wouldn't put it past the old bat to have curbed my cousin's playboy ways so that he might fall for her niece."

I elbow him again, this time quite hard, and both he and Annemette laugh. "If she has that magic, it's certainly gone awry, considering he didn't come for the festival," I say.

"Surely that's Iker's mistake," Nik says, snagging a sweet roll.

"I don't make mistakes, Cousin."

We glance up. Iker is standing in the threshold, his back propped casually against the doorframe. His skin is tan from days spent on deck in the high sun, making his hair seem more bleached than usual. He absentmindedly rubs at the scruff blurring the cut of his strong jaw, something I'm sure Queen Charlotte will insist he shave. I hope he declines.

My heart is beating in my throat as he looks over at me and our eyes meet. He grins.

Don't smile. Don't get up. He promised *he'd return days ago. Stay strong.*

I cave. A small smile creeps up on my lips and, in turn, his grin blooms larger. He strides over, and suddenly I'm afraid he's going to kiss me right there in front of everyone. In front of Nik. He pauses before me and bends down, his fingers grazing my chin as his face moves closer to mine.

Please don't.

Gods, I wish he would.

His lips land softly on my forehead. I breathe out a sigh, whether it's relief or disappointment, I don't know.

"Hello, Evelyn," he says, standing upright again. "I'm sorry I'm late."

Before I can say anything, he strides over to Nik, stealing the sweet roll straight out of his fingertips. "Hello,

Cousin. Glad to see you're looking so well," he says, then takes a bite of the roll.

Nik stands, and the two embrace. "Mother has been in a royal tizzy over your tardiness—I hope you found that king whale you were looking for."

"I wish," Iker replies, frustration echoing in his voice. It's unlike him not to get what he wants. "We chased him past the tip of the Jutland, but he's a slippery bastard."

"I suppose that's why he's named 'king,' Cousin."

Iker grins and claps Nik on the shoulder. "We are a slippery lot, aren't we? Always running to and from the call of duty."

"And you are forever running late in both directions."

"Nothing that can't be fixed with a grand entrance and a daring story."

I raise a brow. "That certainly is your life's motto." The words come out harder than I'd planned, and his smile stiffens in answer.

"I'd say it's worked well for me so far."

"You would," Nik says. He's now standing next to Annemette's chair, his hand grazing her shoulder. "But let it be, Cousin. I'd like you to meet Friherrinde Annemette."

Annemette stands and steps toward Iker. She holds out her hand like she's done this hundreds of times before. He takes her fingers in his and kisses them. "Lovely to meet you, Annemette. I daresay I would've remembered such a gorgeous girl from my travels in the Øresund. Tell me, where did you wash up from?"

My heart in my throat, I meet Annemette's eyes. He's just being kind, I know he is, but still.

"Odense," she says, clearly comfortable despite my heart flaring out my nostrils. "Evie and I met yesterday, and she agreed to show me around. Nik was game enough to join us."

"Who wouldn't be?" he replies. "I'd say yes in an instant." Iker smiles at her, but there's suspicion in his eyes. It's just a flash, but it's there—he doesn't even try to hide it. Nik and I both notice it before his cultivated manners return and he bows at Annemette. "I've traveled everywhere, and there are no two prettier girls in all the world than on this balcony."

Both Annemette and I immediately flush scarlet, the compliment the perfect Iker level of grandness. And, when I glance over, Nik is fiercely blushing too—his eyes have never left Annemette.

Iker's attention spins across the three of us.

"What?" I ask.

Then he shakes his head. "The lot of you won't survive your youth if you don't learn to take a compliment or ask for what you want."

Iker turns to Nik. "Cousin, clearly you can't keep your eyes off the girl. Why don't you ask the fine friherrinde to accompany you as you explore today's festivities? I'm sure there is plenty to learn about her."

Annemette turns to him, a lock of blond hair twisted around her finger. Nik lets out a nervous laugh.

Iker, not paying attention, goes on. "While you're doing that, Evie and I can walk through the gardens."

"Really?" I say. "Don't you think you should ask me first?"

"Forgive me, Evelyn. Would you do me the honor?"

I should say no. After all, what is the point? In a day's time, he'll be dancing with half the komtesses invited to the ball, one of whom will surely become his bride. But I can't help wanting what I want. I look up at Annemette, whose eyes are urging me to go. She needs this time too. Two magical creatures and two princes. I want to laugh. Maybe it's time I stopped accepting what all of Havnestad has deemed appropriate for a girl like me and started acting like the girl they already think I am.

"It would be my pleasure, Iker," I say, getting up from my chair.

Nik suddenly stands, looking very uncomfortable, ears turning red too. "Iker, I don't think that's a very good idea."

Iker's eyes brighten and then drop into the same suspicious glance he gave Annemette. He reads his cousin's face and posture, clearly trying to discern if this is about him being alone with me or about Nik being alone with Annemette or something else altogether. His words from the ship ring in my ears: *I don't like to step on my cousin's toes.*

"I'm not going to defile the girl, cousin, we're just going to have a kiss and catch up." Nik practically scoffs, but Iker just smiles. "Nothing we haven't done before."

Nik's eyes shoot to mine, and I know he knows. It doesn't take much for him to picture all of it—to picture me kissing Iker like all the other girls he leaves in his wake.

I glance down—I wish it wasn't like this. I just can't take Nik looking so hurt.

Iker makes it a point to raise his brows at Annemette, everything in the move suggesting Nik take his girl and be fine with it. A hope I have as well. The girl only has three days. Iker's arm slinks from my waist and hooks about my elbow. He leads me toward the door.

"Follow my lead, Cousin, but don't follow my footsteps."

~

The late morning light is blinding when we step out of the shadow of the castle and into the queen's tulip garden. We blink ourselves down the stone path, stumbling a bit until our eyes adjust, arms and legs momentarily touching—whether by accident or on purpose, only Urda knows.

It's sinking in. Iker is here.

He came back. And he immediately wanted to be with me.

All the disappointment and fears about what was keeping him seem to drain from my body. I try to push thoughts of Annemette to the side, too. *Not everyone is your responsibility, Evie*—Tante Hansa has told me this a thousand times. Annemette is alone with her prince, and I'm with mine.

After years of daydreams, my childhood fantasy is somehow now my reality: holding hands in a garden with Iker. Despite my status. Despite his. Despite the lives that are meant for us. A flash of heat runs up my neck, and my cheeks flush with embarrassment. Iker can never know how often I've thought of this.

But is this real? Am I stuck in dream? Or have I lost my mind completely, and Annemette is a figment of my imagination? Iker, too?

I wouldn't think him real at all if his arm weren't still slung about my waist, drawing me toward him, the two of us walking toward a stone bench beneath a shady oak.

Stop questioning, Evie.

Enjoy the spell while it lasts.

He smells of the sea. Of escape. And I want to be there with him, watching his skin go pink and then brown, whales in our sights and free wind in our hair. He turns to me, both hands about my waist now, face angled down toward mine. A smile curves at his lips as he reads my eyes.

"You were worried I wouldn't come," he says, and brushes a curl from my cheek.

I don't deny it.

"I ran into a problem of sorts," he says, eyes in the

middle distance, voice softening. "I lost one of my men. The sea snatched him overboard in broad daylight after we docked in Kalø. Spent the rest of the day and much of the next searching."

My breath catches. It's awful, though not unexpected on a whaling expedition. The resolute set to Iker's jaw mirrors that—disappointment but also acceptance. But then his gaze brightens and he goes on. "Eventually, we found him, floating unconscious between two rocks. Can you believe it? Barely breathing and beaten up, but alive. It was so strange, finding something you doubted could be possible."

A teasing note then enters his voice. "Just like you shouldn't have doubted me."

"I didn't doubt you. I doubted my expectations."

Iker raises a brow and his eyes are on my mouth. "And what were your expectations?"

"That you wanted to be here as much as I wanted you to be here."

At this, he draws me in until his chest touches my bodice and I can feel his legs through the layers of my dress.

"Don't doubt this."

He presses his mouth to mine, stealing my breath. He is gentle in that first moment, but then sweeps us down onto the bench.

The scent of salt and limes swirls about me as my heart

begins to pound hard enough that I'm sure he can feel it through my bodice and his shirt.

His hands move to my face, thumbs sweeping the curve of my jaw. He holds me there for a second before gently pulling away.

"Proof enough, Evelyn."

He says it as a statement, not a question, a sly little grin returning.

I purse my lips in thought. "Honestly, I'm not sure I've had a large enough sampling to be certain."

Iker's face breaks that sly little grin into something toothy and wolfish.

"I'm free for sampling all afternoon. Nothing princely planned until supper." He forces his features into serious composure. "Will that be enough time, my lady?"

I lean in and dust a quick kiss onto his lips. "It's certainly a start."

FOUR YEARS BEFORE

The visitor stood on the dock, parents fussing behind him, weary from travel, though the journey hadn't been far. Just across the Øresund Strait—a trip he could make with his eyes shut and in his own boat, if given the chance.

And he was planning to take that chance within the year, permission or not.

The day was clear, sun beating down, drying the wooden planks of the dock faster than the sea could make its mark, the waves angry the entire way from Rigeby Bay.

Footmen filed down from the castle, whisking away the visitor's parents, trunks, and duties, leaving him alone with the beach and his thoughts. At fourteen, those thoughts were mostly of girls.

Brunettes.

Blondes.

Redheads.

All of them swirling in his head despite what he knew to be true about his station—his mother and her metaphors constantly in his ear.

"Tulips wilt no matter their beauty; jewels of the crown shine forever."

"Blood lasts longer than a whim."

"The royal vase has room for but one flower, no matter the harvest."

His feet led him to the sand, eyes snagging on two girls prancing along the beach, slim forms moving in time with a song that barely reached his ears.

A few yards more and the girls stopped, eyes and fingers pointed toward a sandbar, belly up in the swirling waters. That's when he recognized them—two girls from the village, best friends always up for an adventure, just like he was, though he got the feeling the blonde was rather difficult to impress. Trailing behind them was a boy, his cousin. Another prince.

Then the girls began to remove their dresses, petticoats suddenly catching the sun's rays in all their angelic white.

He couldn't look away.

Not when they folded their dresses and laid them on the sand. Not when they sprinted into the waves. Not when he realized the current was as strong as it'd been in the strait, though he was too distracted by daydreams of their petticoats to warn them.

It was only moments later, when the prince dove in behind them, that the visitor was rudely awakened.

The visitor's feet told him to run. To help. Neither girl had surfaced—it had been too long. He took five steps and halted. His father in his ear this time, another Øldenburg ruler in a land full of them.

"Do not be a hero, Iker; you are already a prince."

His own kingdom needed him alive. If something were to

happen to him, the future of his home and his family would be in danger. Yet still, another voice, his own, knocked around in his ears.

"But Nik . . ."

His cousin had grown tall of late, at least six feet already, but he'd seen tulips thicker than his arms, harpoons wider than his legs. The visitor was the same height but built with all the vigor of the Vikings. He was strong. He could help.

Still, he stayed rooted to the spot. Holding his breath as his cousin finally surfaced, a black-haired rag doll drooping in his arms. Strong and steady, Nik swam for the beach.

As the two landed in the sand, the visitor breathed again, watching in awe as the boy of twelve did all the right things to expel water from her lungs. Citizens gathered around their prince now, Lithasblot preparations halted, all of them getting a good look at the latest near tragedy in a history full of them, the sea well fed in the whale-wild Øresund Strait.

All the relief he'd felt fled the second his cousin began barking orders to the men standing around, their inaction frustrating him. The men finally dove into the water, but Iker knew his cousin. Knew his heart. Knew what he would do. He was going back too.

These girls had been a part of him for years, one the left arm, one the right. They were both beauties—even Nik had admitted it during his last visit. The raven-haired girl was more his cousin's style, but the visitor knew the blonde was the one who saw Nik in that way—it was obvious.

The visitor watched the prince dive back into the waves, and then he ran, all the strength of his Viking blood carrying him as he tore across the sand.

He yelled at the men swimming back to shore empty-handed, soggy from their attempts at finding the girl. "You there, men, don't leave your crown prince to do the dirty work alone. Back in the water with you—your hope does not fade until Prince Niklas's does."

Immediately, the men turned for the waves, diving in, hope the last thing set in their features. Every cut of jaw locked with the knowledge that this was just how things went in the Øresund Kingdoms. The sea took as much as she gave.

But he wanted them there in case Nik faltered. These men were insurance for the prince. Their shared family could not suffer this blow, no matter how heroic.

"Evelyn, are you all right?" He crashed to her side, palms cupping her elegant shoulders.

"Iker?" She blinked at him as if he were a ghost, those midnight eyes of hers dark with terror. "Anna. Nik—"

"I know," he said in his best prince voice, the one he'd been perfecting in front of the looking glass when stranded in the castle, his heart yearning for the sea.

Iker turned back to Evelyn. Tears welled in her eyes, gratitude in the curve of her lips. He knew enough about the girl to know how she felt about him, how she wanted to kiss him right there. He knew enough about her class—the fishermen, the worker bees—to know that she wouldn't.

Instead, her fingers tightened on his forearm as if she were still fodder for the undertow and he'd rescued her himself.

"It'd kill me to lose either of them."

She glanced down at her hands as if the answer were there, hidden in the web of lines—heart, life, and fate.

"There is so much I wish I could do," she said, her voice still so weak.

That was it. There was so much he could do. Nik was his cousin, true, but he had always felt like a brother. And no matter the correct name for their relationship, he was family. And family did what had to be done.

Iker squeezed Evelyn's shoulders for the barest of moments, and then he was gone, yanking off his boots as he ran toward the foaming undertow.

15

"Oh, Evie, it was wonderful," Annemette says after half falling into the window seat in our room. Her blond waves are as wild as the tide in a storm, spilling at all angles around her shoulders. The cream of her face is flushed with pure joy, deep-blue eyes sparkling.

I'm so happy to see her like this. Iker and I spent the afternoon swirled together in a rush of touches and sweet words, two pebbles in a whirlpool, and I can only hope that she and Nik did as well.

"*Nik* is wonderful," I confirm, but she grabs my hand.

"More wonderful than I could have ever dreamed, but so are you. There is no way I would have had the day I just had without you." Her eyes swell, the skin there growing pink.

I squeeze her fingers. "It's nothing," I say, though I can't imagine the last few hours with Iker would've happened without her either. I can't picture him arriving at the castle and then hiking into its shadow to find me in the tiny house at the end of the lane. It's difficult to imagine grand Iker confined by a home smaller than this entire palace bedroom—even when he's on his little schooner, his personality still has room to burst into the open air of the sea.

"Do you think he's falling in love?" I ask as I change dresses for tonight's Lithasblot festivities.

"I think so," she says. "I hope. More time would help." She smiles weakly.

"The sooner we get going, the more you'll have. Almost ready?"

She fastens up the last few pearl buttons on her pink silk gown. "Almost," she says and then looks at my worn navy dress. "Is that what you're wearing?"

I nod. I could probably conjure up a range of dresses too if I put my mind to it, but that would really send the town chirping. Everyone knows what's in my wardrobe.

"No, no. Wear *this*," she insists, and hands me a deep purple gown embroidered with golden tulips. "I made it for you. Iker will love it."

I take the dress, running the lush silk between my fingers. "Thank you," I say. "It's beautiful, but I couldn't. Can you imagine everyone's faces? Me in *this*? What will the townspeople say?"

"Maybe something nice, for once," Annemette replies with a smirk.

I know she's wrong, but I can barely take my eyes off the dress. It's stunning, the workmanship so intricate, it truly could only have been achieved with a spell. And then it hits me. *We have magic.* "Annemette . . ."

"Yes?" she says, weaving her golden strands into an ornate bun.

"Can't you use your magic . . . on Nik? I mean, only if things don't go as planned. He can love you; I can see it. It's just . . . *three* days—now almost two—there's no t—"

"No," she says, sticking the last pin in her hair. "It has to be real when the clock strikes midnight after the ball. That's it. Magic can masquerade as love, but none has ever satisfied Urda before. These little things, dresses and such, are as far as I'll go. He has to love me as me. No tricks. Promise me you won't do anything to interfere, Evie."

I nod, my lips closed tight. Of course she's right. I don't want to manipulate Nik's feelings either, but the consequences are just so steep.

I step into her gown, the cool fabric sliding over my skin, its shape fitting me perfectly. I barely recognize myself as I stare in the mirror, looking so much like one of the nobles. Perhaps a costume is all I ever needed.

"You look like a princess," Annemette says, giving me a kiss on the cheek. "Let's go. Our princes await."

I grab her hand, and we walk down through the palace and out the gates. This night, the third night, is what everyone always mentions when Lithasblot comes up.

When it is perfectly normal, possibly even a compliment, to toss a slice of rye or a dense roll at your neighbor.

Predictably, Malvina Christensen lives for this night. It gives her a chance to show off, and gods know she would never shy away from that. Not one for needlepoint or whatever komtesses are supposed to learn, Malvina chose to take up baking instead, always underfoot of her cook as a girl. I'll admit, she became rather good, that blue monstrosity aside, though I'll take partial responsibility for its demise. She's eager to tell anyone questioning her that baking is a hobby, even though it's beneath her, an activity more befitting someone like me. "If you feed a man right, he'll be true to you for life," I've heard her say many times. It's strange, she so wants me out of her way, too crude for her class, and yet here she is parading her lowbrow achievements. I guess when you have power, you can be whoever you want.

Though the sun has yet to set and the townspeople are still wandering the offering tables in search of their suppers, Malvina has snagged herself a prominent spot by the bonfire. Around her is a literal sea of treats—petits fours, scones à la Brighton, out-of-season fried aebleskiver, and crusty rolls of rye and soft rolls of sweet Russian wheat, both in the shape of the sun wheel. There's a massive blueberry pie as well, juices glistening from under a golden lattice crust.

"Malvina, my, you've outdone yourself yet again," Nik

says with a royal smile as we come upon her.

The girl beams at him. "Why thank you, Nik. It would be an honor if you enjoyed something before the throwing begins."

Nik waves her off. "That's not—"

"I insist. Please take something, there is more than enough here for Urda."

Training and practice with Malvina's forcibly charitable nature are enough to keep Nik from fighting her one word more. "If that is the case, then yes. Something small would be greatly appreciated."

Her still-beaming smile grows larger as she dips to the blanket and chooses a petit four, done in perfect French style. "There's plenty for your friends, too," she adds as an afterthought.

I'm shocked. Malvina has never offered me anything, and then I realize, she may not recognize me. It's the dress. It must be sewn with the most powerful sorcery to deceive a shark like Malvina.

"How kind of you," I say, taking a scone and watching her pewter eyes for recognition. And then there it is, a slight snarl.

"Oh, Evie," she says. "My, that's quite a dress. Where did you—"

"It was a gift. From me, Friherrinde Annemette," Mette interrupts while plucking a sweet roll. "For being a good friend and the most gracious host." And then she does the unthinkable—she links her arms right through mine and Nik's, pulling us close on either side.

Malvina smiles so tightly I can see the veins in her neck. "Well, from a komtesse to a friherrinde, a word of advice. If you treat your help to such finery, they'll get used to it."

"I hope so," says Annemette. "I have plenty more where that came from. Thank you for the sweets."

And then we walk away. Just like that. Nik seems a little stunned, ever the proper prince, but even he can't help but laugh. "You really do look lovely, Evie."

"Seconded," Iker says, grabbing my hand.

I thank them both for probably the third time that night, and then we walk the boys to the platform for tonight's celebration of the grain crop. Annemette and I take our seats in the little white wooden chairs reserved for the nobility—another new view for me, having only sat on the sand before. As the sky darkens, Nik begins to speak, but I can't focus, my mind on so many things. The Lithasblot festival was always something I knew so well, every year the same, and for a time, I didn't go at all.

The Lithasblot after Anna drowned, I never left the house. Nik, Tante Hansa, and Father all tried to draw me from my bed, sure that a measure of festival fun would go a long way toward cheering me up.

But song and dance cannot close a wound like that. More like it pours salt on it—watching other people sing and dance like nothing had happened, all the while blistered with grief.

I didn't go. Not that year nor the next.

I'd tried to spend the time reading Tante Hansa's spell books—the only thing that'd kept me sane in those days—but even that took too much effort. All the strength I had went to shutting out laughter and song.

It was only last year that I agreed to go with Nik again.

He'd lost his friend too but had to make a show of being at the festival immediately—the day of her death—duty and title forcing him to walk around in his nice clothes and accept the people's offerings to Urda. He didn't have to speak as he does yet again tonight, but it was still painful enough just to stand up in front of everyone while so broken.

We are far from that now—not healed, of course, but with just two days left, this festival has felt like the last one we attended when Anna was alive. Iker came that year, arriving with his parents from Rigeby Bay, fourteen and suddenly very tall. Anna and I mooned over him every night, whispering about his eyes and laughing while huddled up in her mansion bedroom. It would be a year before she told me that she actually preferred Nik to Iker and my mind filled of dreams of us as twin queens, the friherrinde-to-princess and the pauper-to-princess loves of Øldenburg kings on both sides of the Øresund Strait.

Of course, Annemette is not Anna, but I can't shake

the feeling that this is what we could have had. I glance over at Annemette as she watches Nik speak on the platform in front of the bonfire. Rosebud lips slightly parted, she follows his words with the precision of a predator, so intent on remembering everything he says. I never saw Anna look at Nik like Annemette does, but eleven-year-old girls can hide their feelings as much as any of us.

Suddenly, Annemette's lips pull up in a smile, eyes sharpening to something hard, and I follow her gaze up to Nik. He's watching her back, but then looks to me, doing his best to concentrate on the words. Still, his ears begin to blush. Then Iker hands Nik the ceremonial first loaf of bread—large as a cannonball, crafted of dark rye, and braided in the shape of the sun wheel. Nik holds the loaf above his head.

"And so, let us give thanks to Urda with the staff of life—bread. Let us share our gifts of grain with our neighbors. Let no person in need go without. Let the loaves fly to them with the gentlest of care, a blessing from Urda by way of a neighbor's hand."

Nik tears a hunk of bread off the loaf and hands it to King Asger. Another piece goes to Queen Charlotte, and a third to Iker, whose parents stayed home this year. Together, the royal family lines up in front of the fire, bread in hand.

Nik lifts his piece above his crowned head.

"Let the sharing begin."

With that, all four of them toss the bread in the direction of the crowd. Nik's lands gently in Annemette's lap. She laughs, and I'm so busy laughing too that I'm not paying attention when a crusty hunk of rye thwacks me square in the chest, bouncing off my bodice and into my lap. I glance up and see Iker with a vicious grin, hovering over the royal table, snatching more.

I grab a loaf from the table next to me and stand. I rip it in half and give the remainder to Annemette. "Aim for Iker."

Her brows pull together with a moment of confusion. "I thought the bread was for the less fortunate?"

I gesture toward the sky. "It's raining bread. No one will go hungry, I promise."

Annemette looks up to see that, yes, bread of every make and shape is flying through the air. She ducks as a sweet roll screams in from Malvina's direction. It bounces off Fru Ulla with a honeyed thud before a toddler snags it with two chubby hands.

"It's all in good fun," I assure her, and chuck the bread Iker's way. He puts his arms up to shield his face but drops them too quickly and gets clobbered right in the nose by Annemette's piece.

This only serves to make him grin and seize two cherry tarts from the table. He thrusts one into Nik's hands, and they advance on us, eyes glinting.

"Run!" I screech, and grab Annemette's hand.

We snake through the crowd and onto an open stretch of beach. Twined together, we run along the shoreline. But the boys are faster, and tarts whack us each in the back. We fall to the sand in hysterics—something I haven't done in four years.

The boys pull us up—Iker hooking one arm under my knees and the other at my shoulders. He runs a finger along my back until my once class-defying gown is slick with beach-ruined cherry filling and aims it toward my mouth. "Sandy tart for the lady."

I seal my lips and shake my head.

"For Urda, you must."

The absurdity of the look on his face pulls my lips apart, and he seizes his opportunity to drop the filling onto my tongue. I gag and buck, coughing with laughter, and tumble out of his arms and into the sand.

Iker goes down too, landing beside me. His eyes seem to glow as he leans over my body and lowers his lips to mine. I enjoy the kiss, his newly shaven skin baby soft against my chin. I guess Iker doesn't defy all royal protocols; Queen Charlotte won this round.

"Mmmm," he says, licking cherry filling from his lips. "Delicious, though a bit . . . gritty."

I laugh. "Sandy tarts always are."

"Odd bit of cuisine, you Havnestaders."

"Eat up. Nik will expect you at full strength tomorrow," I say.

Iker raises a brow, mischief on his lips. "What if I told him I was saving my strength for you?"

I push him away from me and stand, my back to him, arms crossed.

"I was kidding," he pleads. "Are *all* the games tomorrow?"

I nod, dusting myself off while he still lies in the sand.

"Does this mean tomorrow is when you will shimmy across a log?"

When I don't respond, he stands and wraps his arms around me from behind, trailing two fingers across my navel, having them mimic a stiff jog.

"As promised, my prince," I say, laughing a little. *Why do I always give in?*

"Yes—"

A scream cuts off Iker's answer. *Annemette.* Both Iker and I whip our heads toward Annemette and Nik. They are closer to the crowd, Annemette crouching in the sand, Nik staggering a bit before falling to his knees, clutching his stomach. Standing before both of them is Malvina, hands in front of her body as if they'd just released a dagger.

Iker stiffens, his whole body suddenly rigid with tension. "Cousin?"

Nik staggers to a stand and raises a hand to wave him off, turning toward us. His white shirt and dazzling royal coat are a mess of black, like the tears I've cried twice before.

Iker takes a step toward the scene, fists forming.

But then Nik points toward his boots. Toward the pie plate lying facedown in the sand.

"Urda has been quite generous with Malvina's blueberry pie. The goddess must have decided that my wardrobe and the beach were in particular need of nourishment." With that, Nik begins to laugh.

Immediately, Iker joins him, and I catch Annemette's eye as she rises from her crouch. A little chuckle bubbles from her lips, growing into a full laugh when her attention turns to Nik's doubled-over form. I'm almost too shocked to laugh, having been holding my breath this whole time, but then I join in too.

The only one not finding humor in all this is Malvina, embarrassment but not regret in the set of her jaw. She doesn't apologize as she storms past Annemette—clearly her intended target—and snatches the pie plate from the sand at Nik's feet.

She stands to face him. Nik attempts to compose himself enough to look her in the eye but fails miserably, laughter still wryly present in his features as he lets the blueberry glop and sugar crust slide off his gold-threaded coat and onto the beach.

"I hope you will enjoy this gift in the name of Urda,"

Malvina announces, nose in the air, before pivoting on her heel as best as she can in beach sand, blond hair flying.

When she's gone, we gather around him and survey the damage. The shirt, coat and even his pants are all unsalvageable.

But true to his nature, Nik just grins and presents his sopping clothes.

"Pie, ladies? Urda does insist."

16

I WAKE WITH THE SUN THE FOLLOWING MORNING, STILL warm with feelings of belonging from the night before. Yesterday was a daydream from start to end, and I wanted to never wake up. But in the white morning light, reality becomes stark and my mood shifts quickly.

Annemette is still fast asleep, toes stretching toward the ceiling, arms thrown above her head, tangled within her waves. I lie there for a moment and listen to the gulls before I realize my opportunity. I know a way I can do some real good today.

On silent feet, I head to the wardrobe and tug it open. The first dress on the right is one I wore two days ago when I met Annemette. I can't believe that's all the time that's passed, but in the same breath, I can't believe so much of our time has vanished. Today and tomorrow until midnight, and then it could all be over in the most horrific way possible—or it might be the happiest ending of all.

Annemette still seems confident, and I'm obeying her request that I not intervene, at least not magically, but the thought of losing another friend to the sea is almost unbearable. First Anna, then nearly Nik, and now Annemette, who's only been in my life for a short while, but who's helped open my world in ways I'd never imagined. She's the friend Anna never could be to me, that Nik can't be, either. She's the only one who knows my secrets. Well, most of them.

I've been pushing these feelings down, telling myself this is her decision, that I should instead try to appreciate the life around me, as I'm sure she is, but I don't know how much longer I can feel so helpless.

At least I can still use my magic for one thing. I fish through my dress pocket. My fingers brush past the vial of ink from the other day and curl around the little amethyst, safe and sound where I left it. I can only hope that my morning away from the docks led to just one day of poor fishing, or maybe none at all—the magic is new enough that I don't know what happens if I *don't* do it.

I dress quickly, and, minutes later, I make it to the docks without seeing a soul. The cobblestones are littered with dew-covered crumbs, orphaned the night before, and so far neglected by the Øresund birds.

The docks are quiet too, no ships coming or going, though that will change in a few hours. Today is the favorite among the festivalgoers. The gluttony of the previous nights draws some, the final day of sailing and dancing attracts others, but not nearly as many as those lining up to participate or watch the games today.

Our games aren't exactly as sophisticated as the ancient Olympics Fru Seraphine taught us about in school, but they are more than enough for the people of Havnestad.

Palm out and full, I close my eyes and run the amethyst along the docked ship hulls one by one, mumbling aloud the words that seem to work, mostly because, with no one around, I don't have to say them in my head.

"Knorr yfir haf, knorr yfir haf, sigla tryggr, fanga þrír.
Knorr yfir haf, knorr yfir haf, sigla tryggr, fanga þrír."

The words hit my ear as childish, so much more sophisticated when spoken only in the space of my mind. I suddenly wish I'd trusted my magic enough to create a simple and strong Old Norse command—like something Annemette would do. I'd do it now but I'm afraid of what the change will bring.

My words are like a nursery rhyme—but they will do.

When I'm finished with every ship in port, I stand on the edge of the royal dock—the longest pier in Havnestad Harbor—and face the strait.

"Urda, if you will, bring my words to Father, wherever in the Øresund he may be. Keep him safe; leave him to me. You do not need him. Please don't take him simply because you can."

Anna's face crosses my mind, open and free with laughter before she was taken by the waves. But I push it down as far as it will go, along with my dark thoughts of the morning. I need to live like Annemette, like Iker, and enjoy the day to its fullest.

I turn and head back to the castle.

I don't see him at first, my eyes on the clouds the sun has tinged pink with the rising dawn. But then I hear the soft plink of a guitaren being strummed ever so lightly in the tulip garden. That song again, from the party.

"Nik?" His chin tilts my way, eyes swinging away from the sea. He is on the stone bench under the shade tree, the wrinkled version of his strapping statue across the garden—muslin nightclothes rumpled, unbrushed hair shoved out of his eyes with his fingertips. "Did you come out here this morning to let the birds clean the last bit of pie from behind your ears?"

"I ran a bath last night, but thanks for noticing."

"Then you must have risen early to meditate on a plan to best Iker in the rock carry."

Nik raises an arm and pats his lean bicep. "The only plan I need, my lady."

I punch him on the arm, and we sit quietly for a few moments. The pink of dawn has shifted to salmon, the tone already rumbling toward the golden yellow it turns just before the classic blue sky wins out and the sun is fully over the horizon.

Fingers scrabble Nik's hair back again from his brow, and his face turns toward the stones at our feet. After a breath, he raises his eyes to mine, and I have a feeling I might learn the real answer to his morning meditation.

"Evie . . . ," he starts, and my heart sinks at the mournful tone. *Oh no.* "Evie, have you really kissed Iker?"

My heart skids to a halt and I sit there, jaw tense. I don't know what to say. I'm not ready to talk about me and Iker. Not to Nik, anyway.

I laugh and elbow him in the ribs, hoping a joke can mend whatever is in his voice. "The real question is, have *you* kissed Annemette?"

I hope he'll turn red. Say yes. Admit to it so that maybe Annemette has a chance to stay—to live!—and fill the hole in our hearts.

Instead, his face squishes up as if he's smelled something spoiled. "Of course not. I'm a romantic, but I'm not a cad—I'm not, not . . ."

"Iker?" My voice is angrier than I intended, but there's something in the pit of my stomach. Something hot like disappointment, not only at him for his clear disdain for Iker but for anything *I* do with him.

He stops and starts, and I can tell he doesn't know where to begin. It's rare that I ever get angry with him. Rare that he can't bring order with a princely smile or a knowing glance, his only tools of conflict the royal formalities his mother has ingrained in him.

"I realize it's stupid," he says finally. "I'm sixteen and a prince to boot—I should be having fun. Mother would never let something wrongheaded get so far along. She has plans for me, besides. It's just . . . I like Annemette. But it's not . . . it's not"—he looks at me, and there's something else in his eyes—"as it is in the storybooks." Then he glances up at me, the change in his focus clear in the set of his jaw. "And for *him* to kiss *you* . . ." Nik shakes his head, his posture withering. "God, I must sound a mess—"

"No," I say, air rushing into my lungs just enough to get the word out.

He laughs softly under his breath. "Yes, I do. I sound crazed."

"You sound confused. You can find 'crazed' in those lovesick books we read as children. Those princes who lock girls up in a tower to get their way—those are the crazy ones."

Nik nods to himself. "Yes, Mette is a nice girl, lovely really, and beautiful, and I regret that she'll have to return to Odense, but I don't think I'll ever love her enough to be . . . to be . . . her fairy-tale prince."

My stomach practically collapses. But Nik is just speaking from the heart. He doesn't know there is no Odense for Annemette. No . . . nothing. She's just another girl his mother has forced upon him. What if I told him the truth? Maybe that would change things. *Evie, what are you talking about? Tell him she's a mermaid?* But maybe he'd see how wonderful she is and would want to save her, just like he tried to save Anna. But then this truly would all be on his shoulders. All that guilt. Can love spring from guilt? Is that true love? I don't know . . . how should I know what true love is? No, if I told him the truth, it might ruin any further time she has to win him over. This is all my fault, for trouncing around with Iker while Nik spends precious time worrying about me, taking his mind off Annemette. I have to try something else.

"She reminds me so much of Anna . . . ," I say, feeling as if the words are tiptoeing out.

"Her coloring, yes," he admits, but doesn't go further. Not the response I was hoping for.

"And her features. Her singing voice."

He shrugs and leans back off his knees and straightens. "But you know what's not? The way she looks at me—Anna never would've allowed herself to think of me as handsome."

"That's so untrue! She had a huge crush on you, and you know it." I knock his shoulder, though it feels strange to speak of Anna's private feelings as a joke. I'm quiet for a moment, and then I say, "Give Annemette a real chance, please. For me."

"But what about you and Iker?"

"Stop thinking about Iker, Nik! I'm happy, but I won't let him ruin me, like I know you're so afraid of. I'm smarter than that." He blushes red for a moment, but I keep going. "The only happiness I want you to worry about is yours."

FOUR YEARS BEFORE

The boy dove back in. He couldn't just leave it to these other men to find his friend. He'd saved one; he needed to try to save the other.

Drowning was common in Havnestad—the sea took as much as she gave—but this, this could not be.

Immediately, the water clawed at the damp length of him, the undertow a thousand hands ripping his body toward the swirling sands below.

His father's constant refrain crept into his head. Do not be a hero, Iker; you are already a prince.

He'd said it anytime Nik had done anything particularly reckless. A compliment swaddled in a reminder: You are not just a prince, you are an heir. The lone heir.

And here was his father's voice, nagging as fiercely as the waves.

He crested the surface and shook it all off—the words, the water—and filled his lungs. All around him, men thrashed in the waves. Not a single one held Anna.

The boy dove down again, forcing his eyes open against the salty sting.

Blue. Blue everywhere.

He blinked, letting his vision adjust.

Shadows on the ocean floor became crops of seaweed, moving in dark time. Algae, debris, and the tiniest of sea horses floated across the blue, a mosaic rather than one solidly flowing body.

His eyes swung left, right. His entire body spun around.

She's here. She's here. She must be here.

He surfaced again, not far from the sandbar now. No men yelling. No one sagging under the weight of a blonde in a petticoat.

Back down again, deeper, deeper, the undertow greedily guiding him on.

Eyes open, he scanned the bottom. Lungs burning for breath, he dove.

And there.

One hundred yards away. Down in a crevice. A flash of white. A foot, bare against a huge tangle of seaweed and coral.

Eyes pinned on her location, he shot to the surface—he'd need air to get her. Eight great, heaving breaths.

I can do this. I can get to her.

Down he dove again, eyes open as he plunged, pinned to the sliver of white. So far away. So far down.

The boy's lungs burned. His ears popped. Darkness crept into the corners of his vision.

And still the slip of white was there. But not getting closer. It never seemed to get any larger, any more attainable. It just flashed on the seafloor, so much a star he could not touch.

His mind began to slow, as did his legs and arms, which no longer struggled against the undertow.

You do not need to be a hero, Iker; you are already a prince.

You are not just a prince, you are an heir.

The lone heir.

Breath beating against his lungs, he made his choice.

The prince pushed himself deeper.

His life didn't matter more than hers. He was the one with the chance to save her, and that chance shouldn't hinge on the blood in his veins.

Legs burning, he kicked, no breath left in his lungs to propel him. But he was so close. He could make out actual toes now. Head pounding without air, blood spiked with pressure, he kicked again, his arms pulling against the water.

But then came a pressure on his foot. Yanking him back— up. Pulling him until, for a heartbeat, the weight was gone. As soon as it disappeared, it was replaced with elbows hooking under his shoulders. A chest at his back. And force, so much force, propelling him to the surface.

In that moment, his lungs finally sputtered for breath and he involuntarily inhaled, water still surrounding him. A deep mouthful of the sea hovered above his windpipe for a split second before he spit it back into the water.

Out of breath, out of time, water closing in, he broke the surface. The air was so fresh it burned; as his lungs heaved, his tongue swelled from the salt he'd inhaled.

Coughing, breathing—finally breathing—he opened his eyes again, water streaming into his eyes.

He couldn't see well, but he knew the face before him.

"No! Iker—" he began, coughing. Coughing so hard. More salt water streamed out of his mouth. Dribbled down his chin. He wiped at his mouth with a sleeve so wet, it just smeared the water around with more water.

"I've got you, Cousin. I've got you. Don't worry. You're safe."

"I—" He coughed again and took a breath, long and deep. "I have to get her."

With air in his lungs, he tried to shrug off his cousin.

"She's gone, Nik. She's gone. And you were going to be too."

"No! She's down there. I saw her. You had to have seen her too. She's right there, right down—"

"Don't be a hero, Nik." Boat-strong biceps pinned the prince in a hug—his arms stuck at his sides, his only recourse to kick, but that just propelled them closer to the beach. Farther from her.

"Iker, please. She needs us. Anna needs us. We can rescue her. We can—"

"We can't." His cousin's newly deepened voice cracked as he said it, and there was a hitch in his kick. "We can't."

"We can! We can get her!" He was yelling, even though his voice was rough and sloppy.

His cousin only squeezed harder. His lips came to the prince's ear, his voice smaller than seemed possible. "If you die rescuing her, it won't give solace to your parents or your people. It will only give Havnestad another body."

"But she's not a body. She's not. She's there. Right there." But even as he said the words, he knew it had been too long now. Ten minutes, though it felt like a hundred.

And then he started to cry. Salty tears running down his cheeks and into the harbor. He didn't wipe them. He let them run. Let them join Anna at sea.

17

THE ANNUAL LITHASBLOT GAMES BEGIN IN THE SWEL-
ter of noon. Havnestad citizens and onlookers from across
the Øresund Strait spill onto the main beach, ready for
games of skill and sport to take place from the mountains
above to the seas below.

It's the first time in days the boys aren't properly gussied
up in public. To be sure, they're both clean-shaven—the
easier to show off their game faces—but they are also
wearing simple cotton work pants and shirts rolled at the
sleeves. This change of dress is tradition too.

Today is about demonstrating skill. I wasn't lying
when I told Iker our games were useful—they were indeed
born out of utility. Rock climbing and trail running in the
mountains. Log running in the stream that feeds into the
harbor. Swimming in the mouth of the sea. Vital to life,
every one of them. Useful—right down to the rock carry

along the beach, which mimics laboring to bring cargo ashore.

And each citizen in Havnestad has an equal shot to compete. Be you ninety-five or still flush with baby fat, if you can walk, you are allowed to have a go—with the royal family cheering you on, or possibly acting as your competition.

After plates of samsø, rye bread, and peaches, Nik is instructed by his father to oversee the mountain events first. Those sports have the fewest competitors, and King Asger would much rather view the action on the beach.

And King Asger gets what King Asger wants—even from his son.

True to his nature, Nik bows—no crown atop his head—before grabbing another peach and a flask of water and tugging Annemette toward Lille Bjerg Pass.

I side-eye Iker when he doesn't make a move to follow.

His strong hand gently cuffs my wrist and pulls me close. In a breath, I'm an inch away from his lips. The depths of his eyes are striking in the high sun, clear and merry after a good night's rest in a real bed and not a ship's dank quarters. "Let's just stay here alone."

I shift my eyes to the beach. "Alone—with five thousand of our closest friends, including your aunt and uncle."

Iker laughs and gently fingers the curls that have blown forward over my shoulder. "So many people that not a one of them is watching . . ."

No, they're watching. I can feel it. He's just used to it.

I pull away, shifting the arm he's snagged so I'm grabbing his wrist as he clutches mine. I tug him toward Lille Bjerg Pass. "There are many side trails along the pass, thick with brush."

He raises a brow and finally takes a step forward. "It would be a shame if we were to get lost."

"Such a shame. Nik would be so disappointed."

"Only if he's lost in the same brush we are."

It's true. Nik returned a different person after our early morning conversation, focusing on Annemette with a renewed intensity.

With tangled hands, we march up Market Street. We are several lengths behind Annemette and Nik, though they are moving at a snail's pace—Annemette has yet to see much of the town outside of the festival, and she's poking in every doorway and picture window to see the wares. The sweetshop man already handed her a lollipop, which proceeded to turn her tongue a grisly shade of red. She dared to show us a block back, sticking out her tongue nearly down to her chin. It was quite the picture, a bloody maw beneath the face of an angel. Of course, she thought it was the funniest thing. I thanked Urda that Malvina wasn't around to see it.

Nik laughed too, endearment written all over his face. He has no idea how far she's traveled to see these things we walk past every day, to stroll down the street with him.

"I have been to Odense," Iker starts, sun lines crinkling around his eyes, "and it isn't Copenhagen, but it isn't a one-horse village either. By the way she responded to the sucker, you'd suppose she'd never had a candy in all her life."

"Showing delight isn't a crime, Iker." And it isn't, though I know that answer won't atone for Annemette's fierce sense of wonder. Thus, I turn it back on him. "Not everyone is as difficult to amuse as the salt-worn prince of Rigeby Bay."

His lips turn up and his eyes flash my way. "I laugh deeper than anyone and you know it—whether I've lived on only salt herring for three weeks or not." His fingers squeeze mine and I kiss his shoulder. "What I mean is, there's just something unnatural about her level of delight."

My heart starts to pound and my temples grow hot. This line of thought is no good. No good at all. I change tactics.

"Imagine it her way." I sweep my free hand out in front of him. "She arrived at Havnestad with a chaperone green with illness, knowing not a single other soul. And despite it all, she's been taken in, given a bed in a beautiful palace, and the dashing prince she's come to meet clearly believes her to be something special." I swing up our tangled hands so they're within view. "That is a whirlwind of delight, is it not? The curl was nearly blown out of my hair just by being a bystander."

160 —

He gives me a courtesy laugh and snags a wayward lock of hair with his free hand, tugging it completely smooth. He lets it go and watches as it bounces back into a spiral. "That would've been disastrous. Even the salons of Paris would not have been able to reproduce these."

My cheeks run scarlet as we reach the end of the cobblestones and the trailhead of Lille Bjerg Pass. Annemette and Nik have already disappeared around a bend. I step in front of Iker onto the single track, and our hands drop.

"I'm just saying," he says, "what do we know about Annemette? How do we know she is who she says she is?"

I laugh, trying to make it seem as if he's being ridiculous, and not appropriately concerned. "What, do you think she's some con artist on the run, stealing crown jewels one Lithasblot at a time?" It's the most absurd thing I can offer, except for the truth.

"No. No. She's a sweet girl . . . there's just something about her I can't put my finger on. And I don't like that feeling—especially when it involves family."

"I know what it is," I say, hoping to finally put this to rest—for Annemette as much as for myself. "She looks like Anna."

His step hesitates behind me. "Your friend who drowned?"

"The very one."

"Sure. She had blond hair."

"Yes. And blue eyes. And creamy skin. A heart-shaped

face—all of it. The resemblance about bowled me over." And I can't help it: tears well in my eyes. "I'd thought I'd seen a ghost."

He stops moving forward. I turn around and he's watching me, brows pulled together and serious. It's just as he was on the balcony, suspicion slinking across his skin as fierce as the sunlight.

"Are you sure there's no way this girl could have known that? Picked the name Annemette on purpose? She could be preying on the both of you—using your memories against you."

The slope of the trail puts us face-to-face, and he presses his thumbs to the corners of my eyes, wiping away the tears that have welled. I place my hand on his chest. "Who are these scoundrels you meet on the high seas? Does anyone in the world really do such awful things? Do you not have any faith in your fellow man?"

"Evelyn, I am aware that you are not naïve, but I feel as if I should remind both you and my cousin that people aren't always who they say they are."

"You're not wrong." I take a step toward him and touch my forehead to his, our lips a breath away, our eyes locked. "And while I find your concern incredibly endearing, I'm through talking about this. Annemette may not be Anna, but she *is* my friend. I have not been duped."

I close the distance between us, our lips meeting. He

sinks deeply into me, hands wrapping around my back, fingers in my hair. We stand like that for several moments, but it isn't until he's so taken he closes his eyes that I know I've finally won this round.

"Taking the long way up the mountain?"

I push away from Iker and see Annemette standing a few feet from us, Nik surely around the bend. Her brow is raised, but there's a smirk on her black cherry–stained mouth.

"Haven't you heard? I'm never on time." He grins a bit at his own self-effacing jab, but I swear I still see a skeptical look in his eyes as he stalks past her.

Annemette grabs my hands, and we both burst out laughing. It really does feel like Anna is here.

We make our way up to the games, but by the time we reach them, Nik and Iker have already been plied into competing in the mountain run portion of the games. Royal duty and gamesmanship mean Annemette and I have been left behind to hold court on a fallen log. Normally, I'd run too—I'm swifter than I look—but Annemette's feet are already bothering her, the burning she felt yesterday more painful than before. Instead, we'll watch the rock climbers from afar while waiting for the boys to rumble back down the mountain, sweaty, dusty, and full of new tales.

"How do you do it?" she asks quietly.

"What do you mean?" I reply.

—163

"Get Iker to kiss you like that?" she says with more than a hint of exasperation lining her voice. "It's silly, but I was watching you—"

"For tips?" I want to laugh—the idea of someone watching me for my alluring abilities is ridiculous, and I still have my doubts about whether there's actually any love behind Iker's kisses, but Annemette seems so desperate. She *is* desperate.

Annemette's cheeks flush, though the pink is tempered by the mountain light. "I've done everything I can to show him how I feel, and still no kiss! But I do think he likes me."

"He does. I know he does!" I push this morning out of my mind entirely. Nik has heeded my words. I know it. It's going to be all right.

She is quiet for a second, her features mellowing with thought. "My father, the sea king, says that when everything is as you hoped, you are blind to the imperfections."

Somehow, I'm stunned silent that the sea king in our childhood tales is as real as the mermaid before me. Finally, I nod. "Your father is wise."

"But I'm not blind. His wise words ring in my ears when I should be enjoying every moment. Instead, I look past the perfect couple we are on the outside and see all the reasons why Nik isn't in love with me."

"I know what you mean," I say.

"No, Iker loves you."

I shake my head. "I would like Iker to love me. But Iker has a reputation for kissing any girl whose knees go weak at the sight of him—and I'm not the only one in the Øresund Kingdoms with trouble standing. Iker and I are not forever, and I'm trying to be all right with that."

She looks at her feet. "So, he has other girls he treats like you?"

"Yes. Or he did. I don't know." I can feel my face flushing. "The point is, Nik does not! There is only one fish in his sea and it is you . . ."

"That is a ridiculous analogy, Evie."

"And here I thought it was clever, given your situation."

Annemette squeezes her eyes shut, and I regret making a stupid joke at a time like this. "My situation. Yes." She huffs out a sad little laugh. "Such a situation—love at first sight with a boy who won't even kiss me. I was so sure he was going to lead to a lifetime of happiness, not . . ."

Neither of us wants to say what her life will be otherwise.

18

WHEN NIK AND IKER RETURN, THEY ARE EAGER TO prove who is the strongest, the fastest, the most agile, their egos sorely bruised after both losing the mountain run. It seems the tailor's son, little Johan Olsen, is not so little anymore.

"I've never seen someone run like him," Nik admits as we make our way over to the Havnestad River, which slices through the mountains before emptying to the sea. "It was a sight to see."

"You want to see a sight?" says Iker. "Challenge me to a log run, Cousin. I could beat ten of that Olsen boy, and you, too."

I look over at Annemette, who has plastered a smile on her face and is laughing along with the boys. And, because I'd love to see Iker dunked in the Havnestad River, I am totally encouraging it too.

Nik chuckles—a royal chuckle, but an actual chuckle nonetheless. As we reach the riverbank, he's still contemplating. He props one foot up on the tail end of the right log. There's an open one to his left, ready for Iker.

"If I'm not mistaken," Nik says, "I heard you came to this Lithasblot extravaganza with the promise of a certain raven-haired girl scampering across a log, and it wasn't me, Cousin."

Nik! How could he? But I laugh an Iker laugh, head thrown toward the sky. Nik is losing it too—chortling so hard that his foot has slipped off the end of the log and he's nearly squatted to a sit on the thing.

Annemette, though, has her wits about her. I right myself just as she glances my way with a wicked little grin and a gleam in her eyes. "How about this compromise? Nik and Evie race. The winner faces Iker."

Iker's brows climb his forehead and his eyes sparkle, clear and thrilled. He claps his big, strong hands together. "Yes. That's it. The lady has the perfect idea!"

I shake my head. "Yes, the perfect idea to keep herself dry."

Annemette shrugs and backs into the small crowd that has gathered, lined along the rocks and logs. "I'm just a spectator."

Nik laughs and manages a long lunge to nudge her sweetly with his elbow. "That's what I thought, too, my dear, and now look where it's got me."

I cock a brow at him. "Yes, as my first victim."

"Hey, now, what makes you so sure you'll win?" Nik says to me, a smile playing at his lips, though his tone is attempting to sound indignant.

"Sometimes you just have a feeling, my prince. You're sure to be a loser, Asger Niklas Bryniulf Øldenburg III."

As the spectators and competitors chant Nik's name, he plants a foot on the log across from me. Both logs are suspended just above the current, tied by ship ropes on either side to keep them straight and somewhat steady—to keep the competition fair, not to create ease.

It is twenty-five feet from one end to the other. We must race to the other side, touch the bank, and then make a return trip. The first one back or the one to stay out of the water wins. If we both wind up in the river, then it's a draw, no matter who fell first.

Our classmate, Ruyven Van Horn, squashed ginger hair, elephant ears and all, is there between us, the official start on his lips. "On your marks . . . get set . . . go!"

We lunge onto the logs. Nik's legs are much longer, and he's ahead after a step, but his center of gravity is much higher, and he immediately wobbles.

"Unsteady so soon, Cousin?" Iker laughs in the background.

I can't see him, but I'm sure Nik is smiling right back. "Jeer me, and you only serve to anger me."

In the time it's taken him to steady himself and answer Iker's ribbing, I've already made it five steps. The logs are slicked over, but mine is the perfect size for my feet. Planting each foot in a turnout à la the French ballet, I can move quickly to the center point with shallow steps. Beside me, Nik hasn't altered his stride, daring gravity to take him with every long step, but using his strength and coordination to stay steady.

I make it to the end of my log and tag the ground on the other side, earning me a flag raise from Ruyven's counterpart.

"Excellent, Evie!" Annemette cheers.

I get both feet back onto my log just as Nik lunges off the end of his and safely into the dirt.

"Mette, you traitor," Nik yells, mounting his log a bit too quickly. His arms windmill through my periphery in a grand arc—the crowd gasps.

"Less jawing, more movement, Cousin. Evie's smoking you!"

"You only root for me because you're stupid enough to think you can beat me in the next round. Against her you won't have a chance, and you know it."

I'm still in the lead but just barely, my steps slower and more careful now. Over the years, I've seen many a competitor fall in the river a yard from the finish because his mind was already on land. I could easily whisper one of

Tante Hansa's spells and dry the log without any notice, but I won't do that. I'm not a cheat. So my heart stills as I concentrate on the log before me, the sound of rushing water the only thing in my ears.

Nik is beside me, but my tunnel vision has drowned him out—if his arms are flailing or if he is steady and slowing too, I don't know. All I know is that when I touch dirt, Ruyven raises my arm, and when I look over, Nik is there too, hands on his hips, breathing at a good clip.

"The lady, by an inch!" Ruyven says. Annemette is clapping and Iker, too, though his game face is already sliding into place. The rest of the crowd is mostly silent until Nik raises his hands above his head in thanks—then they go wild.

"Well done, Evie." Nik squeezes my shoulder. Then he leans in, for my ears only. "Ignore them. They only cheer because they have to." Then, to the crowd, he says, "Let's hear it for Evie!"

Slightly heartier applause chases his exclamation, but—not shockingly—also some boos. And then all eyes swing to Iker. His gaze is locked on my face, the glee in the blue of his eyes already hardening to concentration. If Iker competes in the grand way that he does everything else, I'm going to need much more than an inch.

I turn and place my foot on the log.

"Are you sure you're ready to exert yourself again so quickly, Evelyn?"

"Quit stalling, Romeo. Let's go."

I glance over to Ruyven, who is having a fine time laughing at our expense. Ruyven meets my eyes, his normally dough-pale face now plum red, and raises his flag for a start. Iker is still a step or two away from his log, turned around, playing to the crowd. I settle my footing, calf muscles tense beneath my dress.

"On your marks . . ." It takes Iker almost a second too long to register the words. Ruyven is onto the next part before the crown prince of Rigeby Bay has time to turn. "Get set . . ." Iker is a yard from his log. "Go!"

I dash onto my log, keeping my chest low, hips square and knees bent. I'm five feet in front when Iker finally mounts his log, but in true Iker form, he takes the lead with just two grand steps.

The surrounding wood is alive with voices, so strong that they rise above my concentration and the babbling of the stream—Iker is always one to bring out the rowdiness in any situation.

"Go get him!" Annemette yells.

"You've got this, Evie!" Nik cheers.

But I don't have it. Iker is already a yard from touching down on the other side of the log, his bold steps risky but not without reward. I am still at least ten careful steps from the bank and the chance to turn around. When Iker's feet hit the dirt, he immediately spins and points to the flagman on the other side and then raises his arms, grand and proud as he addresses the crowd.

"Will no one cheer for the first-place horse? Am I so hideous?"

At this, every girl in the crowd, save Annemette, screams his name. It's the same chorus that I picture when he lands aground anywhere in the Øresund Kingdoms.

Iker's grandstanding costs him, though, and I touch down on the dirt just after he's mounted his log. He calculates that he's made an error in timing and immediately sprints for the other side, half leaping to stay in front of me.

I'm tempted to speed up and take longer steps, but I hold back, the log even slicker than before.

So I take my time. Quick steps, eyes only for the log, breath steady and calm.

I'm in the lead at the midpoint, a second victory in my sights. And that's exactly when someone in the crowd decides a prince can't lose yet again, and a branch whizzes through the air, catching me across the neck.

The pain is sharp, and I lose my balance. I'm falling toward the water and Iker's log before I can do anything physically or magically to stop it. As I'm falling, I think for a split second of Annemette's floating spell, and I almost say the command, but I can't do that here. Still, I hang in the air for the slightest of seconds before I catch Annemette's eyes. I see them shift to the look of concentration I saw in Greta's Lagoon. *Don't do it*, I glare. *Not here.*

I fall into the river and am pushed under Iker's log by

the current. There's shouting above the rush of water in my ears, but I can't make out what's being said. Then comes a flash of white and navy followed by a great whoosh and water droplets splashing upon my face.

The crowd is making a hearty noise, but it's not until strong fingers tuck into the back collar of my dress do I realize Iker jumped in the water. He's clinging with the other arm to the log, in an attempt to keep from rushing downstream.

"Are you okay?"

I nod, somewhat shocked by the water as much as by the fierceness of his voice.

Iker gives me a gentle push, and I swim the final yards to the edge, working hard against the downstream pull of the current. Annemette is leaning over, reaching for me, her beautiful dress hemmed in mud.

Nik is on the bank, yelling. More than that—he's yanking the boy who threw the stick out of the crowd and tossing him from the competition. I've never seen Nik so angry.

Annemette tugs me up the slick bank. Iker follows, hoisting himself up, hands sinking in the mud. We're a mess, the two of us, dripping water and globs of mud everywhere.

The crowd is silent and so are we. Nik joins us and we turn without a word toward the trail. Not even Nik says anything, the anger still simmering off him.

As we walk away, Nik keeps glancing back at me, muttering to himself. He almost looks as if he wants to grab my hand, but Iker's arm is around my shoulders, and so all he says is, "I'll see to it he never competes, never attends again."

I don't know what to think—Nik isn't one to throw around his royal power like this, but I won't deny it feels good. Of course, it'll only make the whispers continue. More reasons for the townspeople to say I don't know my place. I rub at the bruise forming on my neck, a parting gift from the stick, and look over at Annemette. Her expression is withdrawn, her mouth in a line and her brow furrowed. She's walking a few paces from Nik's side, giving him room, leaving him be.

I've done it again, though, haven't I? Found another way to distract Nik from what's important. I just want to be alone, let everyone go on without me, but when we make it to town, Iker tugs me back, taking a moment to scrape the mud off his boots on the jumbled edge of a cobblestone. Boots clean, and Nik and Annemette out of earshot ahead, he grabs my hand.

"Why did you stay here?"

I blink at him. "What do you mean?"

"When I left to go whaling a few days ago—why did you stay where you knew people would throw sticks and say awful things about you?"

Iker could give Tante Hansa a run for her money in the

observation department, but his words also ring hollow. "It's not anything different from before," I say. "Besides, your offer wasn't real. You and I both know that."

He shakes his head, his eyes fierce. "That's not true, Evie. And it's real now, whether you believe me or not. The moment my duties at the ball end, let's leave. Just you and me on my boat. And if we catch a whale, all the better."

It sounds perfect. My dreams flash before my eyes—of freedom, of Iker, of the sea we could conquer together, one whale at a time. But it's too perfect. I can't go, even if it's only for a few weeks—why can't he see that?

But at the same time, Annemette fills my thoughts— she's risked everything for the one she loves and I've risked nothing. Even if she dies—and it hurts just thinking that— she will have lived more in these few days than I ever have.

I look up at Iker. My imperfect Iker. The right choice couldn't be clearer.

"Let's catch ourselves a whale," I say.

Iker pulls me in for a kiss, and I sink into him, my mind already thick with dreams of days on the sea and nights snuggled together with my cheek to his chest.

FOUR YEARS BEFORE

The raven-haired girl couldn't stay on the beach. She couldn't just lie there while the people she loved like family were in the water.

She pushed herself upright but felt as weighed down as if the tide still held her. Her feet stumbled and her lungs seized, and she fell back into the sand.

The townspeople who watched didn't help her up, didn't rush to her aid. They whispered into their hands but weren't quiet enough. She'd heard it all before, and the words played in her ears like memories.

That girl—she's allowed access to the castle and she's dull enough to think she lives there.

The prince isn't your brother, girl.

Wouldn't put it past her to be behind this whole tragedy—social-climbing cow.

The raven-haired girl forced herself to her feet again, eyes on Iker's form, swimming deftly through the water. Her fingers flexed at her sides. There was so much she wished she could do.

She took a step forward. And then another. Moving under her own power, breathing deeply to push herself along. Her heart pounding in time with the names of her loved ones— Anna, Nik, Anna, Nik, Anna, Nik.

And Iker. So strong. He had to save them.

Her toes splashed in the water and she stopped. Fingers flexing again. What she wouldn't give for her mother's inks and crystals, for her aunt's books and knowledge. For a world where she could use their magic—and not burn or be banished for trying.

Iker surfaced. He threw his head back, pulling in a long heave of air, and then dove, his feet splashing over the top of the churning waves.

He'd found one of them. Maybe both of them. How long had they been under? Could it be too late?

The girl looked to her toes, to the minnows swirling about her ankles like the worst thing in the world wasn't happening right then in their slice of the sea.

Like her friends weren't dying and it wasn't her fault.

Though it was. She'd been the one to suggest to Anna that Nik might be impressed by her bravery. That he always seemed thrilled with hers—why wouldn't it work for Anna? Anna, who had such a crush.

It was the girl's own fault. She'd suggested the race. She'd planted the idea of bravery in her friend's head. And now it was all so wrong.

Anna. Nik. Anna. Nik. Anna. Nik.

But she wasn't powerless, was she? A memory crashed forth in her mind and suddenly the words slipped onto her tongue. Old and dark. And worth a try. She didn't have inks or potions or crystals. But she had these words. They were a breath of life.

—177

And they were all she had.

And so, the raven-haired girl stood in the shallows, reciting the last spell her mother ever cast.

Immediately, her skin grew hot, the seawater there evaporating into dry salt streaks. Her blood sang with magic, her back to the people who would have her burned or banished. She knelt into the waves, put her hands in the water—the more of her touching, the more power there would be.

She shut her eyes.

The words continued and she began to shake. Violently. Steam rose from the waves lapping at her petticoat.

A splash. A large splash. Male voices.

Her eyes opened and looked to the faraway surface.

Nik.

Iker had Nik in his arms.

They were yelling at each other, both full of life. Nik's voice cut through the splashes, a single clear word rising above it all, enough to be heard.

"No!"

The girl's stomach dropped. The words stopped. She was too late. They were all too late.

"Oh, Anna. I'm so sorry." She began to cry, the spell dead on her tongue, her skin cooling.

She blinked and saw black. Swirls of dark viscous liquid pooled in her eyes. Startled, she shot to her feet, thick black tears dripping down her cheeks and into the water.

Not again.

The girl scrubbed at her eyes, wiping her hands on her petticoat. And when she could see clearly again, she looked at her feet. Dead minnows floated on the tide's surface, seaweed shriveling black.

She stumbled backward, onto dry land. The magic gone from her lips, one best friend swimming for land, another lying with her tears in the sea. Tears that had killed the life at her feet.

The girl turned to face the crowd, black streaks staining the heels of her hands as she rubbed her eyes again. The magic sinking into the skin.

The collective gasp was unmistakable.

"Oh, stop, it's just sea grit. She nearly drowned!" Tante Hansa. The old woman came toward the raven-haired girl and pulled her close. Whispered in her ear: "We must leave. Hurry, your life is more important than seeing those boys to land."

19

"ARE YOU SURE YOU'RE ALL RIGHT?" ANNEMETTE ASKS as we leave the palace, a bundle of strawberries in our hands. We went back to change so I could put on dry clothes and Annemette less muddy ones. I suggested a snack and a walk so I could clear my head. Everything was just feeling so muddled—did I actually just agree to run away with Iker? But I can't talk to Annemette about any of that.

"I'm fine. It wasn't a big deal. Really."

"I just don't understand why these people are so horrible to you," she says. "You're generous and smart and beautiful and best friends with their prince!"

I sigh and pull my hands away from my eyes. "That's exactly why. You see, I'm poor, but that's okay because nearly everyone is. But in Havnestad, and probably everywhere else, too, the poor do not befriend the royals. They serve them. Being friendly as children was fine, but it should have ended long ago."

"So why didn't it?"

"Tante Hansa. She saved the king when he was a boy, cured him of some terrible illness, and then again years later after a boating accident. My family was rewarded. My father was named royal fisherman, and Nik and I were allowed to remain friends. No matter how much Queen Charlotte protested, even after my mother died in the way she did."

Annemette doesn't push further on that topic, and I go on. "The great irony is that Tante Hansa has never approved of my friendship with Nik, either, but she knows me well enough to criticize yet never to bar. But the people, they just think I'm using Nik to act better than them, to be more than them. They hate me for it. And it'll never change."

We walk by a row of brick cottages, each with a small garden out front.

"Anna? Anneke?" someone calls from behind.

Annemette blinks and I twist around.

Standing there in the lane, weight on her wooden cane, is Fru Liesel—Anna's grandmother.

A crooked finger points toward Annemette, and a smile crosses the old woman's lips. "Anneke, come, give Oma a hug. It's been too long."

Annemette glances at the old woman and then to me.

"Fru Liesel, this is my friend, Annemette. She is here from Odense."

The old woman ignores me. As she always does. "Anneke, come, give Oma a hug. It's been too long," she repeats.

Annemette takes a step toward Anna's grandmother.

Just as I've felt so many times this week, it's as if I'm glancing through a looking glass at another present. One where Anna is alive, well, beautiful, and singing about boys and strawberries before embracing her beloved grandmother in the street.

But for Annemette, this is not a reunion scene.

"Fru Liesel, my name is Annemette, it's so lovely to—"

Stronger than she looks, Fru Liesel ditches the cane and hauls Annemette to her chest with the force of both knotty hands. Annemette goes along without a fight, her face buried against the old woman's heartbeat.

"Anna, my Anneke, why haven't you visited? Where have you been? Your father is worried sick—I'm worried sick."

Annemette pulls herself up and places her hands gently on the old woman's shoulders. Kindness wraps her features. "I've been away, Oma. I'm so sorry. How have you been?"

My throat tightens as I watch Annemette give the old woman what no one in Havnestad ever allows her—compassion.

"Oh, I'm trying to be good, but at my age, I'd rather fly with the witches."

"A safe bet, Oma."

Fru Liesel is still clutching onto Annemette with both hands. Annemette bends a bit and picks up the woman's cane and holds it out for her.

"Here you are, Oma. Now, where were you off to?"

Fru Liesel grabs the cane with her right hand but stays grasping Annemette with her left, all her weight pressed into the girl's side.

"Home, dear. I was headed home."

Annemette catches my eye. "Let us help you, Oma."

I walk a few steps behind as Annemette and Fru Liesel walk arm in arm down the sea lane, up to the castle and around to a row of grand manor houses on the sunny side of the Øldenburg Castle grounds. Fru Liesel is surely guiding Annemette, the way home being one of the few things she likely hasn't forgotten, but Annemette seems so at ease, it's hard not to think there's something else calling her forward.

Anna's childhood home is three down to the right—red brick and clean lines. It was Fru Liesel's childhood home, and she refused to leave it when the rest of her family fled to the Jutland. I watch Annemette's face as Fru Liesel points to it, and I tamp down the little flutter inside me that hopes she will recognize it—that this girl born of the sea really is my old friend in a shiny, impossible package. But if Annemette recognizes the grand lines of the home, it doesn't flash across her features.

"Here we are, Oma." Annemette's voice is clear and

sweet as they maneuver the foot stones to the front door.

"Thank you, child, my Anneke." She rests her cane against the threshold and opens the door. "Let us have some portvin and talk of your travels. I want to hear it all, especially about the young men queuing for your hand."

Annemette laughs gently. "Yes, Oma, we shall. But can we do it later? I have plans with Evie."

"Oh, you and Evie, always running around. Only two fish in your school. Asger's boy always did try to join, but even a crown can be a third wheel." She chuckles to herself.

"That's right, Oma." Annemette pats Fru Liesel's arm, finally freeing herself completely from the woman's grasp in the process. But that freedom lasts only a moment before Fru Liesel snags her hand yet again.

"But you be careful with that girl, Anneke. Bad things follow her. Black death. Minnows floating at her feet." Annemette catches my eye, and I don't know what to say. "That little witch will be the death of you if you're not careful."

20

We are not even out of view from Anna's house when Annemette stops me short by grabbing both my hands, tugging me to a thatch of trees just outside the queen's tulip garden.

"The first time you saw me, you called me Anna. And Tante Hansa mentioned an Anna too. Now this woman insists I'm her grandchild. Who is this girl? How do you know her?"

"Knew her. She's dead."

Annemette's gaze softens.

I swallow but hold her eyes. The tug-of-war in my heart has ended—the little voice in my head has received a chance to be heard.

"She's the person I think you were before you were a mermaid."

She pitches a brow. "What do you mean before I was a

mermaid? Like my soul? What is it that they believe in the spice lands . . . reincarnation?"

"No, not reincarnation—the *person* you were before, the person you were made from."

"I was only made of my mother and father," she says with certainty. "There's no other way to make a mermaid."

"But what if there is?" I flip our grip, and I'm now grasping her wrists. "I know it's crazy, but my best friend, Anna Liesel Kamp, drowned four years ago. She resembled every inch of you but younger—blond hair, deep-blue eyes, freckles across the bridge of her nose. Beyond looks, she loved to sing. She was spirited, she was—"

"Evie, how many blondes have we seen here these past few days? A hundred? A thousand? I'm sure that Malvina has three blond sisters of her own. There are more blondes in Havnestad than under the entire sea. How many girls have blue eyes? Like to sing? Give cheeky answers?"

"I know, but—"

"That's not evidence, it's coincidence." Annemette shakes out of my grasp and points in the direction of the hordes on the beach. "All these people must remember Anna, but except for that ancient woman, your old tante, and you, not a one has mistaken me for her this entire time."

"Because they think you're *dead*!"

Annemette throws down her arms, clenching her fists. Frustration has gotten the best of me, too, and I feel as if I have no measure for how loud my words are. I don't know if I screamed them or whispered them. All I know is that Annemette's face has shifted from annoyed to concerned. I open my mouth to say that Nik and Iker see the resemblance too, but she's already speaking.

"You think I'm her—you have this whole time . . ."

"In the beginning yes, and then, no. It was you I became friends with, Annemette, but has a part of me hoped—*believed*—you were always Anna? Of course!"

The second the words are out, I realize how strongly that belief has been driving me. I haven't just been imagining what an alternate future would have been like with Anna; I really believed it was happening. And is happening now.

I lower my voice and turn my back to the tulip garden. "Anna drowned. Her body was never recovered. And then, suddenly, you pop out of the same water, the spitting image of her. What am I supposed to think?"

Annemette's face is completely buttoned up. Her lips are screwed shut, her eyes closed; a wall of hair shields her ears. I realize she's preparing to answer me, but I can't take the silence.

"How well do you remember your childhood?" I ask. "Do you remember it at all? What were you doing five years ago? Ten? Who is your oldest friend?"

Finally, when she opens her eyes, there is anger there, though her tone is subdued and her words completely ignore my questions.

"I am sorry for your loss, Evie, but I am not your friend. I am not her. I am Annemette." She lowers her voice here, her voice cracking with pain. "Besides, your dream isn't possible for almost the very reason why I'm here."

"What do you mean?"

She's now in my face, the set of her jaw is angry, her nose at a subtle flare. "Mermaids don't have souls, Evie, not like you humans. I couldn't be created from someone who did. Your friend Anna is in a better place, not in this body that will become nothing but sea foam."

Her crushing words hit me one by one, diminishing nearly all my hope. Then one of Tante Hansa's sayings floats across my mind: *The only thing magic cannot do is know its bounds.* Anything is possible. I open my mouth to say more, to argue this one more point, but Annemette puts up her hand.

"Stop, Evie. Just stop. You're only hurting yourself."

I look at her closely. Is she really Anna? And then I hear her words echo from a moment before: *Your dream isn't possible for almost the very reason why I'm here.* My blood begins to rise.

"Why are you here?" I ask, my eyes squinting at her every inch.

"What do you mean? I love Nik," she says.

"No," I shake my head. "You're here for a soul. Aren't you? Any soul will do. So is this your plan, you get Nik to love you, kiss you, and then you steal his soul? Is this all some kind of dark, sick game?" My heart is beating so loudly I can barely hear myself speak.

Her eyes go soft. "No, Evie. You've got it all wrong. I love Nik. And yes, if he loves me and kisses me, I get a part of his soul. I get to live on as human, and then when I die, more. But Nik's generosity is no different from you giving a piece of yourself to him and to all the people you meet and treat with kindness, making them better. I don't have that to give, but I don't think wanting it is a crime, either."

My heart rate slows, but I'm breathing like I've completed the rock carry. How could I have said what I just said? It was horrible. Annemette grabs my hands and pulls me into an embrace, the smell of the sea on her hair, calming me down. I look up when I hear boots clicking on the cobblestones. Iker and Nik are walking down the path. I pull away from Annemette, and I'm sure my face looks like hers, cheeks flushed and eyes red.

"Smile," I say, wiping my eyes. "Our princes await."

Annemette clasps my shoulder, a smile already blooming on her lips. "Thank you, Evie."

With that she turns and runs past me and into Nik's arms, squeezing him close and taking a pink tulip from his hand when it's presented. He's changed too, his mud-splattered boots and sweat-worn clothes switched out for a nearly identical, crisp, clean edition.

"When you weren't where we'd left you, we'd thought you'd run off with some other sailors."

Iker winks. "Well, *he* thought that. I knew you'd find none better."

He hands me a red tulip, and I immediately sink into him. Impossibly, this new shirt smells of salt and limes and the sea despite being freshly clean and scratchy with starch.

Nik glances up the path to the court homes, Anna's house prominently standing at the end. His eyes settle on the sharp red brick, and then move to me.

"That was our friend's house, once," Nik says, his chin nodding in its direction. "Has Evie told you about Anna?"

Annemette nods. "We met her lovely grandmother just now. Poor thing thought I was her."

His thumb grazes her cheek in a delicate arc. "I must admit that you do resemble our old friend, but considering Fru Liesel has accused everyone—including me—of being Anna in the years since, I'd tell you not to worry about what she thinks."

Nik and I allow ourselves a small laugh with the others despite how hard it is still to speak of Anna. And while my body is drained from arguing with Annemette, I can't let go of the hope that somewhere inside of her is that old friend. I can feel it in my bones. In my heart. I'm right about this.

I'm right about her.

Tomorrow cannot be her last day, and if Nik can't or won't help me achieve what she needs, I will find a way do it myself.

FOUR YEARS BEFORE

The hero was too big for the room. That had been happening often of late, his new height making trouble with any doorframe or ceiling outside of the castle. Belowdecks on his father's ships was definitely the worst, ironic considering the Viking blood thick in his veins.

It had been a week, and he had to see her again. She'd missed the entire Lithasblot festival that year, swallowed in blankets and despair. He'd visited her every night before his duties, entering a room cluttered with bottles and incense, Tante Hansa's famous healing skills at work. He'd never been to this room before—she'd always come to him. Her house felt like another world—and it was.

It was weeks later now, August bearing down. And still she kept to her house, heartache confining her to her room.

That afternoon she'd improved a bit, sitting up with her back to the wall, reading some dirty old book in the low light. She glanced up as he ducked under the threshold, sitting at the end of her bed—his proper mother and her opinions about boys and girls far from here.

"How's the world outside?"

"Still moving?"

She flinched. He didn't blame her, he'd nearly flinched too.

Whenever anyone called him a hero for saving the life in front of him, his stomach curdled with the knowledge that he wasn't quite heroic enough. Everyone had seen Iker pull him from the water. He'd been stopped, but everyone assumed he'd failed. Everyone, including Evie. He saw it in her eyes, wells underneath them as dark as this room.

Guilt was there too. It filled the space where Anna had been, just as large and unwieldy as an eleven-year-old girl. His guilt lay in his failure to save her, her guilt in the fact that she'd put Anna in danger in the first place. In some other part of Havnestad's world, there was disappointment there too—that he'd saved the fisherman's spawn instead of a friherrinde. He was a hero, but in dark rooms and hushed conversation, he was a traitor to his class as well.

"As are you, Evie. You're here. There is so much outside these walls."

To put a point on it, he took a tentative step forward into the tiny room. She watched him as if he might bust through the roof. But he made it carefully to the window, pulling back the curtain she had draped there, letting a sliver of sunlight stream in, blinding and white. The girl blinked so hard, her eyes stayed shut. He waited to speak again until she had the will to open them.

"The world is out there. It misses you."

"That's a lie." And it might have been. But he didn't care about the world. He missed her.

It took four more days of those visits, but he drew her out.

They avoided the beach and the cove, sticking to the market streets—at first. Even though he was there to shield her as much as he could, buying honey buns and the sweet man's fresh saltlakrids with all the joy of a summer day. It didn't stop the stares. Judgment radiated out of every street corner and doorway.

"Acts as if she were the one who drowned."

"The sea takes as much as it gives; it's just the way of things, young lady."

"Saved by a prince and still can't put a smile on that lucky face."

Evie's eyes kept to the cobblestones. There was no way she could enjoy the sun with those stares—even with him by her side.

So he took her away.

He tugged her wrist toward the mountains. Up and up they hiked, the trail twisting toward Lille Bjerg Pass.

There, in a clearing, a mile from the cobblestones, he'd found a sturdy log. One with a particular view of the farmlands sprawling out in the valley below, the sea and its troubles at their backs. They'd never truly been alone like this. Not since they were children, and even then Anna had been there nearly every moment.

Paper bag rustling, he offered her saltlakrids and a smile.

"Salty licorice for your thoughts?"

She didn't touch the bag.

"I knew that was how they'd react." She gestured aimlessly behind her, the entire town in a sweep of her palm.

There was no use in denying it—he'd seen and heard it too. He nodded. She went on.

"They were the same after Mother died and Father would take me to the market, unaware of how to buy for a household with Tante Hansa still away."

She was six at the time, the hero knew. Old enough for memories to truly settle. She looked away from him then, out to the summer-burned pastures below.

"I just want to steal a ship and leave it all. I just want to be me—" She almost said more, but then he snatched her hand in his and gathered the treats in the other.

"Come, then, to the docks. Let's go."

She skipped along beside him, her joyful urgency closer to matching his with each step.

"Where shall we go? Copenhagen? Stockholm? Oslo? Amsterdam? Brighton? Name the place you want to be!"

"Anywhere but here."

"Then anywhere it is."

❦

The hero and the girl made it across the strait and to Rigeby Bay that day. The hero's aunt, uncle, and cousin greeted them first with surprise—both at their arrival and that they'd come alone—and then with dinner.

His mother was the angriest when he arrived back at the castle two days later, wearing his cousin's clothes—loose at the shoulders, short in the arms.

Still, his mind wandered to the time they'd had—Evie, Iker, and himself, across the strait—even as his parents dressed him down in the royal apartments, far from where any servant could hear.

Beach walks with hvidtøl (his first taste), his cousin's seafaring stories, and Evie's hair blowing over her shoulders in the bay's famous wind. It was the first time they'd all been together since the day Anna died. His cousin drank enough hvidtøl to become wobbly on his feet; the hero stopped short of a full glass.

"You are twelve and an heir, what were you thinking?"

The three of them collecting sap for syrup in the deep forests, the shadows thicker than clouds under a knot of pine.

"You have duties in Havnestad to your people and your father. You are too old to be running off. Too smart, too important for such whims."

Her grin, crumbs on her lips, at the queen's insistence on butter cookies at every meal to fatten her up.

"Evelyn is a sweet girl, but you care far too much. Believe me when I say you will only get hurt."

His cousin escorting the two of them home, ordering his minder down below as the three of them ran the sails, capable hands all.

"Nik, listen to me. I was young once. I know what it's like to love someone you cannot have."

The hero blinked then, eyes focusing on the queen. "She's my friend, Mother," though he knew the words sounded flat, not at all how he felt.

"I don't think you should see her anymore. It's for the best. It's the only wa—"

"No!" the hero shouted.

"Let him be," said his father, moving out from a shadow in the room. "She is a good girl, Evelyn. Neither I nor Nik nor you, my dear wife, would be here were it not for Hansa. They can be friends. Just friends. Isn't that right, Son?"

The hero nodded. "Yes, Father."

21

THE SUN HAS NEARLY SET, TENDRILS OF GOLDEN LIGHT spraying the beach, when it is time for the close of today's games. The crowd is thrumming with hvidtøl and excitement for the finale—the rock carry championship. The brine of sweaty bodies mixes with the musk of the king's summer wine and the fatty scent of fresh-fried torsk.

Annemette and I pick at the remains of a fruit-and-cheese plate—grapes, a few slivers of rye left alongside crumbles of samsø and Havarti that somehow escaped our lips. We share a cup of honeyed sun tea as well—something I badly need to help calm my nerves.

Iker and Nik are warming up in the inner circle, jogging paces down the course, a hundred yards long. With them are six winners of earlier heats, ready to run one more time today after winning two earlier eliminations to get to this point. The princes, of course, get to run just in the final round. Nik hates the special treatment, but it makes the people happy to see him run, so he complies.

The rocks that they must carry are all beached at the end closest to where we're sitting. They are heavy, each roughly five stone in weight, though they vary in shape.

Little Johan Olsen is getting ready to compete again too. Nik was right: he is a sight. He's so large, he rivals Nik in height and Iker in strength. The oldest of the finalists is Malvina's father, Greve Leopold Christensen. His daughters sit across the arena from our side, Malvina ignoring us, her attention either on her father or the hand pie in her fingers. The other four competitors are fishermen I see on the docks in the morning—in their twenties and thirties, the lot of them.

"What happens if they drop the rock on their foot or some such thing?" Annemette asks, watching Nik practice his start by repeatedly hauling the rock to his right shoulder from a dead lift. She's been nearly silent since the boys left us.

"They pick it up."

"And then what? Drag themselves home on a broken foot?"

"Most likely." I laugh, though it's cruel. "Don't worry, Mette. Nik has done this before. He won last year, in fact. He'll surely have two good feet to dance with you tomorrow night."

He'll also, unfortunately, have two good feet to dance

with the suitors who arrived an hour ago on a steamer so large it could rival the king's. The docks were full of girls, their chaperones, and some parents. Every mark of Øresund nobility was accounted for from equal kingdoms to landholders of each shape—hertug, markis, greve, friherre, and the like.

It's overwhelming, and now that they've filled the rooms of the castle with their trunks and demands, they've crowded around the king and queen on the royal platform. King Asger's expression is unreadable, but Queen Charlotte is soaking up the attention, flitting among the ladies as if each is a tulip lovelier than the next. And Nik, as usual, is being a gentleman, repeating their names, kissing each hand, but still managing to steal some glances our way. Iker is being Iker—loud, grand, princely—but I can see in his eyes that his heart is not in it.

I turn away, finally, after this afternoon feeling confident in what Iker and I have. Annemette, though, continues to watch the chatter. Especially the queen's.

"What do you think the queen makes of me?" Annemette's eyes shift to mine. "She's been friendly with me . . . but then she is just the same with all of these girls." She lowers her voice to just above a whisper. "And she can't be so high that gossip hasn't reached her ears—Malvina's surely not the only one to notice Nik's time with me."

At this I nearly smile from experience. *Everyone's noticed, trust me.*

With the race almost ready to begin, Queen Charlotte has moved to look down upon the competitors, but I know she is only truly seeking Nik for one last wave of good luck.

"She has eyes only for her son. And she wants to see him properly matched."

Annemette's hand presses to my shoulder. I turn to her and find a flash of anger in the depths of her eyes.

"Properly matched? I know we fought earlier, but there is no need to be cruel, Evie. I have as much of a chance as those other girls."

"I didn't mean it to be cruel, Mette. Really. I meant it as a truth. In order to win him, which you know I hope you do, you must know what he is up against. She is quite an opponent." I move into a whisper. "Your father is a king; would he be pleased if you came home with just any boy?"

The anger recedes. "Well, no—" Annemette's face drains of color. "So, it doesn't matter if I stay . . . she'd find out eventually that I can't claim the title I've told her. . . ." She eyes the suitors, all in fine silks and hair ribbons. "Not like those other girls."

"I didn't say it was her choice." I wait until her eyes meet mine and then hold them with a smile. "If Nik is in love, he will fight for you. But it wouldn't hurt to impress her some more. You'll need to show her and these girls at the ball what kind of friherrinde you are."

Annemette laughs. "Oh, I can definitely do that."

The stiff call of a conch cuts off any further conversation, and the race begins. Our heads whirl around to a rush of sand and bodies, lunging down the course. Iker is already in the lead, Nik and Johan right on his tail. Amazingly, Leopold Christensen is fourth, experience making up for his lack of youth.

My heart is pounding as they get farther away, striding one in line with another until they are so far and so in step that it's impossible to discern from our angle who exactly is in the lead.

We leap to our feet along with everyone else, our hands twined in a clasp of nerves, our faces taut with yelling above the din and cheer.

"Go, Nik!"

"Come on, Iker!"

And from my right, "Johannnnnn!"

Across the way, Malvina and her sisters have their hands above their blond heads, chanting, "Papa! Papa! Papa! Papa! Papa!"

As they cross the line, first there is silence. Then a cheer goes up, and the king and queen are applauding. Nik's arms are above his head. He hops atop his rock and claps and waves.

The victory is his.

The other competitors circle around him, slapping hands and patting him on the back with hearty-enough claps that he must check his balance. Iker is the last one to congratulate him, pulling him off the rock, pinning his arms in a bear hug, and running him back to the start line.

The girls on the platform shriek, and the crowd laughs. And the crush of people is so great that it takes several minutes for us to meet the cousins. Both are still breathing hard, sweat slicking their brows, hands on hips. Iker catches my eye and his breath quickly enough to set his future intentions. "Next year, I'll take him. The scoundrel."

Nik's breath is still coming fast enough that he can only shake his head.

"It was close," Annemette concedes, flush with excitement.

"I think your beauty must have made the difference, Annemette. Needed to impress you, the rat."

I wince, though only a little. "I suppose that means we've come past the point where you work to impress me."

"Hardly." Iker leans into me, breath warm in my ear. "I was just planning to impress you in other ways this evening."

Before I can roll my eyes—or better yet, slap him—Nik tugs Iker away from me and regains his voice. "Iker, if you want a night to ourselves, I suggest we leave now." Nik points his chin up at the stairs, where a flock of beribboned girls and the queen are working their way down.

"Well spotted, Cousin." Iker grabs my hand and nudges Nik forward. "Let us away."

22

I LOUNGE UPON THE SAND OF HAVNESTAD COVE.

Above, the stars twinkle, the Lithasblot moon full on this, the fourth night, the shimmering light strong only thanks to the reflection off the smooth waters of the cove. But it is the perfect lantern for the night—bathing everything in a pool of silver.

Iker is lying beside me. The cut of his stubbled chin, the laughing light of his eyes, the sun-kissed pieces of hair curling at his temples fill my gaze. All of it in close relief and profile—my view coming from where I'm snuggled against his chest. It's a perfect moment, and yet my mind drifts to the other side of the cove's rock wall. Where Nik and Annemette are. She is singing, her ethereal soprano lifting toward the stars.

Please Nik, just kiss her.

I don't want it to, but her voice takes me back to that

day Anna drowned, the song we were singing before we dove into the sea. Fru Liesel's words play in my mind: *Bad things follow her. Black death. Minnows* ... No. I stop myself from falling deeper into that hole. I've come too far from that day to take the blame for it and everything that followed. I have enough to live with.

I shift my attention back to Iker. He's talking about our whaling trip. The cities we'll dock in; the sea life we'll catch. Apparently, I haven't been the only one fantasizing.

"What do you think?" he says, his hand tilting my chin so our eyes meet.

"What's that?" I ask.

"Hirsholmene or Voerså Havn?"

"Oh, whichever you think best," I say.

"Where are you, Evie? Don't you want this?" The vulnerability in his voice is a shock, but strangely comforting to hear.

"Of course I do!" I say, and I mean it. "I'm just thinking of how to tell Father and Tante. You know how they can be."

"Tell them a prince wants to sweep you away. That should suffice." Iker's lips lower until they hover a breath from mine.

"If only," I whisper. He closes the distance and I sink into him, all of him. The pad of his thumb runs the length of my cheekbone and he shifts again until both hands are holding my face to his, our breath mingling and eyes closed to anything but this kiss.

Annemette falls into bed in a shower of blond waves. Flecks of sand fall too, bouncing mildly into the air, just forceful enough that I can see them leap and settle in the candlelight as I shake the beach out of my own curls at the vanity table. But something is off. Her eyes are red and her face has gone pale.

"What's wrong?" I ask. "We left when things grew quiet on your side. I thought maybe . . ."

Her shoes are off, her hands running the length of her feet, her face wincing in pain.

"Can I get you anything? Is there a spell that can ease the burning? I may have found something in Hansa's book. Here, I'll show you—"

But when Annemette looks up, I can see that her feet are not what truly pains her.

"I've failed, Evie. I'm going to fail. I know it!"

I swallow hard, because deep down inside, down in the snake pit of my belly, I fear that I know it too. I've been carrying it with me all day. "But there's still tomorrow," I offer, holding out hope. "You can't give up, Mette."

But she shakes her head, almost as if I've made it worse with my insistence.

"We're not supposed to come to land. I should never

have done this! How could I have been so stupid?"

I start to cry, the tears pouring from my eyes. I hold my throat tight so the maids won't hear my sobs. I look up at her—a lost expression on her face, her eyes puffy and dry. And suddenly I realize that she can't cry.

No soul. No tears. No way to truly feel. How is that a way to live?

But if we don't succeed, she won't live at all. And time is running out.

One day left.

FOUR YEARS BEFORE

The one who survived was starting to feel as if she had life left in her.

Most of that was thanks to the boy dragging her out into the sun, to school, up into the mountains.

But there was more to the change of things.

Time. People. Herself.

Winter was at the door, the whaling season at an end, her father home for good, drinking coffee and reading in his chair. They would talk sailing, the young survivor's head spinning with ways to make it easier, ways to make next year more prosperous. Ways for her future self to be successful on her own ship in her own time, far away from the memories of this place.

She spent time with her tante too, soaking up every bit of magical knowledge the old woman thought to share, and stealing any she didn't—tiptoeing into her room and taking one book at a time from her well-worn chest. The lessons could not come fast enough for all she wanted to know about what she would eventually be able to do.

Sometimes she found herself staring at her hands, wishing, as she had that awful day, that she could've saved her lost friend with magic. The failure still ate away at her.

Still, even with Havnestad's archaic rules against

magic—set in place by the same generation of Øldenburgs who'd sent witches fleeing from Ribe more than two hundred years before—the survivor felt it necessary to arm herself so that she would never feel so helpless again.

She knew that with power, the bravery to act would come. The right magic would come at the right time.

And so she read all she could. Begged her aunt for more lessons, more spells. That winter and beyond, her magical education deepened anew, propelled by a desire not just to know herself and her power but what she could do.

The girl even tried to find her mother's words and the history behind them. Digging through the chests for books her father had put away for years. Her tante eventually found out about them and added them to her extensive collection of magical tomes. And then the girl stole them back, one at a time, their dusty covers warped enough that they could easily be hidden within the wrinkles of her sickbed sheets.

And so she studied. And at night, she practiced quick spells with her tante as they made dinner. And then, cozied before a roaring fire, she listened to tales at her father's feet.

23

THREE HOURS LATER, ONLY THE SILVER MOON AND I are still awake. Midnight came and passed long ago, but sleep remains elusive, my mind churning like the angriest of seas. Less than twenty-four hours remain until Annemette's time is up, but I refuse to stand by and watch her become more foam in the sea. I will not be left powerless again.

I slide from the sheets and tiptoe over to my trunk. I open it slowly, revealing my petticoats. Tucked underneath are the amethyst and the vial of black octopus ink. They were in the pocket of the dress I wore at the log race, and I stashed them in here so the dress could be sent to the maids and cleaned—Nik insisted. I gather the two items and close the trunk, dress quickly, then snatch up my boots by the door. Rather than put them on, I pad out into the hall, feeling the cool marble on my bare feet.

I shut the door as quietly as possible and head out-side to the tulip garden. Despite the full guest wing, not a soul passes me, and Nik, Iker, and the king and queen are thankfully two wings away.

Outside, the air is warm, but the sky is black, clouds now covering the moon. Up ahead a guard stands watch at the archway. I can't let him see me. I don't even want to think of the rumors that would spread if word got out that I left in the dead of the night, so I've come prepared. With my hand clasped around the amethyst in my pocket, I focus inward, letting the magic rise in my blood. When I'm ready, I take the octopus ink and pull out the small cork stopper. The smell of the sea fills my nose, and I pause before bringing the vial to my lips. *Greima*, I think, then pour the vial's contents down my throat, the briny liquid making my tongue tingle.

I stand as quiet and still as possible, waiting for the spell to take hold. But nothing happens. *It didn't work.* My stomach sinks. I spent the whole night in bed going over and over this spell, trying to do it just the way I know Annemette would. And now I've drunk the whole vial of ink, and I can't try again. I turn to go back inside, but now my body won't move. My heart begins to pound, and I feel a great pressure crushing my chest. My legs go numb and my vision blurs. When the sun rises, Nik will surely find me lying here dead, another friend gone.

Then, in a split second, it all stops just as quickly as it

started. I suck in a breath of air and bring my hands to my face to collect myself, but I realize I can see right through them. *It worked!* I wiggle my fingers before my eyes, but all I see are the queen's tulips on the other side. I'm invisible—or rather, I'm blending in, my body and clothes camouflaging with the world around me.

I hold my breath and walk as quietly as I can past the guard and out the gate, not risking a glance behind me. Once I leave the castle grounds, I head straight toward my lane, only pausing to put my boots on, a satisfied smile resting on my lips.

At home, I slide off my boots on the stoop, bare feet yet again much more efficient for what I must do. On tiptoe, shoes in hand, I step over the threshold and into the house. Familiar smells of coffee, Tante Hansa's pickling brine, and remnants of boiled octopus ink greet my nose. From Tante's room I can hear her thunderous snores. Father's door is open, his bed still empty until tomorrow night. My room is opposite his, the door shut tight, but that is not where I need to go.

I press myself against Tante's door, the scent of dried roses seeping out with an even heavier round of sound. The knob turns, and I push the door just wide enough for my body. I place a foot soundlessly on each side, sandwiching the door open for a crevice of light.

Eyes adjusting, I step into the room. Tante Hansa is lying faceup toward the heavens. Her eyes are closed and her snores unchanged, so I turn my attention to the reason I am there.

Her trunk.

For Annemette to stay, I must give the magic and Mother Urda something in return—words, gifts, or the perfect combination of both. I just need the right knowledge to guide me.

Tante's trunk is in the corner, ancient moose hide over the top, exactly like it was when I found my amethyst—if she's noticed the stone missing, she's kept it to herself. Just as she has since Anna's death, most likely aware that I've tiptoed in nearly every week, borrowing books to educate myself on all she has refused to teach me.

With careful fingers, I lift off the hide and lift open the trunk. The hinges squeak with a yawn, and the snores hiccup off rhythm. I freeze for a moment before slowly turning to check Tante Hansa. She shifts a bit toward the wall, the weak light from the doorway catching the silver strands of hair braided tightly against her crown.

When the correct rhythm returns, I move again, opening the trunk farther until the lid leans against the wall.

The contents are just as I remember them—bottles of potions on the right, gemstones piled high to the left. And below both of them, what I need.

Magical tomes.

I pick out the bottles one by one, placing them on the hide, then the gemstones, too. As the trunk empties slowly, the books come into view.

I'm unsure which one may have the wisdom I need to keep Annemette here permanently, but I have a decent guess—the one Tante Hansa keeps tucked away at the very bottom. I pull out four books on potions—all near the top, given Hansa's proclivities—before the books with the older, more delicate spines appear. I lean into the trunk from the shoulders on up, my nose a few inches from the covers so that I can read their titles.

The Spliid Grimoire.

I pull the tome onto my lap and I can feel its dense weight on my thighs. It is heavy with pages, but also with power. Inside are hundreds of spells collected through generations. I run my hands along the cover, grazing over the flowers, plants, and symbols that have been etched into its surface. I close my eyes and breathe in deeply, the smell of aged leather, parchment, and ancient inks filling my nose. There's a rush of white-hot heat up my neck, and it's the same delicious feeling that pulsed through my veins when Annemette taught me to spell the oysters—*lif.* The book is pulling me in, calling me, taunting me to open it, when suddenly, I realize the room has gone silent. Tante Hansa's snoring has quieted.

I steal a glance behind me. Tante Hansa has rolled to her other side but is still sound asleep. I don't know how long the masking spell will last, but I'm wasting too much time. I tuck the volume down the front of my bodice, right up against the flat of the ribs under my arm. It bulges, but the darkness should hide it if I become visible. Then I return the other books in order and go to work on the bottles and stones.

I'm just replacing the last stone when I feel a warm dampness against my ear.

"You wicked, insolent child. Stealing from me in the middle of the night."

I pull back, so stunned that my heart is refusing to beat, but Tante Hansa moves her face closer to mine. Her brows are arched down, and her lips are pulled into a sour scowl, the regal lines of her Roman nose and strong jaw made terrifying by an anger I've never seen.

"I'm just borrowing. How can you see—"

She grabs my wrist hard, and I drop the stone to the floor. "Borrowing *is* stealing in the eyes of an owner left in the dark."

In her aging hands, my skin flashes in and out, visible to invisible, until finally my pale arm and my whole body stand out from the darkness as stark as the moonlight. The spell has lifted.

"A witch can always sense the magic that stems from her own blood."

Guilt tugs at my throat. Her room and things aren't a sweetshop, and I'm old enough not to presume so. "I would never steal from you, Tante. I'm just trying to do good—to use your knowledge for good."

"If there's good to be done, I will do it myself. Pride and ignorance cannot learn a spell and save the world; they can only combine for damage." Her fingers twist the skin at my wrist as she goes on. "Why are you here? What are you trying to do?"

I can't tell her. I know she'll believe me, but that's the problem. I promised Annemette I'd never tell anyone who she is. "I told you, I'm trying to do good!"

"No." Tante shakes her head. "This has to do with that girl. The girl who smells more of dark magic than a sailor smells of fish. Annemette, is it?"

I don't say anything. I don't even breathe because it would feel like a betrayal.

I try to stand, but she resists. "You are not blind, child, nor idiotic—though I still believe you to be wicked and insolent in plan tonight. And I believe it has much to do with her. Who is she?" Her eyes crinkle at the corners as she self-corrects. "*What* is she?"

"I—"

"You cannot hide much from this old witch, Evelyn."

No, I can't. But I can deflect. "I just don't want her to go."

"Loneliness is the weakest excuse for magic there is, and it mixes horribly with pride and ignorance." I wince. She nods at the stone by my side on the floor. The one that dropped. "Just because you believe you've stolen from me before and had success does not make you a witch; it makes you a lucky thief."

I should be reeling from her knowledge of all the magic I've done—and the fact that she knowingly let me do it—but my mind is stuck on a single word in that sentence.

Success.

What I've been doing at the docks has actually worked! It was true magic. My magic. Made without anyone's lessons.

I did that.

And I can do it again.

My heart swells. Confidence zips through my veins. The grimoire burns against my skin.

I can do this.

I can save Annemette. If I can reverse the Tørhed, if I can go invisible, I can do anything. I just need the right means.

I press my lips to Tante Hansa's dry cheek and place the fallen stone in her hand. "Tante, I'm sorry. I promise I won't treat your things with such little respect ever again."

"Oh yes, you will, child. They are familiar. One cannot hold respect with the familiar. We forget our boundaries." She moves both hands to my face, snatching my cheeks and forcing me to look deeply into her eyes. "We forget our boundaries with familiar people, too."

I nod. "I am sorry."

"As am I, child."

She lets me go, and it's not until I'm slipping on my boots in the moonlight outside that I realize she didn't mean only herself when discussing the familiar.

She meant everyone familiar at play—Iker, Nik, and, most especially, Annemette.

FOUR YEARS BEFORE

Deep under the splashes at the surface, where the men came in one after another spurred by the boy's orders, five girls with golden hair circled 'round a curiosity from above.

A little girl, tall but with no telltale signs of womanhood, floated between them. Eyes closed. She was beautiful. Just like they were.

One of the five, the oldest, had snagged the girl by her foot as the tow brought her under. There was no way to bring her up safely. Not with the men above. Not with the chance of being seen.

She could only bring the girl down.

The commotion rallied her sisters. Soon, their father would follow. And it would take every one of them if they were going to save her.

"Lida, you must take her back up," the second oldest said. "The sandbar is just there and—"

"It's too dangerous."

The youngest didn't understand. Mermaids could not shed tears but this one tested the boundary, her small hand wrapped around the girl's finger. "You brought her here to die?"

The oldest shook her head in her determined way. "She is already gone. I brought her here to live."

"Oh, Lida," their father boomed, disappointment in his voice. All the girls turned. "We cannot—"

"We can save this one. Please, Father." He didn't approach. "Just look at her face."

Her tone, her face, his gut—all of it forced him swim forward, a king ruled more often than not by the whims of his daughters. So like their mother in spirit, like his Mette, may she rest in the tide.

The king peered at the girl's face. Creamy skin. Blonde hair. Her eyes were closed but her lashes were full and dark, and he knew that open they would be enchanting, no matter the color.

He looked upon his daughters, each of them pleading, each of them touching the girl in some way. Their spirits lifting her up, keeping her from becoming bones in their sweet blue sand. He didn't want to disappoint them but he knew the limits of his magic. He'd reached them when he'd made their mother, Mette, and he hadn't been able to save anyone since. But maybe, with the girls' help, they'd have enough energy for success. Maybe.

He hoped they would.

With a sigh, he nodded.

The girls, all but the youngest, cheered. Those closest to him used a hand to pat his arm or shoulder with approval, but never fully let the girl go. The youngest was confused. She kept her attention on the girl, nearly the same age as she, watching the stillness.

"But how?"

Her father smiled. "Magic."

The littlest didn't blink—long accustomed to the tricks of the older girls. She knew what her magic could do and it was not this. "Magic?"

The oldest answered for her father, already moving to space the sisters at equal intervals along the girl's body. They had to be just right. They had to do this perfectly, or the girl would turn to bones despite their effort. Despite the fact that all but the youngest knew the story of their mother and the gift she was from a great storm many years ago. She was worse off than this, but not by much. "Yes, come here."

The oldest moved to the girl's head, pointing her father to the girl's feet. This made him laugh again—the sea king, taking commands. His daughters did not appreciate it, their serious faces unwavering from the difficulty at hand. They didn't see how much they were like their mother.

When they were set, the oldest finally yielded and he gave the order, gave them the command to say: verða. Then he turned his triton upon the girl, touching the tip to her toes. Immediately, light sprang forth, crawling up her legs to her torso, climbing until it reached the crown of her head.

And stopped.

The light blitzed out like it was never there at all.

The sea king sighed. The girl's pale skin had begun to turn gray. There wasn't much time. If this was to work, they had only one more chance.

"Let us try again." He looked to each of them. Tried to put confidence into his features. Though he knew how the magic *worked. Barter meant a life for a life unless there was just the right amount of magical energy. If he could complete the transaction by himself so long ago, he could do it with his girls. Surely. Maybe. "Concentrate."*

Again, he touched his triton to the tip of the girl's toes. Stared until all he could see was the girl's graying face. "Verða." The girls repeated it, all of them touching the girl, their eyes squeezed shut. Power in their voices.

And again, a light sprang forth, crawling up her legs to her torso, climbing until it reached the crown of her head. Then, as it climbed her cheeks, something dark and old seemed to seep into the water around them, like frigid air hitting the surface and forming ice. The sea king's triton wavered.

But then it came—a flash of light so crisp and bright that it would've been mistaken for lightning up top. And, for the first time since Mette, it was done.

The girl's chest rose. Her eyes blinked open—blue and beautiful as the sea king suspected. She lifted her head just enough to see their faces, her new body, before confusion and exhaustion took her and she fell into a deep sleep.

The littlest knew she was no longer the youngest. That this girl would be a sister. She ran her fingers along the girl's tail, marveling at the fresh turquoise scales, shimmering in the deep water.

"What shall we call her, Father?"

"Mette," he said without missing a beat.

The girls knew what this meant. It made the oldest's spine tingle and fingers shake. She had to say something.

"On the surface, they call her Anna. The men are yelling her name over and over."

The sea king read the faces of his daughters. Glanced down at the sea's newest mermaid. The littlest of his girls. He smiled.

"Annemette. Let us call her Annemette."

24

THOUGH SOFT AND SUBTLE, THE BLUE LIGHT OF THE morning stuns me awake, and the sound of the sea echoes in my ears. *The sea.*

My eyes fly open. Candle still flickering. Book splayed pages down in my lap. My back propped against the rock wall.

I fell asleep in my workshop. *My lair*, I think with a smile. But quickly I snap back to reality. That was not part of the plan.

I grab the grimoire and carefully flip it toward the right page, the parchment delicate and thin. I'm looking for the one with the triton. I thumb through all the pages, but on my first try, I don't find it. It's too dark in here. With a frustrated huff, I grab the book and the candle and pad across the dirt floor to the cave's entrance.

Dawn is just minutes away, the indigo night reaching

past Havnestad to the west while a shade a tick lighter licks at the horizon. Between the coming light and the glow of the candle, I calm myself and read with eyes bleary from a lack of sleep.

Luckily, I found what I was looking for before my body gave in to rest last night. I can almost recite it—but I don't want to take any chances, recalling the panic I felt earlier when I thought the masking spell had gone wrong.

In the brighter light, I focus my eyes on the flipping pages, attention on the upper right-hand corner.

Where is it?

After a few minutes, there it is—the triton. Etched into the page, the symbol of the sea king. I huddle over the page and read.

The sea is forever defined by its tide, give and take the measure of its barter. In magic, as in life, the sea does not give its subjects lightly—payment is required, the value equivalent, no matter the ask. A shell, a fish, a pearl of the greatest brilliance—none can be taken without a debt to be paid.

I know magical barter. I've known it my whole life. I saw it in my mother's eyes the moment before she died, giving her life for mine. If there's a way out of the spell Annemette used to come to land, I'll find it.

I look up at the sun rising.

In eighteen hours it will be midnight.

In eighteen hours, Annemette's time is up.

I can't lose her again.

Blowing out the candle, I hide my book in a crevice in the wall and slide the crate of oysters in front of it.

My fingers dab at the pearl at my throat—*Annemette's pearl*—the light that showed me the way to my own magic. I'm grateful to Annemette, and now, hopefully, I can return the favor.

I make my way to the docks, the winds from deep within the Øresund Strait airing out the crowd of ships with fresh breeze and salt brine. Every spot is full, and half the boats will be leaving in the morning. Half the boats, including Iker's—with me on board. A warmth grows in my heart when his little schooner, towed in and repaired from the storm, comes into view, tied in place to the royal dock.

I press the little amethyst to the hull of Iker's boat for double the time I do any other ship. But I do touch them all, moving swiftly, repeating my words. This magic needs to be done before I test the kind that will keep Annemette home.

In an hour, I've finished. Dawn has risen completely, scarlet and salmon painted in wide swaths about the horizon. It's just bright enough that I squint into the light as I stand on the edge of the royal dock, the one that leads deepest into the harbor.

My heart begins to pound, a nervous twinge climbing my spine. *Seventeen hours.* I know how to exchange words for what I want, but not items, so now is the time to work it out. I place one hand on the pearl and hold my amethyst in the other. My two most prized material possessions. Items I'd fight for—though it's a toss-up as to which one I should use. I squeeze my eyes shut and make my choice.

Then, I summon Annemette's confidence. Mother's magic. My own stubbornness.

There's no reason why this won't work.

I can do this.

I can do this.

"Skipta."

From the tips of my toes to the crown of my head, the oldest of magic crackles through me like Nordic ice ripping through a ship's hull. The sea pours into my veins.

I toss the amethyst into the waters, and I watch it sink.

Then I wait. My heart thuds in my ears, fear mingling with the magic's chill. At my throat, the pearl throbs, frozen. I tell myself to be patient. Remember last night. This is how it works, but after five breaths, the panic is so great in my heart that I drop to my knees.

Fickle sea with nothing to give.

I haul myself over the side of the dock, fingers straining against the weather-beaten boards as I get my face as close to the surface of the water as possible, vision straining for any sign of my precious gemstone.

But all I see is my reflection. Pale and nervous, exhaustion and worry coating my features.

"What have I done?"

Shame bites at my heart. Heat rises in my cheeks, but a chill runs the length of my spine. I whip my head up and fall back onto the dock, curls snagging in the boards. My fingers dab at the pearl.

Tante Hansa was right—I was a lucky thief, but with cheap parlor tricks. I'm not a witch yet—not like my aunt, my mother or Maren Spliid. I'm just a—

Sea spray cuts off my thoughts, shooting straight up from the water like a whale spout just below the surface. My eyes widen as they scan an object within the stream. I struggle to sit up fast enough to cup my palms into position as it begins its descent.

When it lands, I close my grip, protecting it. Protecting the hope that has risen in my heart.

I take a breath and open my hand.

A stone as blue as the noontime sky and smooth as glass sits there, the same weight and size as my amethyst.

Just as sure as the tide, it worked.

I gave. It took. It gave. I took.

Just as I'd hoped.

Clutching the blue gemstone, I hop to my feet and meet the sea's gaze.

"*Skipta.*" *Exchange.*

I drop the gemstone back in the water and hold my

breath, thinking about my amethyst. Hope piling in my heart that I can haggle with the sea to get the exact exchange I want.

"*Skipta,*" I repeat, and then whisper the only Old Norse word I know that's close to what I want. "*Bjarg.*" *Stone.*

Cupping my hands, I stand there, eyes on the horizon. Two gulls play on the water's surface, dipping, splashing, and rising in tandem.

As they soar just above my head, another spout shoots up from the deep. Bigger and stronger, it sprays the royal dock and me with it, but I hold my ground, hands outstretched.

Another item lands in my hands. Palms still together, I run one wrist over my eyes to clear the seawater there, blink the blurriness away, and then reset. Breath held, my fingers bloom open and reveal not my amethyst but something even more radiant.

A stone of deep crimson, jagged crystals a crust on its surface like rock sugar. Its heart is as bloodred as my own, seemingly lit from a fire within.

It is not what I had in mind, but it's blinding with beauty—much more so than my amethyst. But can it do what my amethyst can do? Or will it wreck the spell?

I can't worry about it now. It's clear from the magic's response that it will only trade like for like. The exchange will be the same when Annemette is in place of the stone. And I do not have a body to give the sea.

This *is* a problem.

But maybe the solution has already come to pass—four years before. Perhaps now I can foster the final trade.

"What is it with you and me and mornings?"

Nik.

I turn, holding the gemstone against the folds in my dress, wishing I had the right angle to drop it into my pocket without being obvious.

The twinkle in Nik's eyes doesn't let on to how long he's been standing there. He's fully dressed and clean-shaven, shoulders square and hands on his hips.

"I promise I didn't stalk you to hassle you about kisses again."

"Mm-hmm, that's what they all say."

A blush rises so quickly on Nik's cheeks that I know he's immediately wishing he hadn't shaved before the sun. "I truly am sorry. It's none of my business."

I smile at Nik. "Of course it's your business—you're my best friend."

He takes two steps and sinks to the dock, his boots kicking over the side and dangling. I find a dry patch of wood and sit next to him.

"Some best friend I am," he says. "Always ditching you for duty. And you can't even talk to me about boys—one word about kissing and I become a beet-red gargoyle."

I put my hand on his elbow and use the other to squirrel the stone into the pocket hidden in the gown's folds.

"To be fair, we are talking about your best friend kissing a cousin you treat like a brother."

He nods. "It's true. Why couldn't you go for someone a little *less* close? Say a Ruyven or Didrik or Jan?"

I can't help it: my nose scrunches immediately. "Because Ruyven or Didrik or Jan . . ." *believe I think I'm too good for them.*

"Aren't Iker?" Nik cocks a brow.

Now it's my cheeks that flame up and I point to them, laughing. "This is how you look when we talk about kissing."

Nik laughs, and just the word *kissing* makes him blush too. When our eyes meet, something about his face softens. He brushes a wayward curl away from my cheek—not in the romantic way of Iker, but in the loving way of family.

His thumb and forefinger linger in my hair, and I laugh again because I'm not sure what else to do. After the sound dies, I can't draw in a breath. I can't do anything but hold his eyes.

"Moving in on my territory, Cousin?"

We whip around and there is Iker, fully dressed but not clean-shaven, a ship rope spooled about an arm.

"I can't help it if my best friend is the prettiest girl in all of Havnestad."

Iker doesn't laugh. His voice is as sturdy as his ship. "Wouldn't say that too loudly—I have it on my own authority that you never want to anger a blonde."

I force my features into an overdramatic pout. "Did someone get burned once upon a time?"

A devilish grin spreads across Iker's lips, and that familiar joyous light winks in the icy depths of his eyes. "Yes, and it still hurts." Then he hooks a brow. "My mother always told me a kiss can make it better."

I get to my feet. I can still feel Nik's fingers in my hair. "There's plenty of time for that later."

"There is," Nik adds, putting himself between me and Iker. "Now, let's get back to work. Your ship won't prepare itself."

"That's rich, given you were the one to walk down the dock and not come back."

"Where are you going?" I ask suddenly, worried that Iker might be about to leave without me.

"Father wants to take the castle workers on the steamer for the Celebration of the Sea today."

In my sleep-deprived state and my focus on the ball, I'd forgotten about the Celebration of the Sea, the afternoon party on the harbor before the grand event. It's fun, everyone in Havnestad with their boats anchored a little way out in the water. It manages to bring us closer to our cherished sea, and yet, looking back to the coast, we can see how beautiful our home truly is.

"Anyway," Nik goes on, "Mother plans to have all her special guests and their minders aboard the old three-sail. And Iker doesn't want our party to go with either."

"Stupid as a plastered horse, that would be," Iker grumbles.

"So we made the royal decision to take the schooner."

It's silly, but my breath catches. "Just the four of us?"

"Indeed." Nik nods. "As long as we can ship off before my parents get wind of what we've done."

My heart rises. Just the four of us all day on a boat. Laughing, singing, eating, before dressing up and dancing the night away—a fitting end to our Lithasblot and a fabulous beginning to the new way things will be. The weight of the gem in my pocket tells me this is right.

"Perfect."

25

ANNEMETTE IS AWAKE AND DRESSED WHEN I RETURN, standing at the window, looking out to the sea. Despite the sky and sun pouring in, there's a weight to her silhouette, as there should be. This day—the next sixteen hours— means life or death.

If she hears the door and my footsteps, she doesn't turn. Doesn't ask where I've been. After a moment, she finally speaks. "It's so beautiful, watching the sea from this view," she says, now facing me. "But I'll never be able to go back, and I can't stay here. Oh, Evie. I shouldn't have come!" A sob squats in her voice as she buries her head in her hands.

There's not time for talk like that. No time for wishes and should haves.

"I know what to do," I say.

"No." She lifts her face, furious in the new light even as her voice cracks. "I told you. You can't use love magic,

Evie. You don't understand how this works! What I've done. What I have—"

"Yes, I do." I take a step closer, stubbornness squaring my shoulders. "And if Nik doesn't have the answer, I do. I've found the right spell. Between the two of us, we can keep you here. I know it. I have it figured—"

"No. You. Don't." She lunges toward me and grabs my wrists. Her angelic face blooms with pockets of deep red. "Whatever little spell you've created doesn't matter. The magic won't take anything else. It won't, it won't, it won't . . ." All the fight drains out of her in a flood, and her body sways and then begins to sink. I catch her on the way down and try to soften the blow as we hit the stone floor in a heap of silks and gold thread.

Her head dips into my lap, her shoulders heave in wracking shakes, and she moans. No tears, of course. I know that now. I place my hands gently on the back of her head, combing my fingers through her hair. I take a deep breath and let my voice settle, calm.

"We're spending all day on a boat with Nik. Just the four of us. And then there's the ball tonight. Balls are the most romantic venue in all the world—true love is practically a decoration."

Annemette tosses her head from side to side in my lap, but she doesn't say anything.

"If after the last dance, the magic still hasn't been

satisfied, we'll do it our own way." I wrap my arms around her shoulders and lay my head upon hers. "I won't let you go."

~

Annemette's nerves are as obvious as her freckles as we appear in the sunlight.

She's nervous about the time remaining.

About Nik's feelings.

And, almost more than any of that, she's nervous about being on the water. I know now that when she transformed, she had to let the sea go in every way possible, and it won't take her back, not even to indulge her to enjoy a day gliding on its back.

I grab her hand and give it a squeeze as we spot the boys by Iker's schooner. Iker and Nik each have a tulip in hand—pink for Annemette, red for me.

"Ladies," Iker says, "you're so beautiful today, the mermaids will be fuming with jealousy."

I do a little curtsy, and Annemette bobs with me. "Convenient, then, that we have two dashing princes to keep us safe from their clutches."

Iker cocks a brow and draws me in for a kiss on the cheek. "You're meant for my clutches, not theirs." His arms squeeze my waist in a bear hug.

Blushing lightly at the ears, Nik rolls his eyes. "Is this how it's going to be all day with you two?"

Iker meets my eye. "Probably."

Another roll of Nik's eyes, and then he tugs at Annemette's arm. "Let's go, before it gets so crowded we can't leave the dock." I lift my brows in encouragement at Annemette, mouthing, "You'll be fine." She turns a nervous smile toward Nik.

Iker and Nik hop onto the schooner first and hold out their hands to us—no gangplank available. I step into the boat next and immediately regret not waiting to help Annemette. Her coloring has not improved, and now she stands alone on the dock, both hands gripping her tulip with white knuckles.

"Are you all right?" Nik asks, stepping forward.

Annemette nods, but there's no credibility in it.

"She's a tad nervous—boating accident when she was a kid."

The kindness in Nik's face makes me melt. "I know what that's like. I haven't told you about my recent incident, have I? It was scary, but the best way to beat the fear is to get back on the water. And you're with an expert sailor today, Mette," Nik says, slapping Iker on the back. "The best there is. You're safe here. I promise."

Annemette nods but doesn't move to come aboard.

"Here, jump to me," says Nik. "I'll catch you."

Annemette takes a deep breath. After several seconds, she leaps into his arms.

I stumble back out of the way just in time to give them more room. Nik's excellent balance keeps them upright, and

Mette lands as gently as possible on the little schooner's stern, a grateful smile at her lips as she beams up at him, scooped against Nik's chest. Exactly where she needs to be.

"Summer wine, Mette? It calms the nerves," Iker says, sitting down on the bench next to me. Annemette shakes her head at his offer.

I meet Nik's eyes. "Perhaps some water?" Nik nods for Iker to retrieve it from the chest he filled with chipped ice.

We'd made it to the mouth of the harbor with ease and were now pleasantly floating. Well, pleasant for everyone except Annemette, who can barely look over the rail.

Iker returns and slips the canteen to Nik, who uncaps it for Annemette.

She takes a greedy pull. "Better?" Nik asks, and she gives another unconvincing nod.

Iker grabs a large jug and fills a tin cup with the contents—from the smell of it, hvidtøl.

"Starting early, Iker?" A glint rises in Nik's eye, and he takes a swish of Annemette's water.

"Starting right on time. And who do you think you are, second-guessing the captain on his own boat?"

"Someone who is often in charge and remains sober for his duties."

"This is a festival, and there has been entirely too little drinking for my taste. I am eighteen and a prince. I can enjoy myself on my own ship as I please."

"Iker, may I have some water?" I ask, because they can't continue this way. Not that I'm sure I can stop them, but I'll settle for distracting them as a means to turn this around. It's *supposed* to be a romantic jaunt.

Iker plops down on the bench and takes a long swig from his tin cup.

"If your sober prince wants to share, of course you may."

I eye the flask—most likely Iker's personal water jug and no more. It sits lightly in Nik's hand, a third gone with two measly glugs.

"Not to second-guess the captain, but is that all you brought to drink?"

Iker shakes his head into the cup. "Like I said, there's summer wine," he says before raising the jug in his hand. "And hvidtøl too. I'm not an idiot—I know it's hot."

I roll my eyes. "What about to eat?"

Iker stands and flips open another chest of ice, plunging his free hand into the depths. "Ah, yes, cheese and fruit and not a single thing more. What is this? A garden party? There's not even a herring."

"Mette's allergic," Nik says. He was in charge of packing the food.

"Well, I'm not. And allergy, my arse. She's just being particular to watch you fall all over yourself to accommodate her."

Annemette winces and heat grows in Nik's cheeks, a true argument brewing in his veins. While I'm pleased to see fire from Nik regarding Annemette, it does nobody any good if the boys toss each other overboard.

I place my hand on Iker's forearm. The bickering is too much and almost as bad as the lack of water and food. If it goes on, this day will truly not go as planned. He turns to me and I give him a calming smile.

"We have the sun and blue sky and each other. We have enough."

Iker draws me in to the flat of his chest—the scent there more than salt and limes, a sour note from the hvidtøl ruining the balance. Nik glances down.

"Evie and her quick mouth. Always right, even when she is very wrong," Iker says.

"I *am* always right." I smack him on the arm but let him hold me against his chest, his heartbeat slowing as the fight drains from him.

"Don't trip on that pride, Evelyn. It'll hurt even more when you take a tumble," he jokes.

It takes several hours, but Annemette is eventually at ease enough to unplaster herself from Nik and, dare I say, *enjoy* our time at sea. She stays close to him, to be sure, but she becomes comfortable enough to share some berries and cheese with me, and conversation with us all.

Iker and I sit with our backs against the hull, facing Annemette and Nik at the mainmast. Nik has drifted off to sleep, having had a little too much wine, comfortable with Annemette at his shoulder. Iker has yet to slow on the hvidtøl, and it hasn't made him sleepy as much as it's made him more of a cat, enjoying a sunbeam with his claws out.

"Are you feeling better, Friherrinde Mette?" Iker asks.

Annemette responds with a regal nod.

"Good. Over your fears, then? A changed woman now that your prince is asleep?"

I elbow Iker hard. "Enough," I say. "I don't know why you're being like this. So . . . impolite."

"Forgive me, Evelyn. It isn't polite, it's true—I am a prince, and though I don't prefer it, I follow social norms most of the time. But my family is another matter." His eyes flash, ice blue and hot. "When it comes to them, I am never polite. It is worthless to be polite when something so important is on the line."

Annemette swallows, and I'm fairly certain all three of us steal a glance at sleeping Nik.

I should speak up and stave off Iker, but I can't. Nik is just as important to me as he is to Iker, and an ill-timed defense of Annemette would come off as wrongheaded. It also might put more strain on this day—enough to carry over to our whaling expedition. With a coward's heart, I shut my eyes and let him attack.

"So, yes. I want to know everything about you, Friherrinde Mette. Starting with how you came here—and why you arrived ahead of all the other invitees. And just as much as I want to know those things, I want to know even more how you knew to befriend Evie to get access to Nik."

I wince. Because he's right. But I'm too afraid to open my eyes and see Annemette's reaction. Both to his drunken questioning and to my cowardly silence.

"Thank you for your concern, Cousin." My eyes fly open, and Nik is awake and straightening himself from sleep. Annemette huddles against him while Iker's teeth are bared in something of a smile—but the intent is much fiercer. "But interrogating our guest isn't the way to go about it."

"She hasn't been properly vetted."

"Who are you, my mother? When did we stop taking people at their word?"

"*You* never have that option."

Iker shoots to his feet, and Nik is right after him. They lean into each other, jaws tense and features reddening.

"You are the sole heir to the jewel of the Øresund Kingdoms, the richest fishing village in the strait," Iker spits. "You can't just go throwing your future at a stranger."

"How is that worse than what you do? Throwing your pole in every corner of the ocean, tossing back any girl you catch?"

"If I'm so horrible, why in the name of *all the gods* would you let me be sweet on someone *you love*?"

My heart flutters at the word *love*, though there really isn't a better word for our friendship. Nik stares at Iker for a long time before he answers. "I thought Evie would be enough to settle you down. And, considering you're planning on taking her whaling in the morning, I think she's succeeded."

My eyes shoot to Annemette's. There's surprise in them—as much as I imagine in mine at Nik knowing our plans. There's something else there too, but I can't look long because the boys start up again, hands balled at their sides, color in their cheeks, faces an inch apart.

"This isn't about Evie. This is about the fact that you are so blinded by that thing in your chest that you can't see this girl for what she is—a complete and total stranger with no proof that she is who she says." Iker takes Nik's shoulders with a firm grip. "Her story is thin and her credentials are nonexistent—that makes her motives suspect. I have met many people in my travels and—"

"The fact that *you* are well-traveled does not make *me* naïve." Nik shrugs off Iker and takes a step back, out of easy reach. "And I'd rather be ruled by the thing in my chest than the thing in my trousers—"

A peal of thunder rips through the sky, loud enough to kill the words and anger on Nik's lips. All four of us tense and wrench around in the direction of the sound, to the northeast. A cloud so big and black it appears like night with no end is heavy on the horizon. Just like on Nik's birthday, this storm has come out of nowhere—so sudden it's strange.

But it's a storm, and the three of us know exactly what to do.

Without another word, the boys and I are in motion, working around Annemette, who cowers against the mainmast pole as the boat begins to rock at a heavy clip.

There are far too many ships in the harbor, and we're just beyond it, in the strait and nearly out to sea—much farther out than we were the night of the party, and on a much smaller boat.

The three of us get the ship turned, the food and drink put away, the long oars at the ready. Finally, there is nothing more we can do other than hunker down and row forward—just what every other boat in the strait is doing at the same moment. Well, save for the king's steamer, which is puffing merrily toward the dock, cutting a path through slower-moving vessels.

Ships clog the harbor, and where progress is slow on the water, it's quick in the sky. The storm beats at our backs, wind blowing in the right general direction, but also serving as a warning call. The stronger the wind, the closer the storm.

"Evie!" Nik calls between heavy breaths as he and Iker row for it. "Help Mette."

I leave my spot at the wheel and slog to the mainmast post, where Annemette is huddled, hanging on for dear life. I sink down beside her and press my bodice against her back, shielding her from the storm as much as I can.

The rain begins to pound down, and I feel her shudder beneath me.

—243

"I just want to go home."

"I know, Anna—Mette. Mette, I know."

She doesn't react to my stumble. She just repeats herself. Over and over.

As lightning flashes, something hard and biting thwacks me on the back of the head. I shake it off and turn to where the object has fallen to the ground.

Hail.

My heart drops and I raise my head. White chunks are flying through the air, plunging into the harbor in a deluge, rocks falling as fast and knitted together as fat raindrops.

I scan the horizon. We're at least four hundred yards out, and more than two dozen boats stand in our way of safety. We're small enough to cut around the bigger ships, but even with the boys rowing at full strength, I'm not convinced we're agile enough to not get crushed in the process.

I glance to the left. To the cove—the natural shelter. It's completely open, no ships there.

"The cove! Can we land in the cove?"

Behind me, Iker's voice booms over the rain, pinging hail, and another slice of thunder. "As good a chance as any. Cousin?"

Nik lifts his head, not once wincing as two hailstones smack into his flop of wet hair. "I'm not sure of the obstructions. But it's our best chance."

Taking that as a yes, I squeeze Annemette before

running for the wheel to help steer as Iker adjusts the mainsail to change course.

We get going in the right direction, and Iker turns to me. "Evie, stay. We need you to hold course against the wind."

I take one glance at Annemette. One glance at Nik. Iker's right.

We cut around the queen's three-sail, skip around two other schooners, a sloop, and the tiniest of one-man row-boats, and zip in a line to the cove. The blind part of the beach comes into view first, then the rock wall, and finally, Picnic Rock.

We enter the cove and I take a deep sigh of relief, my arms shaking while holding our line, red welts from the hail rising on my exposed skin.

Then Annemette begins to scream.

"Turn! Turn! Turn!"

I follow her eyes, but I don't see a thing. There's nothing but rough water ahead, our boat still too far out for the footstep islands to be a hazard. "Sandbar!"

Just as the word slips from her mouth, we shudder to a halt—run aground with water on all sides.

I meet her eyes and know exactly how she knew the sandbar—submerged and hidden from sight—would be there.

She's the only one of us to ever swim so far out into the cove.

I wait for the questions to begin. But they don't come. Instead, Iker is silent as he bends over the bow to survey the situation—both how stuck we are and what the damage might be. I truly hope there's no damage. "Time to swim for it, crew."

Nik leans over and confirms. "Yes."

"No!" Mette shouts, still clinging to the mast pole. "I can't."

But Nik isn't accepting that. "It's a hundred yards. I will swim you in. You'll be fine."

Iker drops anchor so that his boat won't float away when the storm ends and the sandbar releases it. He comes alongside me and brushes a few half-melted hailstones from my hair.

"Leap together?" He takes my hand and we step to the edge of the bow. The water is alive, waves at a rough clip, revealing the octopus that has haunted the cove since the beginning of summer, plus schools of large fish and several dolphins. The cove is practically overflowing with more animals than should ever inhabit it—unusual animals. My mind flashes to my spell, my daily call for abundance.

No, it can't be. I didn't do this. It's the storm—pushing sea life out of place.

Before I can think any more, Iker is pulling on my hand to go, and we leap into the cool water.

The hail has stopped, and the thunder has rolled into the mountains ringing Havnestad. Tendrils of lightning still flare in the sky, and the rain remains steady, but the swim isn't the worst I've ever had. Rocky and rough and exhausting, but I make it to shore just seconds behind Iker, pulling myself onto the nearest pile of sand with a great heaving breath. I roll over and fill my lungs again and again with salt air, sand caking the wet folds of my dress.

He helps me up until I'm in a seated position and have a view of the cove, where I watch Nik pull Annemette to safety. He holds her head above water, her body flat against his. My heart fills with love for him all over again, knowing that not long ago, I was the girl in his arms, being swum to shore in a terrible tide.

Nik's stroke doesn't miss a beat, and they are on land soon enough. His breath is thick with effort, hers with fear. In his eyes, I'm sure I see a spark of love—something I hope tonight's ball will truly ignite—and Annemette will be home at last.

THREE AND A HALF
YEARS BEFORE

The newest mermaid simply became another royal sister, her memory in such a state that she believed she had always been there. Everyone said so. Even if she had the nagging feeling that her life felt like one big conversation entered years too late.

She was just a little mermaid, swimming in the collective shadow of her five older sisters—Lida, Clara, Aida, Olena, and Galia. Blond and fine-boned all, full of cheer and manners. Together, the six girls were the pride of their grandmother, the Queen Mother Ragnhildr, or as she preferred, Oma Ragn.

The little mermaid loved Oma Ragn with a special fierceness—she felt at home when she was with her. At home, folded into the long white waves of her hair, against the warmth of her skin, the song she hummed under her breath just louder than their collective heartbeat.

But Oma Ragn was more than a comfortable lap and soothing voice. She was their guide to life in the palace. Their tutor. Their example. Their goal. Days began with lessons in policy, lessons on how to rule, followed by the sciences and the arts. Nights were filled with music and magic, the lessons shifting with the shadows in the water, becoming less definitive, more dreamlike.

To the little mermaid, this was how it had always been. How it always would be. Until something happened that she hadn't predicted.

One morning, there was a great fuss, her third-oldest sister, Aida, at the center of it all. Her room had been done up in garlands of twisted seaweed with sparkling shells twined throughout. The little mermaid swam through, admiring every last detail, but she didn't know what it was for.

The little mermaid found the ear of her sister closest in age, twelve-year-old Galia. She settled in so that they were shoulder-to-shoulder and whispered as the others circled around Aida, adjusting ribbons in her hair. "What is this?"

Galia opened her mouth as if to speak and then snapped it shut, finding the correct words a few moments later.

"It is the fifteenth year since Aida's birth."

The little mermaid thought this might mean a celebration. Galia read the confusion on her face. Again, Galia seemed to choose her words carefully, tugging the little mermaid farther into the shadows.

"On the fifteenth anniversary of a mermaid's birth, she can go to the surface."

The little mermaid's eyes grew large. "The surface?" It had never occurred to her that this was even an option—she'd been told many stories of the dangers above, humans with their harpoons and nets a terrifying reality. It wasn't something she wanted to get close to. Ever. But Galia was smiling.

Smiling.

As were all her sisters and Aida herself. Beaming *might have been a more appropriate word.*

The littlest mermaid got the distinct feeling this was something she should've remembered—two of her other sisters would've already celebrated in this way. Instead, her mind held endless black upon black, no remembrance shining through.

Still, she waved away her own question as if she'd known all along. "Oh, yes, of course."

It did not do to make waves.

26

NIK AND IKER DEPART DOWN THE HALL TO THEIR WING in a soggy mess, tired, calling for the kitchens and a hot bath. We will see them in three hours—standing at the palace ballroom's doors, welcoming guests into the Lithasblot Ball.

It's a grand end to the festival, but it's not just for the nobles. Everyone is invited to partake in the music, dance, and great feast—all of Havnestad equals for one night.

Normally, Nik only has to choose from local noble ladies and common girls to dance with, ever the egalitarian prince, giving each girl a chance. But things will be different this year. Aside from Annemette, there will be dozens of the queen's girls waiting, fighting, and grasping at their chance to dance with him.

Those girls must still be aboard the three-sail, probably down below, protected from the hail and rain.

Protected, unlike us.

Annemette and I shuffle down the guest hall in enough of a state that I really don't want to know what I look like. I thank Urda that the queen is not here to pass judgment. But what I see of Annemette does not give me hope. Her waves are tangled; deep-red welts cover her arms, every shard of hail having left its mark; and the pre-storm sun made its presence known as well, flushing her forehead and nose as pink as the natural blush at her cheeks.

I can only hope a bath and the three hours we have to dress will improve such matters for both of us. It's difficult to have the most romantic evening of your life while resembling ghosts of the bubonic plague.

We reach our room, and Annemette immediately falls into bed, sodden clothes and all. She bounces as much as the down mattress will allow before settling in a heap of hair and rags.

"Are you all right?" I ask, sitting on my bed across from her.

She answers with a smile. "I am more than all right— Nik has asked me to open the ball with him."

I gasp. Each year the king and queen take the ball's opening dance. And now that Nik is of age, it makes sense that he would dance alongside them—something even I didn't know. Something maybe Nik didn't know until his mother's guests arrived.

"That's amazing." If that invitation doesn't show

blooming love, I don't know what does. And after a night of staring into her eyes, there's no way Nik won't fulfill the magical contract.

"It is," she agrees. "Though I am thoroughly exhausted. We have time for a nap, don't we?"

I catch my reflection in the length of the window—red spots on a pink sea and a bird's nest of curls. Iker hasn't asked me to open the dance, though surely he will dance too. Maybe he doesn't think he needs to ask me. Maybe he thinks it's implied.

"I don't know—it might take all three hours to mask this and—"

"*Ljómi,*" Annemette says, and a frigid breeze flows over my head and down my arms. It's cold enough that my eyes snap shut for a moment until it blows over.

When I open them, and see myself in the mirror, I'm completely different. My hair is clean and bouncy; my skin is glowing, all redness gone. I am radiant. My clothes are still a mess, but the rest of me is better than before. And again, I'm reminded that Annemette is more at home with her magic than I ever will be. She *is* magic.

"Thank you. . . . How long will it last?"

"Not forever, but long enough for Iker to have trouble remembering." She yawns. "I'll spell you a new gown later. Now, I need to sleep."

"Mette, you can't—we have less than eight hours until midnight and I need to teach you to dance."

Annemette shuts her eyes. "I'll figure it out. Mermaids dance more than we swim."

No. No. No. What is wrong with her? "Dancing with your legs is a lot different, Mette. I mean, I know you're graceful, but do you know the Havnestad waltz? Every girl in that room will know it backward and forward. If you don't do it right, everyone will know your story is false. The king, the queen . . . Nik. It could all fall apart before your time is up."

Annemette sits up and smiles. "All right. You win. Sleep can wait until after I have his heart." She lifts her arms for me to grab her hands, and I tug her into the center of our gilded room. Somehow, she's spelled herself without me seeing, her skin glowing, her hair cascading perfectly over the shoulders of her dress, now dry. Mine remains wet, but I won't ask her to change it. Not yet. I can't distract her from this. We're almost to the finish line. And the ball is more important than any moment we've had yet.

I place her hand on my shoulder and take the other out to the side. My hand goes to her hip. I'm intensely glad Queen Charlotte never succeeded in making les lanciers the dance of choice at the ball—I'd never be able to teach a quadrangle to a mermaid by myself.

And we begin. "One, two, three . . . one, two, three."

She adjusts her hand on my shoulder, clearly bothered by its damp state. *"Purr klædi."*

My dress dries instantly as we spin around the room.

Annemette steps on my toes and corrects but doesn't apologize.

"Just you wait for the dress I'll make you for tonight. If I'd known the last one was going to get covered in Malvina's pie, I wouldn't have spelled one so fine, but I'll have to go all out on this one. Really show the town up—and the queen's girls, too. Iker won't be able to keep his eyes off you."

I smile at her as we spin in circles. "Thank you," I say. And I'm grateful. This afternoon with Iker was difficult, and I'd love nothing more than to get back to where we were this morning.

"You'll look just like a princess."

"But you've already done that once," I laugh.

"Oh, now we're getting picky, are we? Fine, I'll make you look like a queen!"

I laugh so hard, it's practically a royal snort. Then I lead us into another turn, holding her hand tight.

SEVEN DAYS BEFORE

Aida's birthday had unlocked something within the darkness of the littlest mermaid's mind. She couldn't see what was there, couldn't access it, but she'd felt the click of the key settling in. She knew something lay in the endless black, hiding. Waiting to consume her whole, like a shark in a reef.

And with this shift, she noticed something else. A fatalistic obsession.

Humans.

She knew they were dangerous. That they plagued the sea, stealing lives with abandon. Upsetting the balance of things by killing too many or too few. The natural give-and-take forever ruined by their greed, their ships, their nets, their harpoons.

If the "legend" of merpeople were ever proven, they would be mercilessly hunted by humans. Made a sideshow. Sold to the highest bidder.

Confirmation of their existence would be the death of them.

Yet, as she approached her fifteenth year, she began to daydream more and more about observing humans above water. She often left the confines of her father's castle at night, looking for ships to float next to, listening and watching for any signs of what people were like, these trips becoming more frequent the closer her birthday came.

A few days before the special day, she came upon just her type of boat. One without anywhere to go—a monolith simply floating in the tide. Even better, this one had funny little windows in the hull. She'd seen those a few times before, leading to little below-water spaces where humans played cards or stored their treasures, depending on the type of ship.

But these windows were dark. All the people were above, playing music loud enough that the sound drifted below. The little mermaid had always loved music, and she swam along to the lingering notes, swirling and rolling through the water just below the surface.

But then, after a few hours, a light appeared behind the windows. Brighter than the mermaid had ever seen. Light made by more than an ordinary candle. Maybe several candles. Or something larger—a torch.

The little mermaid stopped drifting to the music and rushed to the nearest window. She pressed her face as close to the glass as possible.

And saw into her past.

The girl beyond the window struck her like a bolt of lightning.

Suddenly, all her mind's darkness was illuminated, and she could see everything. The memories in her mind surged forth through the blackness, one right after another in rapid succession, physically knocking her back with their force.

But not before she'd made eye contact.

The girl had seen her.

The girl had recognized her.

Evie. The girl's name was Evie.

And her name—it wasn't Annemette. It was simply Anna. Anna Kamp. Friherrinde Anna Kamp.

And the king's son.

Nik.

Nik, with his sweet face and dark eyes. Stately despite being slim, elegant, and graceful. A lover of music and the arts. So kind. The first memories of him came to her in a golden cloud, as if he'd filtered sunlight itself and bathed in it.

She had to see him.

The mermaid gathered all her strength and pushed forward, back to the little window. Evie and Nik were always together. If Evie was on this ship, Nik was too. She knew it deep in her bones.

But he wasn't there. And Evie was ascending the stairs. Leaving her alone.

If Nik was there, he was above.

Where they were laughing and dancing and singing.

Without her.

And that's when the dark memories crawled forward. Burning so painful she had to squeeze her eyes shut.

That day. Evie and the heavy waves. The dare. The undertow. She would still be alive if Evie hadn't suggested the race.

The little mermaid began to sob—this time very aware that she could shed no tears as a mermaid like she had been able to in a past life. And, oh, how she craved that release.

She'd drowned that day.

Or nearly drowned—she was clearly alive, though her life had been stolen away. Her father—the sea king—must have saved her, or he wouldn't have kept her for his own.

He'd lied to her. They'd all lied to her. Told her she was one of them. Kept her in the dark.

The little mermaid sobbed again, her eyes stinging as she watched the ship float along, the life she could've been living happening above.

And then the last chunk of blackness evaporated. The last images she'd seen as a human surged forth.

Evie drifting down toward her.

Nik's lithe form racing toward her friend's limp body, drawing Evie up to the surface and away. Evie first. Always first.

Then, several minutes later, his shadow returning, his eyes landing on her own body, prone near the seafloor. Him bobbing back to the surface.

Him swimming back down but then stalling out. Caught in the waves by another boy. The one Evie liked—Iker. Another prince.

Nik could've fought, but he'd let Iker pull him up. He'd given up.

Their friendship, the way she felt about him, her life—none of that mattered.

The golden glow around her memories of Nik and her human life with him evaporated. Her fond memories of Evie, the girl who was like the sister she never had, gone. Her happy memories of Iker, always a handsome distraction, no more.

All that was left was anger.

Fury.

Ire.

She wanted to break it all. Shatter it all. Ruin it all.

She wanted retribution for all that had been stolen from her.

She wasn't human anymore because of the choices of these three. She was magic, though. A being of intense and beautiful magic. There was no place the magic ended and she began. She didn't have her rightful life, her soul, but she had her magic and her anger.

And she wanted to use them.

"Veðr."

Storm. Yes. Storm.

"Veðr," she repeated, feeling the magic surge in her veins, saturate her skin, tingle behind her eyes.

She was magic. She was the storm.

"Veðr." Above a clap of thunder rolled, loud enough to shake her waves. It was the most beautiful music she'd ever heard. Yet she wanted to see this happen. See the destruction. Endless waves, and yet she'd suddenly felt so confined.

But she wasn't. A light went on in the darkness, and she knew she could go above.

The day she'd been told was her birthday—three days from now—wasn't her birthday. It was the day she'd lost her *rightful life and been reborn, but not the day of her true birth. She'd shared that day with Nik, so if this was his birthday, it was hers as well. She was fifteen. She could go above.*

The little mermaid repeated her command as she pushed for the surface. Lightning was growing, the wind was picking up, and the waves were rocking. The boat's hull swayed and suddenly filled with light. People running from her power. Hiding below.

But not everyone.

As she crested the surface she saw the three people from her memories—from that day—up top. She knew they'd be there—always acting like heroes.

Except when it came to her. Their bravery had a limit.

And she would make them suffer.

The boat lurched as Evie and Iker tried to steady it. Nik took orders from his cousin—of course he did—and went to the side of the ship to cut free a little attached schooner.

It was her chance.

"Veðr."

Waves rocked the ship and the prince faltered, hanging on with all his strength. And just when he seemed to settle into his balance, the little mermaid sent the largest wave yet—bigger than the wall of memories that had struck her, bigger than any she'd seen with human eyes—right into the boy who hadn't saved her.

The ship tipped. And over Nik went, into the sea.

His eyes were shut when he appeared before her—his

head striking the hull of the schooner on the way down. No blood. Just Nik, floating before her, looking almost as if he was sleeping.

Peaceful.

The little mermaid took his face into her hands. He looked older now, the beginnings of a beard scraping against her fingertips.

"Why didn't you fight for me? Why?"

Nik answered in bubbles, his lungs failing him.

She thought to let them fail.

She thought to let him become bones in the sand. Her revenge. Yet somehow that didn't feel right. It didn't feel great enough. It wouldn't get her what she wanted back.

And so she brought him to air. Swam him ashore. Her mind churning with possibility as his chest rose and fell in her arms.

The sea king had made her a mermaid—not her choice, not what she wanted. The little mermaid wanted to live above the sea. And she would find the magic to change herself back.

Then she would get her revenge.

27

THE RECEIVING LINE FOR THE ROYAL FAMILY SEEMS TO be a mile long—it curves through the hallways, down the staircase, and out of Øldenburg Castle. It doesn't make it down the exterior stairs and into the tulip garden, but it would have if they'd waited another five minutes to open the ballroom doors.

We stand at the end of the line. Several schoolmates of mine are closest to us—including Ruyven and Didrik. Malvina is ahead of us. As usual, stares come from all sides, cold and dismissive, whispers of conspiracy on warm lips. They all think I have a plan—that everything I do is to assert my place in the palace, where I don't belong.

This time they would be right, I suppose. I do have a plan.

But it's not for me.

If a kiss doesn't do it, I will. I'll take Annemette to

Havnestad Cove and tell the sea what I want. What the magic owes me—owes us. The sea took Anna. I deserve Annemette.

And Annemette, well, she thinks I deserve some of the magic she has tonight. She spelled the dress I'm wearing—an enchanting Havnestad blue, netted with black lace at the bodice. Hers is the same color, but accented with ivory. With our matching pearls and tresses left down and flowing, we're a study in contrasts—light and dark.

I try to take a deep breath in, my nerves piling high, but my bodice is a little tighter than usual. "Pride must suffer pain," Annemette had whispered in my ear as she tied the bodice. I'd think about how tight the queen's bodice must be, but laughing would only hurt more.

People line up behind us as we move forward at a steady but slow clip, the line snaking forward in a constant motion but with the velocity of a centipede. When we wind down the hallway, the entrance to the royal ballroom is finally in sight. I spot King Asger's tall form, crown atop his dark head, sapphires glittering beneath the great chandeliers that light the hall with a golden glow.

I glance to his left and see Nik and his less ornate prince's crown. One more spot and two inches down and there's Iker, wearing, for the first time this trip, his own crown, decorated with the rubies of Rigeby Bay.

Almost there.

Up front, the visiting girls dawdle, finally getting the attention of both princes. The queen is all smiles, and so is Nik—he'd never let these people down. Not in a million years. Iker has on his Prince Charming face, playing up to his reputation with winks and bows and kisses to each girl's hand.

After another long spell, we come to our turn with the king.

"Evelyn, my, you look more beautiful than ever tonight."

"Thank you, your grace," I say, shaking his hand.

"Yes, quite beautiful," adds Queen Charlotte, her eyes narrowing. "Your gown is lovely."

I'm sure she's wondering where I got such an extravagant thing, whether Nik purchased it for me, or worse, I stole it from one of her precious visiting girls. She's too careful to say anything here, though I'm sure whatever rumor she spreads will reach me later.

I take her hand and curtsy.

"Evie, you look fantastic," Nik says when I move down the line to him, and I'm surprised his attention is on me when Annemette stands behind me, looking even more striking. As I turn to him, he takes my hand and kisses it. My breath catches.

"Yes, she does. Hurry up, Cousin," Iker says, irked.

I draw in Nik and give him a peck on one blushing cheek before squeezing his hand. He is simply dashing in his sleek black suit, hair combed and lying perfectly under his crown.

Next to us, Iker clears his throat. Nik gives my hand one last warm squeeze before we part, and he bows to Annemette.

Nik and I joke about Iker's status as Prince Charming, but Iker certainly lives up to it tonight in every way. My heart was already pounding, but seeing him now causes the blood in my veins to grow hot.

Sweeping navy trousers top high-shine black boots. A crisp white shirt peeks from underneath a pressed coat that glows with golden thread and the crest of Rigeby Bay. The sun-kissed highlights in his hair shine in a way that only serves to make the ice blue of his eyes more stunning. The ruby crown is a symbol of his status, yes, but even in rags— even in nothing at all—he would look like a prince.

Iker takes my hand and kisses it, as he's done with all the girls in line. His lips are gentle; the rasp of stubble at his chin makes my skin tingle and the flush deepen.

He straightens to his full height, broad shoulders back, a smile tugging at the corners of his mouth—a subtle movement that makes my knees weak. "I am very much looking forward to dancing the night away with you, my lady."

There's a mischievous look in his eye as he leans into my ear. "Tonight you are the spitting image of a komtesse, but you have the grace of a queen. And in your blood is the sea woman I have fallen for."

It's all I can do not to kiss him right there, in front of everyone. But there will be time for that after all of this. After tonight is the rest of our lives. Together.

SIX DAYS BEFORE

The difficulty wasn't in surviving the humans—it was in returning to the sea castle, slipping into her old life like nothing had happened, when everything had changed.

The little mermaid knew who she was. And as she swam through the sea castle's ornate coral doors, past schools of fish new to this water, she could only think of one thing.

How to get herself back.

She hadn't had magic on land. That much she remembered. But Evic had. She hadn't seen it when she was a girl, but now that magic coursed through her own veins, it was easy to spot in her friend's home, especially with that peculiar aunt of hers.

Oh, what a delicious secret that would been for Anna to have known. Ever the loyal friend, she wouldn't have told anyone.

Magic existed, but it was illegal. A danger to the balance and order of things—at least in the eyes of the Øldenburgs.

Which made the little mermaid's revenge easy. Obvious.

She'd use Evie's magic against her. Force her to perform magic in public. And even better, force the people she cared about most to lay down the punishment.

Nik was trickier. Evie's punishment would torment him, she knew, but it wasn't enough. Evie's punishment would be the start of his, but it wouldn't be all.

And Iker, well, his confidence might kill him before anything she did would touch him, the oaf.

But before any of her plans could fully form, she needed to learn how to go above. She knew the stories of "their" mother. She'd been human once too—a witch they tried to drown off the coast of Hirtshals. But Father—the sea king, not her real father—had gotten to her first. Made her his queen. He said it'd been something he'd never been able to do before and hadn't done since.

He'd lied.

They'd all lied.

Which meant there were more secrets. And she knew just where to look.

The day her sisters had turned fifteen, the sea king had made a big show about writing their names in the large ledger he kept on his desk—the kingdom's official listing of every merperson allowed to go topside. The sea king ruled with order and regulations as a way of protecting his people from discovery.

Thoroughness was his safety net, and so far, it had worked.

He made note of every magical transaction. Thus, if there were a way to get topside, it was likely he would have recorded it.

And so, with the scent of Nik still upon her skin, the little mermaid returned to the castle and immediately snuck into her father's chambers. He kept his business papers in a particular parlor room, one with a view of the great reef below, the million colors of his kingdom shifting in the ocean light.

His snores drifted in from the bedroom. She didn't know how he could sleep so soundly. Not only because he'd lied but because of the chaos taking over his waters. Magic had upset the natural course of things. A spell of abundance was pushing faraway creatures into their seas, creatures who were devouring the scarce resources already eroded by a strange sickness that had attacked the waters only a handful of years ago. The black plague, they'd called it. Most believed it had been magic too.

But the little mermaid knew that soon the sea's problems would no longer be hers.

Quietly sweeping past the sea king's copious bookcases, the little mermaid pulled herself up tight to his grand desk. With deft fingers, she opened the ledger and paged to four years before.

It had been no one's fifteenth birthday that day, so there wasn't a name. Simply a few entries from the sea king about that day's regulated magical activities. On the very bottom line of that day, written so plainly it shocked her, was her birth.

Annemette joined us on this day, her eleventh birthday. Her sisters and myself brought her to the kingdom with the same magic that brought me Mette. For the first time in thirty years, that spell found success.

If this was written, why had they lied? The truth was there and everyone in the kingdom knew it. Why hadn't they told her?

Just as fury began again to creep up her spine, the little mermaid realized exactly why they'd lied to her face.

They knew I'd want to go back.

So there's a way back. There has to be.

She skipped forward, stopping for any longer entry, hoping for details of how he'd done it.

But she found nothing. Just page after page of dull business—"brought down a ship, the tally is twenty-two men, five barrels of oil, seventeen casks of wine, and ten pallets of silk."

The little mermaid racked her mind for a better guess. Any guess.

A shot in the dark: she turned to thirty years before, looking for the entry marking the "birth" of the dead queen, Mette.

She found the passage dated February 17, 1833—an awful time to drown anyone. Hypothermia might have killed her before water claimed her lungs. In the three-page entry, the sea king went on and on about how the magic he'd used to save Mette had worked, but nearly killed him, leaving him so weak he could barely hold an inked feather to document it all. The magic had indeed been a typical exchange—he asked and he received—but the toll was so great, he'd nearly died.

And in his weakness and burgeoning love, he'd told Mette how she'd come to be a mermaid. He wanted the beautiful stranger to recognize his personal expense in having saved her—maybe that would make her love him, too. Instead, his admission initiated a flood of memories—memories that left her yearning to go back right away.

She'd been a witch. She'd known magic above. And he knew magic below.

And because he already loved her, he told her she could go.

The little mermaid's heart began to pound. Fingers shaking, she turned the pages.

Finally, after lengthy paragraphs documenting weeks of the king's recovery, she found what she wanted.

Today Queen Mette began testing a spell to bring mermaids to land in human form. In previous weeks, the queen had run tests on loyal subjects but failed to send them topside, as the magic stalled out, exhausting her and tormenting them, despite all her knowledge of the ways of magical barter. But this morning, she had an epiphany.

This spell is unlike any other. The magic needs assistance—the energy it uses is too great and deadly otherwise.

Only a life added to the exchange will fill the void. I was powerful enough to save her without sacrificing myself—and love may have pushed me through—but another try could kill me. Which means that to go above, she needs to take a life—a human life.

There were no entries for three days.

And, after that, no entries about it at all. The little mermaid paged ahead.

More than a year later, a new entry with shaky writing.

A storm brought a man into our path today. Mette saw her opportunity—though she'd come to love me, she missed home. She wanted to try the spell.

My queen could not kill a human. But this man's life was over. Laying her hands on him, she repeated her spell.

"Líf. Dauði. Minn líf. Minn bjóð. Seiðr. Seiðr. Seiðr."

The human's eyes jerked open as his lungs released. His skin glowed where she touched him, and soon the glow was bright enough that I could see neither of them.

In a flash the light was gone, the man was fully dead, and there was Mette, just as I'd found her— with legs and lungs, struggling for air. I swam her topside, found her a piece of the human's shattered boat to hang on to, and then swam her to the nearest shore. I am not sure how long the magic will hold, or what will happen when it runs out. Or if I will ever get her back. Mette is on the hunt for

a witch to help. She knows of a powerful one in
Havnestad—one who will keep our secret.

I fear I will lose her. I fear our people will suffer.

The little mermaid turned the page. Nothing.

She turned the page again. Nothing. The sea king must have spent days waiting for his queen to return. The little mermaid knew she had, for she was the true mother of the girls who she, herself, called sisters.

On the fourth day, a new entry.

I have heard from my dear Mette! The
Havnestad witch gave her four days at most.
After that, I would need to change her back into a
mermaid or she'd be lost to both the sea and land.
I told her I was too weak. That I couldn't, but the
witch simply smiled and told me I underestimated
love's effect on my magic. Mette hadn't loved me
when I'd transformed her the first time, but she
loved me now. And that made all the difference.

The little mermaid skimmed the rest. There must be a way to keep her legs longer than four days. That couldn't be it. If she had to kill a man, she needed to know she could stay on land forever.

She skipped ahead. Nothing. Nothing anywhere.

Frustrated, she shut the book, careful not to let it slam,

though she wanted to slam it. She wanted to throw it across the room. She raised her arm to do just that when she saw the queen's bookcase across the way. She lunged for the shelf. Thumbed through the spines. And stopped when she saw what she wanted. The queen's diary.

Heart pounding, she flipped to that year. To that day. The day the queen had returned with the sea king's help.

The queen wrote that she had known what it would take to remain on land. Love wasn't just the answer to return; it was the answer to stay. True love would break the magic, the witch had said.

But so, too, would something else—death. A sacrifice so worthy it would make the magic stand up and listen long enough to create a human life.

It was right there in Mette's looping script. The answer to the little mermaid's quest. A way to get both her life back and the perfect revenge.

28

THE BALLROOM IS BRIMMING WITH MERRIMENT.
Beyond the doors, a sea of people—young and old, of
Havnestad and not—mill about, their laughter and cries
of delight adding to the general hum as the king's band
strikes a lively jig in the corner.

For once, Nik is not with the musicians, stealing their
instruments and the show. Tonight, he does that from the
dance floor.

King Asger has just finished a speech—one he didn't
foist upon Nik—and takes Queen Charlotte's hand. "And
now, the first dance."

Nik steps forward, in line with his parents. The weight
of the room is upon him as a statelier tune starts up. Wilhelm van Horn, Ruyven's father, stands in front of the
orchestra as the king's official announcer. He reads from a
scroll, stamped with the king's seal. All of this is so formal,

so unlike us. A prince coming of age is serious business.

Wilhelm clears his throat. "Crown Prince Asger Niklas Bryniulf Øldenburg III invites for his first dance . . ." The drums kick up for a minute. Annemette grabs my hand. "Friherrinde Annemette of Odense."

I squeeze Annemette's fingers just before she steps forward into a sea of applause. Every eye in the room is upon her, this beautiful creature. Fru Liesel is proclaiming loudly somewhere behind me, "My Anneke, my Anneke."

Annemette curtsies, graceful. The queen looks pleased. The king too. Nik looks slightly embarrassed, ears red. He glances to me, but I'm not sure how he can take his eyes off her. She's the sun and the rest of us are ordinary stars.

She glides toward Nik. He extends a hand and takes hers and they stand to the side, a nearly identical image to the monarchs next to them. One generation and then the next. My heart heaves. After this exhausting, disappointing day, we might have a happy ending. For all of us.

Iker steps forward next. My heaving heart begins to pound, vibrating like a rail tie under an oncoming train.

This is the moment.

Wilhelm clears his throat yet again. I can already feel eyes settling upon my silhouette.

"Crown Prince Christian Olaf Iker Navarre Øldenburg invites for his first dance . . ." The drums begin, and I can't separate them from my own heartbeats. "Friherrinde Oda of Kalø."

My heart skips a beat.

Who?

Iker extends his arm in the direction of an icy-blond stranger.

The girl steps forward, the women around her frozen with excitement. Iker doesn't so much as glance my way. He watches the girl as if she's a prize pony, sauntering forward. The queen looks pleased. *So pleased.* For once, the rogue prince has done her bidding.

My cheeks burn while my heart and blood grow cold with stagnation. I should have known all along. Iker could never dance with me here. Just like he'll never be able to dance with me in Rigeby Bay or anywhere else. Whether our whaling trip is real or not, it won't be anything more than those few weeks. I close my eyes and let the wave of embarrassment wash over me.

When I open them, Malvina's smug face flashes before mine, as if there's a spotlight on her from across the room. This is what people like her have been waiting for ever since Nik, Iker, and I became friends—my ambition slammed down in front of them all.

And here we are.

I'm just as bad as the townspeople say I am. Always expecting something from these princes whether I deserve it or not. Nik drops Annemette's hand and takes a step forward. As if he can save me. But I meet his eyes and hope our special language spans the distance and the weight of so many eyes.

My heart is broken, but his is more important in this moment. These next moments could mean life or death.

Yet Nik is still reaching for me, until Annemette grabs his hand and whispers something in his ear. He immediately moves back in line, his eyes in the middle distance.

When the music begins and the dance officially starts, all I want to do is run away, but I'm trapped, forced to watch the three royal couples, a fake smile plastered on my face.

Nik's crown is a beacon in the very center, everyone else floating around him. The smile on his face is unavoidable, the brightest thing in the room. Brighter than the queen's diamonds. Brighter than the king's sapphire crown.

Annemette's long waves sweep around, swinging with each spin, a flash of butter-blond moving at a happy clip across the inlaid marble.

Many of the older townsfolk hang by the dance floor with more enthusiasm than even the youth, standing close enough to soak in young love at its most enchanting.

The song ends, and each couple takes a bow before other couples swarm the floor, clapping them off as a new song starts up. The royals are swallowed by the crowd, almost everyone dancing. I sink farther into the background, finally settling into a chair pushed up against the wall. Almost immediately there's a hand on my shoulder.

"I didn't give the announcer that girl's name." Iker's voice is low and hushed. Strained. "Please dance with me. Please, Evelyn."

"I—"

He takes my hand in both of his. "Let me right this wrong. Please. That girl means nothing to me."

The icy-blond girl is nowhere to be seen. She's not hanging over his shoulder. She's not anywhere. His dismissal after one song must have been more than disappointing.

I make the mistake of looking into his eyes. He's spelled me as deeply as any magic I've ever known, using memories as much as the present. But I can't dance with him. The embarrassment of rejection will double if the townsfolk see this as a pity dance. I shake my head.

"Please," he begs. "I can't bear to dance with any of these girls. I need you, Evie. Only you."

I look around at everyone enjoying the evening. Dancing, spinning, laughing. Why shouldn't I have that? *Let them talk.*

Finally, I nod, and he draws me up and sets one hand upon my waist. My hand fits neatly into his other palm. Like it's meant to be there. The band plays at a sweeping clip, and we make our way onto the floor. I feel as if the entire world has blown away and only Iker and I stand alone, pressed together in an invisible, swirling tide.

"My aunt must have put that girl's name on the scroll,"

Iker whispers in my ear. "It has to be. Yours was the one that I requested."

I want to believe him. I do. But I know his reputation. His habits. And somewhere deep in my gut I wonder if he and that girl had met before. He didn't look my way when her name was called. Not like Nik. Iker only looked at her—like he knew her.

"Please, Evie—" Iker leans back so I can glimpse his face as we sweep through traffic on the dance floor. The strain in his voice has reached his eyes.

"Iker, it's fine," I say. Even though it's not.

He twirls me past the king and dodges Malvina and Ruyven. We pass Nik and Annemette, and a prickle of magic shoots through my blood. I wonder if Annemette has used a spell to keep her feet from tripping up. For all her grace, even after an hour of practice, her legs weren't doing what she wanted, her exhaustion too great.

Iker follow's my eyes. "What?" he asks.

There's not much I can say that he'll agree with. "Nik and Annemette—they're just so . . . this is just so . . ."

"Questionable?"

That was not the word I was thinking of. The specter of his anger on the ship rises. I haven't seen him have a sip of hvidtøl tonight, but his true feelings are on display again in that single word. I smile, hoping it will soften the edge in his eye. "Romantic. That was the word I was going for. Romantic."

Iker laughs, bold, in his way. The few heads that weren't watching our drama unfold turn at the sound, and he makes a show of plucking a wayward curl off my face before leaning back in to whisper in my ear. "There is not a single iota of real romance in that relationship." His voice is light, but I know he's not kidding.

"Have you seen them?" I shoot back, my voice as cheery as possible, though there is irritation crawling across my heart. Why can't he accept that Annemette could make Nik happy—that we could *all* be so incredibly happy?

"Evie, you are as brilliant as you are beautiful, strong and ship worthy; your wit is a marvel . . . but"—and my heart drops here, made worse by the fact that it feels as if his eyes are seeing through me—"all this time with Nik, and you still don't understand that royal duty is duty to the people? We are walking symbols—ones who can dance and sing and perform. We do those things for our people, whether we want to or not—symbols do not have a choice."

We whirl around in another circle, and he moves to the other side of my face, pressing his cheek into mine. "That romance you see is just passing. It cannot stay—the crown won't allow it."

And just like that, Iker confirms everything I've known all along. He may be angry at Annemette, but his same rules apply to me. It's been sitting there right below the surface the whole time we've been together. And in each chance that I've had to walk away, I've willingly fooled myself into denial, his smiles or promises changing my mind.

But the cruelest thing is that he thinks I should just accept this, which is why the words fall off his tongue as if they're a passing phrase. He can beg me to dance, to sail away with him, be at his beck and call, be his . . . plaything. And I'm supposed to accept it because *he* has responsibility, *he* has his duty? No.

I want to break free, but we're spinning, one turn after another as his painful words swirl around me. His grip is so tight.

"Don't you see how exceptionally dangerous she is, Evie?" Iker goes on.

"There's nothing dangerous about love, Iker," I say, the heated words sounding cold.

"Everything about love is dangerous. When I look at Annemette, I see a person I don't know who has incredible interest in my cousin. Considering his status, his responsibilities, and his heart, that isn't innocent. It's predatory."

Predatory? Maybe only in the plainest sense: Annemette has to win Nik's love to stay. But considering she's invested her life in this, considering my magic is insurance, considering she belongs here—I know deep down she is one of us—predatory is the wrong word.

Fate is the right one.

This is fate. It is fate for this to succeed. For our world to be righted again.

"And do you see me as a predator?" I finally ask. "I'm a girl without a title. But I wanted to be with you."

At this he smiles, and for the first time I'm not sure if it's for me or for the couples surrounding us, swirling across the marble. Iker as a symbol—Prince Charming. His role.

"Of course not, because *I* asked *you*. And *I* know that *you*, of all people, see how this works."

He's right. I always have. And under the light of the hundreds of candles decorating the chandeliers above, there are no more dark spaces to hide away this reality.

And just like I can never truly be with Iker, Nik can never truly be with Annemette. When he finds out she's not really nobility, it'll be over, and never mind if he ever finds out what she really is. If she was truly Anna, maybe. Maybe. But Anna is dead, and no spell can fix that. I don't know what I was thinking, asking Annemette to believe that Nik would fight for her. That he'd ever be able to defy the queen. I guess I just wanted to believe it for her as much as I wanted to believe it for myself.

I look for them, twirling at the center of the room. Although she only needs true love's kiss, and not a proposal of marriage, I worry that Nik may never let himself give one without the other.

I try to catch Annemette's eye. We should go. I can do my spell and she can stay, and we can be friends. New love will eventually find each of us. But instead I catch Nik's. For some reason, he breaks rhythm and leads Annemette our way, cutting through the couples, against the tune.

"Cousin, how is the dancing?" Iker greets them, as jolly as ever.

"Magnificent," Nik answers. "Though I wondered if we might switch partners for a song."

He doesn't give a reason. Just meets my eyes again. The same weight hangs in their dark-brown depths as when my name wasn't called.

My stomach blooms with warmth for the shortest of moments before a tiny sound from Annemette breaks the hold Nik has on me. I draw myself together and look to her. Color has rushed to her cheeks, her blushed lips hanging open—it's clear the last thing in the world she wants is time with Iker.

"It's so hopeless," she says, a sob cutting into the air.

She gathers her skirts and shoulders past us, toward the balcony. Toward privacy for tears that won't come.

Without a second thought, I chase after her.

FOUR DAYS BEFORE

The little mermaid knew she wouldn't be as lucky as her name-sake queen. She knew the death of another was the only way to get her soul back.

The only way to stay.

Love wasn't an option. Not for her. Not with the hate mounting each moment in her heart. Her hate had replicated itself until there was no room for another emotion. It had become her blood and breath and flesh and bone. It engulfed her, the pressure filling up without release. If she could cry, she knew that her tears would overflow the sea. Destroy all in its path. Wash away the world's coasts in one fell swoop.

She wanted destruction—not only of the world above but of the world below.

Everyone involved in taking her from the life she'd loved deserved punishment. She would ruin them. All of them.

She had a plan for revenge—on Nik, on Evie, on even the sea royalty.

And the first step was right before her.

She'd stalked the coast of Havnestad in the days since her discovery, waiting for her chance. Her family thought she left the castle often because she was nervous about going up for the first time—that she needed to swim to clear her mind. She let them think that.

On the morning of her supposed birthday, her family saw her off with songs and merriment. Galia, the sister closest to her in age, offered to come with her for company's sake. The little mermaid told her no, she would do it by herself. Galia didn't push.

And then she was free.

The little mermaid went to Havnestad Harbor, searching for ships on the move. Easy bodies to snatch. It wasn't a matter of taking a life. She knew she could do that. It was a matter of not taking too many.

She spied Evie on the dock that morning, magic in the girl's wake, like perfume trailing a noble dressed in silk and lace.

The mermaid shook it off. She needed Evie to be alive for this to work.

But Evie's father . . . She watched as the man prepared his ship, ready to sail. And she thought it might be the answer—something else to cause Evie pain—but then she spied a better option.

Iker.

Iker, who was kissing Evie in the open. Like she wasn't a peasant. Like she had a chance.

Death finding him might be more painful for Evie than death finding her father—love was strange that way.

It was Iker who kept Nik from reaching her the day she drowned. He'd been her death.

And she would be his.

The little mermaid followed him aboard the same ship she'd stalked that night—the one with the little windows. His little ship was being repaired in the yard. It was simple to stay in the big ship's wake, following through the Øresund Strait and up toward the Jutland, waiting for her chance.

The second day, it came.

The ship docked on the island of Kalø. There wasn't much there but a ruined castle, she knew. Why would a fishing expedition stop here?

But soon she understood why.

A girl boarded, her chaperone and attendants following, carrying multiple trunks. The little mermaid's memories were full of her own noble family and kin—she knew this was the daughter of a high house. She knew the trunks would be full of clothes, something she would need once she got to land, when she'd be too weak from her transformation to cast her own.

The elegant girl met Iker the same way Evie had left him— with a smile and a kiss. Just a sweet one on the cheek, but a kiss all the same. They knew each other. The playboy prince, living up to his reputation.

The elegant girl left him to go below, looking back as if she expected him to follow. He didn't—and the mermaid wondered if Evie actually did have a chance. Instead, Iker directed his men to raise anchor.

The mermaid waited. Thought of using her powers to bring about yet another storm. She hoped Iker would get drunk. Teeter too close to the rail. Make it easy for her.

And just as she lost hope, a better idea struck.

Iker's kiss did mean something. Even if he didn't follow the girl belowdecks. It meant he'd be able to hurt Evie more alive than dead.

And Evie deserved pain.

Iker would pay later.

The little mermaid stole a trunk. She spared the ship's captain, for the moment. Then she set out to find Evie's father.

29

I FOLLOW ANNEMETTE OUT ONTO THE BALCONY AND pull her around to face me. She looks as though she's about to melt into tearless sobs. I squeeze her hands. We are close enough now that our pearl necklaces catch the same lantern's glow, and they light up like twin beacons in the night.

"Please, Evie. Go. Let me have this peace."

I won't. She knows I won't.

The distance and whispers won't guarantee us privacy, but they're the best I can do. I keep my voice quiet yet confident. "Remember, I have a plan."

Annemette rips her hands from mine and presses them to her face. "It's useless! Neither you nor I have magic powerful enough to stave off what is to come. Just go!"

My words are barely audible. "I'm powerful enough," I

say, the words coming out strong and clear. "Please believe me."

She sob-laughs. "You are so ridiculously stubborn." Annemette swipes at her eyes, but doesn't go on. I take her silence as an invitation.

"You know magic is barter—despite how different we are, we both know this. Magic with the sea is no different. We give to the sea, it returns you to land in kind." Annemette doesn't say anything, her features closing tight—trying to make sense of this. I quietly hurry into more of an explanation. "I've tested this. I know my magic is rigid and book-learned, but it's right. And tonight, on the last night of Urda's festival, our magic is strong. Stronger than any night of the year. Don't you feel it?" I touch my pearl necklace, whose throbbing has grown as the days have gone by. "We are at one with Urda; we are balanced, and that is what magic is all about—balancing our inner power with the forces around us, giving and taking. It's Urda's way, and she and the sea both require like for like. They took Anna—"

"I am not Anna," Annemette says plainly, clearly annoyed. "If you keep believing that, whatever you have planned won't work!"

I shake my head. "I know you don't remember. Maybe you never will, but this is something I can feel. I can feel Anna inside of you. But it doesn't matter, Annemette—I care for you just as you are. Our friendship can be so much more than mine with Anna's ever was. You and I are the same!

"Look," I go on, trying to keep my voice as steady as possible, "the sea took Anna from me four years ago. And even if that girl only lives on as a memory in you, the sea took her soul. You did not keep it." At this Annemette flinches. "And that's what you need to survive. Anna's soul is one portion of the exchange. The sea took from us and now it owes me—*you*—a soul in return."

But she doesn't consider a word I say. She only turns and raises her voice, and I realize both princes have followed us out—what they've heard, I don't know.

"I must leave tonight, Nik," she says.

Nik glances at me, but then returns his attention to Annemette, taking a step toward her. "Now? But the ball isn't over yet," Nik says, sadness in his voice. Behind him, Iker cocks a brow.

"I have to go. I'm sorry."

Nik is about to say more, but Iker barges into the conversation, taking a few steps until he's towering above both of us. "I wasn't aware of a midnight train to Odense, and no carriage will take you that far. Surely you aren't going to walk."

Nik shoots Iker a look of warning but doesn't say a word. Instead, he takes both Annemette's hands. "If you need to go, then go. I understand."

"So, you're going to vanish in the middle of the night? What a plan!" Iker's eyes flash and he steps away from the wall. "Break his heart but not his spirit, return again in a few months and he'll be so happy, he'll just throw himself at you—title and all? Too bad you failed at the first step—"

"Enough, Iker! If she needs to leave, she needs to leave," Nik shouts. I don't know why Nik isn't suspicious too, but I have a feeling it's because he trusts me. And I trust Annemette.

"I really have to go," Annemette says, rushing to Nik's side. "I'm so sorry." She moves to kiss him on the cheek, when Iker grabs her by the arm.

"Witches are creatures of the night. That's it, isn't it? Is your cauldron about to boil over? Do you have toads that need simmering? Brew to bottle?"

"Iker!" Nik shouts, and pushes him off her.

But Iker keeps going, turning more and more into a monster than the man I love. "Or is it simply that your broom has arrived and you mustn't leave your favorite mode of transportation waiting?"

Annemette's calm cracks wide open, her teeth bared in the moonlight. "I am not a witch, you ox!"

"Then what are you? A fairy? A ghost? Or maybe just a con artist, like Evie once suggested. Foreign trash finding an easy mark in our Nik." Iker's teeth are gritted in that feral grin as he twists the knife.

I latch onto Iker's forearm, and Nik moves protectively in front of Annemette, but neither of us can stop Iker's momentum.

"How many lonely boys have fallen for your tricks? Five? Ten? Twenty? Whatever the number, I'm sure this one here would make quite the feather in your pointy little hat. He's definitely got enough gold to retire on."

"Stop!" Nik shoves Iker away, and though Iker barely budges, I lose my grip on him and stumble into the table.

Iker stands his ground but holds out his hand to haul me up. His eyes flash at Nik. "Look what the witch has made you do." I push his hand away and get to my feet.

"She isn't a witch," I say.

"I am not." Annemette's voice is firm. She's done backing down. "And I must go."

"Doesn't he deserve to know why?" Iker says then points a hand toward Nik. "The man you've been tossing yourself at out of *love* for three straight days? If you aren't leaving in the middle of Havnestad's biggest ball for nefarious purposes, surely you can tell him the reason. At least give the man that."

Annemette doesn't look at Iker. Doesn't look at me. Or even Nik. She just spins for the door. The boys freeze in shock—the both of them unused to not receiving a reply to their questions—but I whir into motion, running after her, snatching her hand just before she opens the French doors.

"Evie, it's almost midnight! Let me go. There's nothing you can do. Nothing Nik can do!"

But I won't let her die like this, and I hang on to her arm tightly. In her struggle, Annemette gets turned around enough that I can look her in the eye. "If you won't let me help, then tell him what you did. He'll understand. Maybe he does love you and just needs a push. Isn't it worth a shot? Tell him—"

"Tell me what?" Nik asks behind me.

Annemette clamps her lips shut and shakes her head as she tries to buck away from my grip.

He places a hand on my shoulder. "Evie, what is it?"

Annemette catches my eye, pleading.

"I won't have you leave us, Annemette. I won't," I cry. Her breath hitches, but I am strong, and I know this is right. I raise my voice just enough that the boys can hear it but nobody beyond the balcony.

"She's a mermaid." I turn to Nik. "She saved you on your birthday—dragged you from the sea."

Shock registers on his face as his eyes meet Annemette's.

Iker huffs out a great laugh. "Sure she is. And I'm the ghost of Leif Erikson."

I hold his smiling eyes. "No, I saw her. Before you scrambled over the rock wall. She was on land with him. She was—"

"Singing." A smile touches Nik's lips as he says it. A smile just for Annemette, whose expression only shows a brewing anger. "You were singing. I thought it was Evie, but she doesn't sing. It was you."

"I can't believe you did this," Annemette growls at me. "We had a deal."

My stomach sinks, my betrayal tearing at my insides.

"Annemette, don't!" I shout, but fury flashes in her eyes as she turns to the boys. "I am a mermaid, it's true. But, Evie . . . Evie is a *witch*! Her aunt is a witch! Her mother was a witch! She does magic every day right under your proud Øldenburg noses!"

She wrenches out of my hands with a shove that sends me to the floor.

Nik is staring at me, his face in a complete state of shock. "A witch, Evie?"

But before I can respond, Iker moves in front of me. My Iker. Strong, protective, stubborn, loyal Iker. The look on his face is one I've never known. Then, without so much as a pause, he bares his teeth and shouts, "Guards!"

FOUR DAYS BEFORE

The ship belonging to the royal fisherman of the sovereign king-dom of Havnestad was easy enough to find. Just up from Østerby Havn—far enough from the Øresund Strait to sight the best whales, but close enough to home that the ship's captain would make it back to Havnestad by the final night of Lithasblot.

The sun was failing, twilight setting in late, as was usual for a summer night this far north. Despite the hour, there was a flurry of activity aboard the Little Greta, *the crew cleaning up after a long day. Evie's father was moving about too, not leaving the work to his crew—on a ship so small, everyone had to carry his own weight, most of all the captain.*

In the shadows, the little mermaid considered the best course of action.

She could call a large wave, as she had to claim the chest of clothes now trailing her through the water, kept in tow with a simple spell of binding magic. Or perhaps a storm more power-ful than the one she'd used to pull Nik under—wreck the ship and claim the whole crew. But no, she wanted Evie to feel the agony of her father dying when others easily survived. A sharper pain, that.

She knew firsthand.

And then, the little mermaid's attention snagged on a way

to drive in the knife even further. A way to hurt Evie the most.

Without a moment's hesitation, she reached out through the distance, sending her magic snaking through the Nordic depths.

"Hvalr. Hvalr. Koma hvalr."

In short order, the edges of her power hit upon success, and her plan began to unfurl, a fat pilot whale steaming toward her like a locomotive on new track.

When the whale arrived, it was glassy-eyed under her command. But the sailors wouldn't see that. They couldn't smell magic—they would only smell a chance at another catch for His Majesty.

She looked the great animal in the eye. Her lure. And promised it it'd be safe. Then, she gathered her magic anew.

"Rísa, hvalr. Rísa."

The whale did as it was commanded, rising to the surface like a gift from the sea king himself.

The little mermaid skipped the whale across the water, dancing it across the surface.

Tantalize. Trick. Catch the big fish.

The commotion above was enough that she could pick up the sounds of men sprinting and shouting from her spot below. Smiling, she surfaced in the shadow of the portside bow, and saw that, yes, the fish had taken the bait.

The men scurried about, readying nets, spears, and, optimistically, a huge knife—a mønustingari—for severing the spinal cord. Amid it all, Evie's father did exactly what the little mermaid expected.

He readied the harpoon gun. The innovation Evie had fashioned for a better kill. They'd discussed it that day on the dock. She was clearly so proud. And he of her.

Pride must suffer pain, Evie.

As the whale danced on the edge of her fingertips, the little mermaid called a storm with another tendril of her power. "Veðr."

The storm gathered, wind gusting over the crew as they darted about, ignoring the lightning crackling on the horizon, their sights only on the catch.

The little mermaid got in position, watching and waiting as the father worked the dart gun, stuffing the harpoon into the barrel. Hauling it around, so that it might aim at the whale.

Aim right into the storm.

And in that moment, the father shot the dart gun. The harpoon exploded into the rough air, hurtling toward the whale as it crested another leap. A rope trailed the harpoon, attached to the gun stand, so that it might be easier to haul in, whale and all.

But it would spear no whale.

With a sweep of the little mermaid's hand, the storm unleashed a gust of wind strong enough to change the harpoon's course. It skipped off the rocking water, swinging around, past the whale, through the air, reversing course until it shot back toward the ship's deck. Deadly end pointing back the way it came.

It was so surprising, so unnatural, that his reflexes failed Evie's father.

He didn't move. Didn't flinch. Didn't even cry before the harpoon speared him through the stomach.

Another wave of the little mermaid's hand, and the harpoon bucked wildly, pulling itself and Evie's father into the rumbling deep.

The little mermaid moved then, surging below the surface to catch him before his crew regained its wits and tried to haul its captain up by the gun's rope.

She pulled him off the spear, blood flooding in the water, and as she did so, he opened his eyes. Not yet fully dead, despite the gaping wound.

In them flashed the slightest hint of recognition. That he was not only nearly dead, that he was not just seeing a mermaid, but that he was seeing his daughter's dead friend before him.

"Anna . . . ," he said, his voice but a whisper and a gurgle.

"Yes," she replied.

The light in his eyes flickered, and the little mermaid reached into her hair, pulled out the coral knife she'd fashioned into a decorative comb, and plunged it into his chest, right in to the soft spot between his ribs and sternum where it would pierce his heart.

More blood in the water.

The light left his eyes.

Finally, the little mermaid felt a release. Just a small amount. A crumb could not satisfy such a hunger.

Not yet.

She gathered the corpse, called to the clothing trunk that had been floating down below as she worked, and swam as fast as she could to Havnestad.

The little mermaid arrived close to midnight, heart pounding after so many miles. She immediately ducked into the cove, placing her trunk in the shallows behind the great rock wall that divided the beach, leaving Havnestad blind to her catch. She'd search it later for the perfect gown and then toss it back into the sea.

She returned to Evie's father, whom she'd left under the watchful eye of a giant black octopus who had made the cove its home.

"Later, beast. He's mine to start."

The octopus slunk away in a puff of indigo ink to a small cave in the rock. The little mermaid returned her attention to the dead man. His olive skin was tinged white and the whole of him had begun to bloat.

She hoped the spell would still work without him being freshly dead. Hoped that because it was she who had killed him, she already possessed what the magic needed. That it was bottled inside of her with her hate, ready to explode. Ready to enact her plan.

The little mermaid took him by both hands. Shut her eyes. And asked for her life back.

"Líf. Dauði. Minn líf. Minn bjoð. Seiðr. Seiðr. Seiðr."

A warmth immediately filled her, running from her fingertips to her head to her heart down the length of her tail and fin.

It spread like the mouthful of summer wine she'd stolen with Evie on her eleventh birthday. It spread like the way Nik had made her feel in those days, his dark eyes lighting up her soul.

It spread like life. Líf.

In a flash and shock of pain, the little mermaid knew a change had been made. Where once she had a tail and fin, she now had legs again. But she didn't have her soul back. Not yet.

She dropped Evie's father and pushed her way to the surface, her arms tired no more. And when she reached for air, her lungs couldn't get enough. The fresh night flushed through her, warm and free. Knocking loose a little bit of the hatred that made up her fabric. But not much. There was so much left.

And as she found her swimming legs treading water, she spied a girl on land. Leaving the beach for the step bridge of rocks leading into the cove.

Evie.

The brand-new girl smiled from her spot in the tide and adjusted the comb in her hair, the knife's edge hidden among the damp waves.

Yes, my plan will work.

30

I BURST OUT OF THE CASTLE DOORS AND INTO THE TULIP garden, hot on Annemette's heels. I took off after Iker's command and haven't looked back, but I can hear them coming.

"Annemette, please!" I shout. I know I betrayed her, but even if she despises me for sharing her secret, she can't deny I did it out of love. Although her own betrayal felt more like spite than love, it doesn't bite. Not really. Because all I can think is how I can fix it. I can do it. I will do it.

If I can save her, we can use our magic to run away, far from here. It pains me, but it's the only choice left to make.

My lungs heave to keep up with my pace, pure adrenaline propelling me forward as I tear down the cobblestones. I take a hard right through a gateway of stiff black rocks and onto the soft sand of the cove.

The moon shines heavy here, reflecting off every

surface in a pearlescent glow. Annemette has stopped running, brought to her knees in the sand, an inch from the lapping tide. The gold thread of her dress catches the moonlight as her shoulders heave in a dry sob. She's not far from where she rescued Nik—on the beach side of the cove, the stone wall jutting over the blind side.

"Annemette," I call tentatively. The sand slows my progress, already inhibited by my heavy ball gown. She doesn't move—chin tipped down toward the tide—nor does she seem to hear me. I'm about to repeat myself when she makes it clear she knows I'm there.

"Go away."

"I'm sorry." I settle onto the sand beside her, leaving more distance between us than I ever have before. "I let hope take over my words. I thought telling Nik would help us satisfy the magic."

She doesn't look at me. "It did not. It's over. I'm over."

"We're both over if we don't go now. The guards are coming. Let me help you, please."

When she doesn't answer, I move to stand. "The sea will give me what I want. And I want you to stay."

Here, she finally glances at me. The look in her eye is all questions, but she seems relieved. I think.

I step into the water. The sea is crisp, and immediately it takes my boots, stockings, ankles, hemline—all of it—as its own. Grounding me in its power.

A shadow falls over us, and I look to the sky. Another

sudden storm has swallowed the moon, the whole cove bathed in a shimmering silver darkness—the curtain drawn before the magic begins.

I measure the clouds. There's lightning in the distance. This is good. I'll need all the energy I can harness. My heart begins to pound as that familiar crackle sparks across my veins, warming me from my toes to the top of my skull. I raise my hands above my head, feeling the brewing storm's charge on the edge of my fingertips.

"Evie, STOP!"

I turn. But only because the voice is Nik's.

He's standing on the sand not ten feet from us, all the finery woven into his jacket and the crown atop his head sparkling brightly in the moonlight. Shifting his weight, Nik lifts his chin, his stance so much like the one he uses in public appearances. It's his practiced armor, and I recognize it in an instant. The next words are not his—they're the crown's.

"The guards are on their way. Annemette, if you are not gone from Havnestad before they arrive, they will forcibly return you to the water. You are a threat to Havnestad and all of the Øresund Kingdoms."

Nik believed me. He remembered. As soon as my words tumbled out he must have seen his rescue—her tail.

And it's ruined Annemette. And me as well.

There's not a prayer of him helping us now. Even if my magic is able to keep her here, he'll want nothing to do

—305

with her anyway. But if he believed my truth about her, he should believe her truth about me. And I know he does, deep down. He'll want to protect me, but he can't.

There are boots on the cobblestones now—*thud, thud, thud*—King Asger's guards approaching. Coming for us. Annemette's eyes return to the sea. Her shoulders begin to heave again, dry sobs coming fast, but she refuses to move.

I take one last look at Nik, standing there so regal, so good, so kind, but I've already made my choice. I turn to Annemette, my hand outstretched. "Get up! Let's go! Don't you want to live?"

Nik lunges toward me, his façade crumbling. "Evie, please don't do this." He grabs my hand, and I'm pulled to face him as much by the desperation of his movement as by the look in his eyes. He knows that if he sees me perform magic—confirming Annemette's accusation—then he won't be able to protect me. We're truly on opposite sides.

But we have been all along—I was just the only one of us to know it.

"Evie, please don't do this," he repeats, and I nearly push a finger to his lips to still the tremble there, despite my frustration.

"Nik, you forced me into this magic. Annemette will *die* if I don't do it," I cry. "If you'd given her your heart, it would have been so simple—"

"Evie, you don't understand. My heart is not mine to give."

His hand tightens, and despite the want in his eyes I expect him say something next about nobility, duty—all the things the Øldenburgs hold dearer than their own feelings. But he doesn't.

"My heart has been yours, Evie—always. Since Anna's death. Since sandcastles and stick princesses." His voice cracks and tears threaten his eyes. "I have always loved you. Every day. My heart is not mine to give because it is already yours."

The truth crashes over me like a winter wave.

All this time, I've known. But the truth—the truth is always something I've struggled with, whether I'm lying to Nik or myself, or both. But his truth is the truth in my heart, too.

Then I'm kissing him.

Quick as a lightning strike, I press my lips to his hard enough that he takes a step back to keep us from falling to the beach.

In that brief moment, everything surrounding us stops—the sadness, the magic, the boot strikes on the cobblestones, the entirety of it.

His lips are warm, his hands gentle as they fold themselves over mine. He is delicate and strong at the same time, matching caress with intensity in a way I didn't know was possible. In a way I don't want to end.

I do love him. I've loved him as long as he has loved me. I've just spent so much of my life, so much of the last week, pretending it wasn't true. So that we wouldn't be hurt. That we wouldn't suffer at the hands of class and expectations.

But love doesn't work that way.

And with a sudden dip of my trembling heart, I realize I doomed Annemette from the start. I've taken her true love's kiss.

"Step away from him, witch."

Iker's voice slices through my thoughts, and it's Nik who pulls away, though the order was meant for me. Iker doesn't need proof to know what I am; still the abandonment cuts deep.

The world comes flooding back in—twenty rifled soldiers on the beach, standing at attention behind Iker. Behind the only other boy I've kissed. Iker has vengeance in his eyes and armed men who can do something about it.

Nik's hands clamp around mine again as he plants his feet to shield me from his cousin. I glance quickly to Annemette. She's standing now, in the water. New clouds tightening, the wind has picked up, tossing her hair in long tangles, the coral comb nestled within them barely holding anything in place. There's something in her face—fear, anger, urgency—that has hardened what had been just a resigned puddle.

"End your spell over him!" Iker's eyes are ice. It's as if he's already forgotten who I am. Or that he didn't care in the first place. I refuse to believe either—and twine my fingers around Nik's so he's not just holding me, I'm holding him.

"She doesn't have a spell over me!" Nik shouts. "You know it as much as I do!"

Iker doesn't blink. Doesn't acknowledge him. "Witch, the king has given orders to shoot you on the spot."

I look to Annemette. I hope she'll understand what we need to do. That she won't slow us down.

I squeeze Nik's hands, willing my fingers to remember his touch, no matter what happens.

Then I whisper into his ear.

"I love you, Nik."

And as soon as his name hits the air, I shove him onto the sand with all my might. I grab Annemette's hand, and dive into the water.

"To the sandbar."

As I say it I see the shadow of a wince, but then Annemette takes a deep breath and hurtles forward. Anna and I never made it to that other sandbar, but I know Annemette and I will make it to this one.

We swim out past Picnic Rock, entering the open water of the cove as Iker and the guards pull Nik to his feet, all of them shocked into inaction. They're slow to set their rifles, bullets unchecked—no one was expecting a witch hunt tonight.

I assume Annemette will cling to me, as she did to Nik

earlier in the day. But the situation has given her strength, and she has new resolve, the fear gone. She kicks her legs, swimming as if she truly knows how.

We cross the distance in a bare minute, the guards finally getting off shots, bullets pinging through the water. A single bullet grazes my shoulder, searing heat and blood draining into the water as I paddle forward.

But I am stronger than the pain.

We reach the sandbar. The moon is just right and I know we only have moments now. My heart is pounding and my left arm is awash in blood from where the bullet struck me, but I try to stay calm. I haul myself onto the thin strip of packed sand and pull Annemette up. Half the soldiers have charged into the water now, daggers in their teeth as their counterparts reload.

Placing my hands on her shoulders, my eyes go to the sky. "Ready?"

She nods, watching me, hope daring to creep into her blue eyes.

"*Skipta.*" I channel Urda and the power of the waves churning beneath us. *Exchange this life for the soul you took.*

A breeze lifts, and a flash of far-off lightning answers.

"*Skipta.*" A peal of thunder.

The charge of the storm seems to radiate from my hands, the zip of energy surging all the way to my heart.

"*Skipta.*" The wind picks up. The thunder and lightning

close in. I can feel the magic in my bones. Annemette consumes my thoughts, all of my concentration on her. On shifting the sea's hand—forcing it to deliver my request.

"Skipta."

"Child, what do you think you're doing?" Tante Hansa screams from the beach. I hear her over the guns. Over the men splashing in the water. Over the thunder. It's as if she has an amplifier aimed straight for my ears. Still, I do not turn.

Annemette. I want Annemette. I want my Anna back.

"Child! Evelyn, listen to me. Listen to my age and mistakes. Magic born of pride and spite is unwieldy. It is far too much for your little hands!"

My hands are not little—they are powerful.

I am none of those things, Tante Hansa. I come from a place of love.

Thunder pounds and the magic singes my veins with every crackle of lightning above. The magic is in my palms.

This is right—it will be enough.

From the beach, Tante Hansa shouts again, though her words no longer register in my ears. The men with daggers are almost upon us, the charging waves of the storm keeping them at bay just long enough.

I order the magic a final time.

"Skipta."

I see Anna's face at eleven. I see Annemette in my future.

I'm focused on all of it so tightly. All of my concentration. All of my power.

Everything I have is aimed at Urda. Determined. Ready.

The storm rages. My concentration is flawless.

But then a flash of lightning rips across the sky, so bright my eyes spring open.

And I see Annemette is smiling.

Not just smiling.

Laughing.

Her hands cup my wrists and pull them off her shoulders. Her strength is surprising. Her lips twist into a smirk.

"You studied, you tested, you planned, and your solution is to simply ask the magic for an exchange? Like you want a blue dress instead of a red one?"

Magic surges until it is swirling around us. It sparks and undulates. I realize it's not mine. Not all mine, anyway. The storm was never mine—it has the same feel as the storm on Nik's birthday. On Iker's boat earlier that day. The storms are Annemette.

I am blind for the briefest of moments, and then I feel her cool magic welling up from the pit of my stomach, through my lungs, and clutching at my heart. When my vision returns, a cone of water surrounds us—shielding us from the beach.

They're going to think I did that.

Annemette's grip tightens as she leans into my ear, as close as Nik just minutes before.

"You know what I think? I think you didn't really want to save me. You didn't want to save me any more this time than you wanted me to survive four years ago."

A gasp escapes my lips. *Anna.* My Anna. But there's a knife twist in her words that my Anna didn't have.

Between Nik's love and Anna's resentment, my heart stops beating for a moment.

It thuds back to life, tears stinging my eyes as I try to grab for her face, her hair, my friend. I've missed her for so long. Even with all my personal loss, I can't imagine her pain. But her grip only tightens more and I can't touch her. "Anna. Oh, Anna, I wanted you to survive. I did a spell that day, but I—"

That smirk twists into a sneer. "Failed. You failed because you didn't understand, and you wrecked that too." Her teeth are bared—I don't recognize her face anymore. The torque of her grip on my hands is cutting off my circulation. "Instead of protecting my life, you caused the black plague with that magic."

The Tørhed. The minnows at my feet, faceup and inked black, flash in my mind. Dead by my tears. My black tears. The look on Hansa's face as she saved me. The Tørhed didn't just start that summer; it started with me that day.

I did it.

She's right. I know she's right. I've known it deep down for a while now.

"I tried to fix it. This year, the sea life has returned—"

"The sea life you've ripped from where they truly belong? The spells of abundance you unleashed on the sea, killing faster than the black death? If they aren't dying in nets, they're dying of famine. Because there are too many." Her hands grip tighter, her cool magic ringing my wrists along with her fingers. "The sea can't take more of your kindness, *witch*."

"Let me try—"

"To fail again? Oh, no. No. Tonight is about success." Despite the cone of water, a swimming soldier gets a hand on the sandbar, but with a lift of her arm, Anna sends him back into the deep. We can't see the rest of the guards, but I can feel her magic surging forth, pushing them all back and out of striking distance with a mere word under her breath. She doesn't even break eye contact. Her eyes flash, and the cut of her teeth finally resembles something of a smile.

"Tonight, Anna Liesel Kamp reclaims her life."

I try to move, try to touch her, implore her, but she's done something, and I can't move my arms. My feet. Anything. Even my magic won't budge, frozen in my veins. My heart begins to sink, the only thing Anna cannot control.

"Anna, please!"

"Oh, no, you will get no pity from me." Again, she

laughs. The sound is guttural, mirthless. "You stole my life. You stole it with your dare. You stole it with that stupid hold you have over Nik. He chose you. He saved you. He failed me. Because of you."

"Anna—"

"Nothing you can say will give it back. Nothing you can do will give it back."

She removes a hand from my shoulder and thrusts it out behind her in the direction of the rock that divides the cove. Though only one hand remains, I'm still powerless to move. My magic feels like sludge under my skin. If only I knew more about how it all worked. If only I'd studied harder. Practiced more. I'd felt so powerful moments ago, and now I'm completely helpless.

The wall of water surrounding us parts, and something bursts through into our space. Not a guard, no . . . it's misshapen, gray, bloated, a dark hole through its middle.

But then in a blink I recognize it. I gasp and start to fight against Anna's restraints. I need to touch him. I need to make sure. But I know when she starts laughing again that the nightmare before me is real.

The thing before me is my father. *Was* my father.

"While your solution was an exceedingly juvenile spell, the idea was right. A life for me to be here, a life for me to stay."

I see it all so clearly now. True love was never going to save Anna—not with what she's become. If it was even a solution to begin with. There've been so many lies.

There's a rumble from somewhere in the clouds, and something surges deep within the water surrounding us. And I know my part in her revenge before I can see the outline of the wall of water.

Our sea didn't claim me that day, though Urda's choice was there. Now, Anna is giving the water another chance.

"And I'm to be the life you take to stay." I force myself to look at her as I say it. My father paid the price for Anna's vengeance and now I must do the same.

She smiles—the most soulless thing I've ever seen. "Oh, no. Your life isn't valuable enough for that."

Anna's grip releases. Suddenly, I'm aloft, next to my father, floating. I'm still immobile. My muscles, fight, magic, all useless.

With a twist of her hand, a gust as strong as a cannonball strikes me in the chest. Father's body and I shoot back through the wall of water, arcing toward the stormy churn of the cove.

As I fall, I inhale my last breath. Close my eyes.

And then I am one with the sea.

ON THE SURFACE

The little mermaid was smiling. Smiling and crying—salt water was the perfect cheat for tears.

She would be crying real tears of joy soon.

"Hold your fire!" the boy called as the guards raised their rifles to the little mermaid splashing past the footstep islands on her own two feet. Behind her somewhere, Evie had taken her last breath. The approaching guards, too, dead in the deep; she couldn't let them ruin this next part. She didn't have much time, but there wasn't much left to be done.

She just had to hold on for the final piece of her plan.

"Nik! Nik! She did it! She did it!" The little mermaid crashed onto the beach—the princes and the remaining guards were the only ones nearby but at the mouth of the cove was an entire ball's worth of gawkers. An audience. This was perfect. "She did it, and I remember!"

The little mermaid grabbed his hand. Pointed her practiced smile at his stunned face. "I'm Anna. Anna Liesel Kamp. I'm Anna!"

From the sea lane above, the little mermaid heard her batty old oma, right for once. "Anneke. My Anneke—you're sopping wet! Out of the water with you! Out!"

A few titters came after the old woman's outburst, but then

Iker's voice thundered over them all. "Cousin, step back. She's no better than a witch and you know it. She's worse. Move away."

"Not this time, Iker," Nik said, touching the little mermaid's face. Reading it. Confirming the suspicions he should've had since the moment he set eyes on the "traveler from Odense."

"If you're really Anna, tell me this: What happened on Lille Bjerg Pass when I was ten?"

The little mermaid didn't blink; rather, her answer brimmed with joy and urgency. "You bashed your right leg on a rock, you've got a scar as long as your shin bone. Evie and I had to carry you down the mountain."

Those dark eyes of his widened and he grinned. "It's you—it's really you." But then he broke her gaze, his eyes searching the waves for the girl she would never be. He couldn't even give her this moment of attention. Yes, he deserves this.

"Where's Evie? There was a wave and—" His eyes broke from hers, scanning the water.

"Niklas, what are you doing? Step away from her!" The queen—the little mermaid almost smiled again. The queen and her piety. The king and his nobility wouldn't be far behind. "What are you waiting for, cowards?" she yelled at the guards, porcelain features cracking in fury. "You have guns, use them."

The guards advanced—but Nik was prepared. "Stay back. That's an order." He turned to his mother, looking over the little mermaid's head. Holding her tight. "You too, Mother."

"Overruled," the king answered, his voice stern. "You are of age, my son, but as long as I am alive, your orders will still be

those of a child." He faced the guards who were left. "Seize the prince and kill the girl."

This time, the guards didn't hesitate to advance, their bayonetted rifles pointed squarely toward the little mermaid. The prince stepped in front of the little mermaid, shielding her from the guards. From view.

The time was finally right. And with not a moment to spare.

The little mermaid pressed into his back as if cowering. Then she swept a single hand through her hair. Her fingers wrapped around her comb, the point glistening with seawater.

"Nik!" That voice. Evie—she'd survived, the little witch.

The prince turned toward the water. Looked toward his true love.

The little mermaid smiled then—the prince had yet again made the wrong choice.

It would be his final one.

With all the strength remaining in her body, the little mermaid plunged the knife straight through the prince's back and into his heart.

31

MY EYES OPEN TO DARKNESS. EVERYTHING ABOUT ME IS
midnight. Sad and colorless. Time does not exist.

So this is the sea.

The true sea.

The only light from above is the moon. As my eyes
adjust, it gives the blackness a little color—a hint of blue
in so much dark as I sink beneath the waves onto cool
sands. My father lies next to me, his eyes sunken and gone.
The hole in his middle—it's the size of a harpoon. From
my dart gun, surely. I want to scream as my heart aches.
The cove's octopus sweeps into view, even larger than I'd
thought.

Thought. Thoughts. I have thoughts.

I'm alive.

My lungs scream.

Wait.

I'm alive, and I need air.

I test my arms. My feet. Anna's magic has somehow gone—I can move.

Suddenly, my feet are kicking and my hands are clawing at the water in an upward stroke. Pain radiates up my arm from where blood seeps into the water.

I was shot. Yes, I was shot by the king's men. And I survived.

I survived what Anna had planned, too.

And now I must warn Nik. Anna isn't our friend anymore—she's something else entirely.

She is rage.

My heart quickens, pounding harder with each foot gained toward the surface. Blood clouds every stroke, my shoulder threatening to fail.

My vision breaks the surface, and with a heaving breath I'm already moving forward, swimming and then lunging toward the beach once my feet gain purchase on the submerged sand. I try to breathe in deeply, but my necklace is too tight, the pearl still throbbing. With every ounce of energy I have left, I tear at the magic thread until the pearl bursts free, landing with a plunk in the water below.

I am free now too. I can feel my connection to the old Annemette fade away with the waves. She must have had a spell on me this whole time, or perhaps I put the spell on myself.

Water streams from my hair into my eyes. *Nik.* I have to find him.

He's standing tall and regal on the beach—protecting Anna from advancing guards. My heart beats fast. He's alive. But not for long. I know now his is the life she plans to take.

He's standing too close.

"Nik!" I scream.

I get his attention. But then I also get Anna's. And the guards'.

Shots ring out, and a sudden burst of pain rockets through my chest. I flail back but manage to keep my momentum. I bring my fingers to the wound along my ribs and wince. It's hot and wet, and my breathing grows shallow, each intake bringing a fresh stab of pain. But I have to keep moving, slogging through the water, now almost waist-high.

Nik is stunned still, but Anna is not. Her hand reaches for her hair.

A knife is in that hand, the blade moving straight at Nik, who is watching me.

"NO!" *You will not take him! You will not!*

Now Iker is yelling—running. He sees it too.

Despite the blood. Despite the pain. Despite the distance, I surge ahead as fast as I can, water just above my knees. Wet, my gown weighs more than the rest of me, but that won't keep me from him. Nothing will.

Five yards away. Four. Three.

But it is too late. Annemette's blade is already in a downward arc. The sharp coral pierces Nik's back just as Iker grabs him, wrenching him onto the sand.

Nik's blood is on the beach.

Spilling in a trail from where he was to where he fell, staining the sand.

Oh, Urda. No. Not Nik.

Even after everything, I can't believe Anna has done it, but I have no pity for her. If she thinks she's the only one who will get her revenge, she'll be sorely wrong.

"Niklas!" the queen wails, and dashes forward. The king runs too, finally coming to their only son's aid.

The onlookers go still—recognition, terror, and fear frozen upon faces I've known my whole life. Malvina. Ruyven. Every member of the castle kitchen staff.

Anna's beautiful features twist as she dips her toes in Nik's spilled blood, laughing. *Laughing.* "You ruined my life, and I've ruined yours, *my prince.*"

I dive for her feet, knocking her to the sand. I move on top of her, pinning her hand that still holds the knife, red with Nik's blood. I scream for my tante. "Hansa! Nik—you must heal him!" But two guards hold Hansa back, my magic enough to condemn her, too. I reach out to the only person with the power to change their minds. "Iker, let her do her work. Please! She can save him!"

My heart stutters as Iker immediately does as I

say—family over everything. "Let the old woman go!" he commands.

The guards comply. But I can't watch her act. My heart can't take it if she fails. She's known as the Healer of Kings, but tonight she'll have to save my prince.

As Hansa works, Anna's magic tugs at the edges of my strength. Overhead, storm clouds gather. Pinned beneath my body, Anna's suddenly laughing again. I want to slap her, but I don't want to lose my grip. "Shut up!" I scream. "How could you? He loved you! *I* loved you!"

She spits in my face. This person I no longer know. This person I don't recognize. This person who tried to take Nik. This person who took my father.

The wind picks up, and lightning sizzles in my peripheral vision. Thunder crashes. Her magic rolls over us, and I do everything I can do to keep her down, my magic sparking in spurts as I bleed.

Now she's laughing so hard that she's crying. *Actual tears.*

They flee down her blood-splattered cheeks, wet and real. Terror claws at my heart as it struggles to work under the weight of the blood streaming out of my shoulder and chest.

No, she can't be human. This person doesn't deserve a soul. She can't have won. Nik isn't dead.

He can't be.

Yet her tears are there. And with them, her eyes roll

dramatically up to where I have her hands pinned to the sand. Where the knife is pinned—*no.*

No.

Screams sound from the sea lane. A mass of bodies rushes forth. The guards, too. All to a single body, prone on the beach. Knife sticking out from a strike dead center to the throat—the last of Annemette's mermaid magic used to hit its target.

Not Nik.

His father. The king, dead on the sand.

It must only be royal blood that matters to the magic—Øldenburg blood, passed down from the witch-hunter king—because before him is Iker, pulling himself up from a crouch. He'd been just low enough that Anna's blade missed. It was meant for him—the final player on the day Anna drowned, but the king would do.

The queen's voice, shrill and high, echoes above the chaos as she sinks to the sand. *"Kill them!"*

The guards spring forth. Anna continues to laugh, her human legs kicking at mine. My blood has stained her dress, her skin, her hair. It only makes her laugh harder. So hard she doesn't even try to escape—she's reveling in it too much.

Over the noise—the laughing, the lockstep of the guards, the screaming townspeople, I hear it. The voice I've always known as well as my own.

"Evie."

Nik.

He's crawling toward me with Hansa's aid. The look in her eyes tells me her healing cannot help—he'll soon be dead, like his father. Nik knows it too, his voice shaking. "Evie, I love you. I'm sorry I didn't say it until today. I'm sorry . . ."

"Tante, hold Anna still. Please. Don't let her up." Hansa's magic is strong and she uses a binding spell like Anna used on me. One I never learned.

Still, only when I know Hansa has Anna pinned do I let go. Anna is screaming at me, struggling against Hansa's magic, but I drown her out. My hands find Nik, and I bring his bleeding body to my chest. "I love you, too. And I won't let this be the end."

Confusion crosses his face. The skin there has lost its color. His breath comes in pants, his lungs struggling against my bodice. The blood from our wounds runs together, like finding like.

I shut my eyes, my mother's words coming to me. I don't need octopus ink. I don't need gems or potions or charms. I just need the words and the will.

I am a witch. I am and I always will be. The magic is in me and it is enough—I suppose Annemette taught me that.

"I love you, Nik," I repeat, and then I start my mother's spell. The words coming like I've known them my whole life, and maybe I have.

"Líf. Dauði. Minn líf. Seiðr. Minn bjóð. Seiðr. Seiðr."

My skin begins to burn, white hot, heat radiating from my bones outward, steam in the air. Tears come to my eyes, and I know they're black—Mother's eyes didn't do that, but I'm my own kind of magic. They drip onto Nik's skin as I begin to shake. My eyes roll back for a moment, and the last thing I see is color returning to his skin, his cheeks pinking like we've been together all day at sea.

I force my vision to clear. I need to see him. I need to.

His eyes flash open. He knows what's happening. He knows it like I did the day my mother died.

I will see to it that he is safe.

That he lives a long life.

That he can rule his people without fear.

I will see to it.

With the last of my strength, I leave Nik and push my failing body onto Anna's, tight as a corset. Tighter than the magic Hansa used to paralyze her. My tante steps back, tears in her eyes, and helps Nik to his feet. He's almost completely healed. He will be fine.

Anna is the only threat left, but I have plans for her.

With my last breath, I take ahold of her—this girl I loved, this girl who came back to me. Used me. Ruined me. Ruined every person who ever loved her so that she could be human again. Ruined for revenge.

I get to my feet and heave her toward the water. My hands burn fingerprints into her skin as she tries to pull away.

"What are you doing?" she shrieks. I can feel her heart beating wildly against her bodice. Against my heart—still in my chest.

The clouds are clearing overhead. The wind has died down. The lightning vanished. Her magic is leaving this world, and soon she will too.

Her blue eyes grow wide. She's realized that she'd gotten what she wanted. She's just a girl, like she was before—and it's made her vulnerable to people like me.

I smile at her, and there's no pity in it. No joy. Nothing but rage.

"This life is not yours to live."

With that, I do the only thing I can to reverse Anna's final magical act. To keep my loved ones safe. To stop her threat cold.

I return Anna to the sea.

BELOW THE SURFACE

The tide claimed the two girls, one with curls of raven black, the other with waves of butter-blond. Its water was crisp, despite the summer night. All veins of magic swirled under the surface, mixing with the blood and death that bound the girls together.

The raven-curled girl's heart was failing. Her time was up, spent on the boy above. The one she'd always loved. Always protected—even from herself.

But she would win—the blonde's lungs were seizing. The raven-curled girl could feel them sputtering and shuttering as she held tight to the girl's chest, driving them both down, down, down. As deep as the cove would allow. To the bottom, home to that bewitched octopus, her father's corpse, and the fresh bodies of the guards the blonde had killed with a sweep of her fingers.

So many dead, but the prince was alive. Her boy. Her own borrowed breath in his chest. She'd sacrificed herself for him again.

As the cool remnants of magic swirled around them, the girls plunged to the sandy bottom. The blonde's back lodged in the cove floor, the raven-haired girl's body flushing streams of blood into the water, more of her life fleeing through bullet holes.

Light was failing as fast as their bodies, the strong moon barely reaching these depths. Still, the raven-curled girl wouldn't give in to the darkness. Her heart was barely beating, but her eyes were open, watching the blonde struggle and fail to break free.

She wouldn't die first. She couldn't.

She had to know her boy would be safe—her family, her home—from the monster beneath her fingertips.

Just before the raven-curled girl's heart finally stopped, the blonde went still. Her blue eyes stuck wide, blank. Her rosebud lips forever parted, water seeping in.

The girl had really drowned this time. There'd be no coming back.

The raven-curled girl opened her mouth and accepted the ocean. Let it sweep in and claim her along with the magic still singing in her veins. Still skimming over her skin—it would live longer than she.

Then, a darkness fell across the pewter light of her vision. The end, pulling the curtains shut.

No.

The octopus. The giant one. The one that haunted the cove. Her beast—a product of her spell of abundance. A mistake. An aberration.

The animal was swift. Vengeful. Spiteful.

"Lif . . . lif," the girl started, the words dying in her mouth, drowned in salt water. She wasn't sure what to say other than to tell the octopus to go. Live. Live away from this battlefield. Let her rest with her father in peace.

But the octopus smelled the ink in her veins and the magic it held, and it began to feed. The beast's tentacles trembled with power as they slithered across her wounds, mingling with the water, with her blood, with her spell that controlled its life for the past few months. The girl's eyes rolled back into her head as fresh magic entered her veins.

"Lif. Lif."

Suddenly, a great spasm of white light shot up between them. Connected them. Magic as old as the sea itself threaded the octopus's life and hers.

The light drew the great beast closer to the girl's prone form, barely alive. Barely anything at all. The tentacles reveled in her blood. Tried to capture it. The magic between them was a magnet, pulling all of it to all of her.

"Lif . . . ," she repeated again, no breath in it. Seawater washed the word down her windpipe, pushing the oxygen out of her heart, her blood. Until she was one with the sea. Her soul water itself.

The light flickered and grew, engulfing both the girl and the octopus in its warmth, shooting past the water's surface, to the moon and the magic still hovering in the air above. With the light came an equal darkness, seeping across the cove in a sheet of black.

The people on the sand scattered then, knowing it wasn't safe. All but the boy and his cousin, still watching the water as if the girls might resurface. So many questions on their lips as the black water feathered out toward the Øresund Strait.

And down under the surface, the water roiled and turned until great whirlpools twisted from cove bottom to top. Scalding gas from deep within the earth shot up through the deadened sand, violent geysers forming between the whirlpools. The cove's sand began to rot, all the color washing away until nothing but gray remained. And when the light faded to nothing but the obsidian of the ocean, something peculiar happened.

The girl with raven curls was no longer a girl.

She still had her raven curls, her beauty, and the upper body of a woman, but where her long legs had once been were eight tentacles, onyx black and shiny as silk. They plunged from her waist, unlike anything the ocean had ever seen.

And, with magic swirling around her, through her, from her, the creature opened her eyes.

EPILOGUE—
FIFTY YEARS LATER

THE SEA KING AND HIS PEOPLE CALL ME THE SEA witch—though I'm still surprised to be anything at all.

I was prepared to die that day in the water.

I'd given my life to Nik. I knew what that spell would do.

But something happened in the swirling magic—mine, Mother's, Hansa's, what was left of Annemette's. The octopus haunting the cove had something to do with it too. All combining to leave me with the body I have now.

Not the body of a mermaid.

Not the body of anything else seen in these waters.

I am my own magic.

I spread out my tentacles beneath me: eight, shiny and black, and as voluminous as one of Queen Charlotte's gowns, each plucking a shrimp from the seafloor. I am quite the sight, though very few have laid eyes on me. I am tied to the cove, something keeping me here. Magic or memories, or both.

My lair is a sunken cave, surrounded by bubbling mire—turfmoor—and violent whirlpools. The water here is a flat black—Havnestad Cove now a sunspot on the sea.

Around my cave, strange trees have grown from the bones of Anna and the guards, though my father's bones never changed, buried gently as they are. These trees—polypi—are half-plant, half-animal, like serpents rooted to the pewter sand, a hundred heads where branches should be.

The Tørhed died in the magic that made me this way, the sea rid of both drought and abundance. And so, the whirlpools draw fish into the polypi's clutches, keeping me well fed without ever having to hunt.

Feeding on my strange forest's catch, I study magic. I've learned everything I can about the sorcery beneath the waves, though new mysteries present themselves to me daily. And so my power has grown, but so has my reputation.

The merpeople are frightened of me—time and tales building upon each other. They've been told to stay away from the witch powerful enough to ruin the sea as soon as save it. The sea king knows of the magic I've done—of the black death and then the famine—and he also knows of me and his Annemette, memories of her resurfacing when my name is spoken aloud. But that is rare. No one dares.

It, too, has been long enough that no one on land knows me as Evelyn. Evie. That girl.

They know the story of the mermaid and the witch

and King Niklas. They know of—and dare to visit—the strange cove with ink for water and sand as gray as steel. Now they forgo the bonfire and toss their little wooden dolls into the cove every Sankt Hans Aften. Presents to the witch who saved their kingdom.

But they don't know me.

My people are long gone, or so I've heard from pieces of conversation floating down from above over the years.

Tante Hansa was taken by age, having lived out the remainder of her life in Havnestad despite her magic. Safe from banishment because of her role in saving Nik on that awful day. Hansa sent me gifts until the end—enchanting her own magical tomes to be waterproof before hurling them into the deep. All the secrets that she didn't dare teach me when I was a girl, now at my fingertips. Almost as if she knew I were alive beneath the muck. And maybe she did—though I cannot surface.

Iker: lost in the North Sea. Victim to the king of the whales, who grew tired of being his prey.

Nik is gone too, but he lived out his days as he should have. How I had hoped he would. Marriage, children, a successful reign, and beloved by all.

I miss him. I miss everyone. I strangely miss her sometimes, too—Anna, Annemette, whoever she was.

Alone, there is a quiet under these waters that no one above will ever know. A quiet that makes me miss even the most painful of sounds.

But one day, I receive a visitor. Not from land, but by sea.

A little mermaid. Brave girl, with golden curls topped with a wreath of sea lilies and a complexion as clear as fresh milk with cheeks blushed at the apples. Her eyes are an earnest blue—as icy as the fjords up north.

As icy as Iker's once were.

But rather than the confidence that flashed in his, her eyes hold a determination warring with fear. For such a fearsome creature I've become.

So immediately I know.

Yes, only one thing would cause a mermaid like her to brave my presence.

I stare down at her as she approaches, tentacles mounded beneath me—a throne if ever there was one—a web of ghost-gray curls swirling about my face. Her tail swishes under the weight of eight oysters, each showing her rank. For a moment, I think she will retreat, but instead she holds out her arms, which had been clutching a bouquet of bloodred roses.

"Please accept these flowers grown in my garden, a gift for the great sea witch—"

All it takes is a shake of my head, and her voice immediately cuts off. I glide toward her, and to her credit, she stays still.

"I know what you want," I say, and the girl's eyes blink with my words. Her arms flutter down, the roses sinking to the seafloor. "You want to chase the love of a human boy on legs of your own."

Her answer is immediate. "He already loves me, this I know."

Dubious. "And do you know this boy's name?"

"Not his official name—it is long and drawn out, five names in one—but the other sailors, they called him Niklas."

Crown Prince Asger Niklas Bryniulf Øldenburg V.

Nik's grandson.

I grit my teeth and set my jaw, glancing down my nose at the girl before me. A princess. One of the sweet singing girls who perform often at the palace. Shows to which I'm never invited. I can hear the music, though—the sea king's castle isn't far. If I squint past my strange forest, I can see the peculiar blue radiance surrounding the palace grounds. It looks almost as if a piece of clear sky fell from the heavens to the navy depths of the sea and mingled with the brine.

"Please," the girl starts when I say nothing. Though she's desperate, there's a thoughtful quality to her face— both her head and heart are feeding her bravery. "You are the only one with the magic to change me—it's been banned for so long. Please, even if it is just for a day, I must see him. My heart cannot bear to be away from my Niklas."

Looking in her eyes, I am sixteen again, learning of

Nik's love for the very first time on that beach. Kissing him before our lives changed forever.

But now I am old enough to know better than to listen to my memories.

And I know she doesn't know what she is asking. The price: the cost to her family, her loved ones, the magic. The pain: physical, mental, familial, magical. It is too much.

"The heart can bear many things, child, and love is one of them."

The little mermaid reaches for my hand, but thinks better of it at the last moment. As if my touch will burn. Maybe it will. "Please—I will do anything."

I again think of Nik. His laughter. His love. How long it had been there, waiting for me to see it. There in his dark eyes.

Before he passed, Nik would visit me sometimes, walking the cove's edge, fancy boots marked by my black water. Then he'd tell me stories of the world above, trusting the tide to carry his tale. Maybe he knew I was alive too. A friend, a love, to the end.

I hold the girl's stare. Her eyes are no longer fearful, determination and need filling them in a rush. It is impressive, I suppose—no one has ever braved my lair with such a request. She wants this, more than anything.

More than anything she can promise me.

But I will need something more in return. The magic may no longer require a life, but it still demands a sacrifice.

In the years since, I have learned this, and much else.

And I know what I must take.

"I must know that you will only tell the truth above," I say finally.

The little mermaid is so surprised that it takes her a moment to understand what I mean: that I will help her. When she does, her reply is immediate.

"I will—"

"Do not answer so quickly. What you ask is a serious request." The girl concedes, her lips drawing shut, thoughtfulness sewn tightly into her skin. Good. "Once you have become a human, you can never become a mermaid again. You can never see the palace again. Your father. Your mother. Your sisters. Everything you know and love—save for this prince—will no longer be yours."

The girl blanches. Her blue eyes fade to the middle distance. For all the time she spent thinking before making her request, plucking those flowers from her garden, summoning the courage to swim past the polypi and above the turfmoor, this is something that never crossed her mind. I had heard that the sea king had destroyed the ledgers with the story of Queen Mette, hiding history so that it could not become the future. This girl proves that. If she could have researched more, she would have.

After several moments, her eyes return to my face. Resolute.

"I will do it."

"Very well. But I must be paid also—and it is not a trifle that I ask."

The girl lights up. "I can give you whatever you want," she says. "Gems, jewelry, the finest pearls—please." Privilege and *things* define the life she hopes to leave.

I don't need pearls. The one from long ago had held enough false promises for a lifetime.

"I only ask for one thing: your voice."

The girl's fingers immediately fly to her throat. "My voice?"

"It is imperative that you do not tell a lie above."

"I won't lie."

I cock a brow at her. "You won't without a voice, will you? And if you write a lie while above, your fingers shall fall off."

The girl swallows hard. "If the price is my voice—*though I shall not tell a lie*—how . . . how . . . ?"

"You'll have your beautiful form, your graceful walk, and your expressive eyes," I say, lowering my intonation in the way of Tante Hansa so long ago. "Surely, if you are willing to brave my dark magic and leave your family and friends without a word, you can communicate to your true love without a word as well."

The little mermaid's lips snap shut, her mind working furiously for another way.

My brow arches higher. "Unless you fear his love is not true?"

"It is! It is. He is my true love. Take my voice! Take it! It is worth the cost!"

I slither a tentacle to her face and tip up her chin. There is something else in her eyes—not just fear or longing or love. "Do you really love him or do you love the idea of being human?"

The girl's pupils bloom and her jaw stiffens. Finally, brave thing, she speaks without looking away. "What is it like—to be human?"

I won't give her a bag of saltlakrids and tell her a magnificent story—I am not her grandmother.

If I were, I could tell her that it's like the tang of summer wine and the ring of voices as a new ship docks. Like the scent of salt and limes and the twinkle of a boy's eyes just before a kiss in the moonlight.

But I don't say that. I can't.

If she loses her voice in proving her love, then so be it.

"Very well." I slide my tentacle to her waist and pull her even closer. And suddenly it's as if the girl's voice is already gone, her lips dropped open, no sound escaping. I place my fingers to her bare throat, luminous and elegant even in the bleak light of my home—a pearl shining in the murky depths. Her pulse thrums beneath her warm skin, the first true heartbeat I've felt since Anna's faded in my grasp. "Tell me exactly what it is you love about this Niklas."

"You . . . you just want me to talk?"

"You will have your voice for only a few more moments,

my dear. Use the time wisely."

The girl swallows again and then takes a heavy breath.

"I first saw Niklas on the day I turned fifteen. It could be called love at first sight—but I'd seen his face before. In a statue I've had in my castle garden since I turned ten. Those red flowers I brought you, they grow—"

"Yes, the Øldenburgs love their statues," I say, sounding again very much like Hansa. "There is yet to be love in this story. Only coincidence and horticulture."

The girl licks her lips and recasts. "I stayed beside the boat all night, watching this boy. Then, after midnight, a great storm came, waves crashing down so hard, the ship toppled onto its side. The sailors were in the water, but I didn't see the boy." Here, her voice hitches. "I dove down until I found him. His limbs were failing him and his eyes were closed. I pulled him up to the surface and held his head above water. We stayed like that the whole night. And when the sun returned and the ocean calmed, I kissed his forehead and swam him to land."

Reflexively, my tentacle tightens around her waist as I'm reminded of Annemette, even though I've read enough to know this story by heart. A storm, a shipwreck, a savior.

"And?" I ask.

"I placed him on a beach beside a great building. I stayed to watch, hiding among some rocks, covered in sea foam. Soon, a beautiful girl found him and sounded the alarm. I knew then that he would live. He awoke, and was smiling at the girl."

"No smile for you?"

"No." The determination returns to her voice. "But I wanted that smile—I want it now. I want him to know that I saved him. That I love him. And I want him to love me."

Ah. She's lied to me.

"But you said he already does."

The girl looks away, caught. Finally, she continues. "For the past year, I've watched him. And I *know* if I could just be human, he would love me. He thinks he's in love with the girl from the beach, but I saved him. I saved Niklas."

Like Anna, this girl believes she deserves something and she's willing to risk her life and all she knows for it. But this girl doesn't crave revenge.

She wants a happily ever after.

And for that, I cannot blame her. Even after all these years, I still wish for my own.

"It is very stupid of you," I say finally, "but you shall have your way."

And so, I recall my mother's dying spell. The one she used to save me from myself.

"*Gefa.*"

The little mermaid's eyes spring open. She shirks back—getting nowhere in my tentacle's grasp, pale fingers flying to her throat. An invisible heaviness settles within my hands—her beautiful voice weighing on the lines webbing across my palms. Heart, life, fate.

I release her and turn to my cauldron, fashioned from sand and magic.

In goes the girl's voice, a brilliant white light in the dark.

The cauldron glows. I retrieve a swordfish spear from my cave, and hold it over the spring, sterilizing it. I am lonely, but I am clean. Then, leaning over the bubbling cauldron, I prick the skin of my breast, just above my heart. A life is no longer needed, true, but this dark magic still feeds on sacrifice. Like anything of power.

Blood as black as midnight oozes into the murk. Molasses slow, it slinks into the pot, slithering through the white light of the girl's voice. As they mix and mingle, they heat the pot together, pushing the temperature up until the cauldron itself is a fireball, a comet come to rest at the bottom of the cove.

Steam rises, curling above the brilliance. As it does, it swirls and dances, forming shadows like the worst of night. The polypi forest parts for the horrid shapes, wanting no measure of their magic.

I prepare the words I've learned, the ones Anna used to regain her legs and seek revenge. Ones that won't work for me, strange magic that I am, tied to this cove.

"Líf. Dauði. Minn líf. Minn bjoð. Seiðr. Seiðr. Seiðr."

The cauldron begins to tremble, the contents swirling round and round under great pressure. Coming on like life itself.

An explosion like a dying star rockets forth, rippling through the cove with such heat the water evaporates in a plume of smoke and steam. White foam settles around us in a swath running the length of my home. It all smells of sulfur, the stench heavy enough that it burns my nose and the back of my throat. When the foam and light clear, I see the little mermaid has turned away, arms flung over her head in protection. I don't blame her.

I dip a small bottle—another long-ago present from Tante Hansa—into the vat. The draught shimmers like moonglow and sunlight trapped under glass.

"There it is for you," I say, holding it out to the girl. She drops her arms at the sound, whirling around, so afraid that she didn't realize what was happening until I spoke. "Drink it down, and you will gain legs for four days. If your love is true, so much so that your prince loves you with his whole soul, you will stay in human form for the rest of your days. If you do not win his love, you will become but foam in the tide."

The girl's lips drop open to respond and her tongue begins to move. It takes a few moments before she remembers that no sound will ever come from her mouth again.

Regret floods into my chest, but my tentacles float into view and the feeling immediately disperses.

Lies ruined my life as much as they ruined Anna's. Nik's.

With shaking fingers, the girl takes the bottle. Fear has returned to her eyes, but the deed is done. Only her determination and love will do.

"Take the draught in the shallows. It would be a waste if you drowned before you could get to land." The girl nods. "Go now. Visit your family one last time. You won't regret the good-bye." Again, she nods, and I know she will do it. Losing them was more of a surprise than losing her voice. Maybe even her life.

She turns to go, but then I call out for her to stop.

No one knows me, it's true, but I am still Evie. And for all my fearsome reputation, for all my years and loneliness, I'm not heartless.

I retrieve from my cave a gown from long ago—one from a trunk I found submerged in the cove after I arrived. Back then, the cool scent of Annemette's magic still draped across the wood and latches, and maybe that was why the fabric remained undamaged. I quickly whisper a spell that will keep it dry until she surfaces.

"Take this with you. It will help if you look the part."

It is all I can do.

Hopefully the magic is kind.

I know the magic well enough now not to expect a

happy ending. The fairy tales of my childhood are the exception, not the rule. It's a wonder there aren't more creatures like me in this world.

And so, I return to my cave, the new silence ringing in my ears. Somehow, it's more painful than before. As if hearing a new voice, regaining the shortest moment of humanity, has torn open the wound that is my loneliness. Leaving it gaping. Festering. Infected.

But in truth, I am not alone. No, the polypi are living and breathing in this murky place, fashioned from the spirits who tried to kill me. My dark life tied to their souls.

Lining the cauldron is a smear of shimmering light, what is left of my payment. The girl's voice. Only a drop was needed for the draught, her body paying the price for the remainder of the magic.

I scour my hands across the cauldron's belly, collecting the voice until its weight has returned to my palms. The white light dances, its glow reflecting across the cove, illuminating my forest, my cave, my own dark form.

It is truly something special.

Maybe it's the new silence or the memories that swirl in the front of my mind. Maybe it's simply that enough time has passed.

But I know exactly what I will do with this gift.

And so, I turn to the largest polypi. The one planted next to my cave. The last body to drift below.

When I give the command, I know the magic will

isten. That it will know what I want. I feel its power surging from the tips of my tentacles to the roots of my hair.

"*Líf. Líf.*"

The girl's voice sweeps forth, floating up, up, up, until it settles into the top of the strange tree's trunk where the branches shoot off into the flat black murk.

It settles and becomes one with the polypi. And, after a moment, there is a deep breath, all the heads in the branches inhaling seawater in time. And then the little mermaid's voice speaks with the thoughts of another little mermaid from long ago. One tied to me here silently, fifty years since I sprouted tentacles from my waist.

When the voice comes, it's direct and focused on what just occurred. She has centuries left to dredge up what happened when we were human.

"She will fail. He loves another. That mountain will not move in four days."

"I know." And I do. I hope she will not fail, but I also cannot forget what my mother did for me. What I did for Nik. What Anna's family would've done for her had they been given the chance. "But her family will not let her go so easily." They'll come begging for a way to save her.

When I return from my lair with a deadly length of coral, Anna understands. "Make it sharp. The blood must fall on her feet—if she will use it at all."

And so, I prepare the knife. Because though magic can shape life and death, love is the one thing it cannot control.

ACKNOWLEDGMENTS

Ever since my parents introduced me to *Cat's Cradle*, I've always been drawn to the idea of Kurt Vonnegut's "karass"—a group of people cosmically, inextricably linked together. Yeah, I know it's a term coined as part of a fake religion and sort of silly, but I do think the fates put people together for a reason. Call it a karass or something else entirely, but the following human beings are in my life for a reason, and I love them in their own ways. Without them my life would be considerably less full.

To my lovely editor, Maria Barbo, whose magical imagination made Evie's world possible. I can't thank you enough for your faith in me.

To Katherine Tegen, our fearless leader; Rebecca Aronson with her queries and smiley faces; copy editor Maya Myers for her sharp eye and grace in weathering my hatred of the Oxford comma (journalists unite!); production editor Emily Rader for her steady hand; Heather Daugherty and Amy Ryan for their beautiful book design; Anna Dittmann for her stunning/haunting/perfect rendering of

Evie; and to the rest of the Katherine Tegen Books and HarperCollins team.

To Rachel Ekstrom, my agent/cheering section/ grounding force, who always greets myself and my work with enthusiasm and guidance. And to the rest of the IGLA family, most especially Barbara Poelle, for their support, humor, and belief in me.

To Joy Callaway, my ray of forever sunshine—you've made a difference for me every single day. You know exactly when to text, call, make me laugh. Your grace and friendship are truly inspiring.

To Renée Ahdieh, leader of my pack—wisest, chicest, most altruistic rock star in the world. You're part sister, part fairy godmother, and 100 percent diamond dust.

To Rebecca Coffindaffer, who has a habit of murdering off my characters before I even realize there should be blood on my hands. To Natalie Parker and Tessa Gratton—my coven elders, who vetted my magical system with wisdom, wit, and cold LaCroix. Additionally, to all the Kansas writers I'm lucky enough to know. Our time together is like the best of college—nights spent dissecting the art of writing in the most delicate and interesting ways. Plus, you all have amazing taste in snacks.

To Julie Tollefson, Christie Hall, and Christy Little for the hours upon hours spent huddling with me in the freezing-but-delicious confines of T. Loft. To Marie Hogebrant for pinch-hitting in Old Norse.

To Kellye Garrett, my fictionally murderous sister-in-arms, always one text away. To Randy Shemanski, keeping me sane over email for twelve years and counting. To Whitney Schneider, Nicole Green, Laurie Euler, Coleen Shaw-Voeks, Colinda Warner, and my passel of Trail Hawks for the endless sweaty miles and even sweatier hugs. To Jennifer Gunby and Cory "Cass Anaya" Johnson, who awoke my imagination early and never let me get away with a boring scene.

To Ricki Schultz, Danielle Paige, Zoraida Córdova, Dhonielle Clayton, Brenda Drake, the Sarahs—Lemon, Cannon, Jae-Jones, Smarsh, Blair, Fox—and everyone else in my life, for their various cameos during this journey over the hill and through the woods. In ways big and small you kept my sanity with humor, love, and light.

To my parents, Craig and Mary Warren, for being the best dream enablers out there. You kept me in construction paper when my "books" were stapled-together crayon drawings, and never let up when actual words found their way to the page. I'd be nowhere without you. To Nate, Amalia, and Emmie, and the stories you're unfurling before our eyes. To Meagan, our missing piece. So it goes.

And, finally, to Justin. My IT department, my chocolate pretzel supplier, my kid-wrangler. My heart. Without you, literally none of this would be possible. I'm so glad you're here with me on this journey. I couldn't imagine setting sail with anyone else.